"Let's just concentrate on one pie for now."

Quint crossed to the sink and rolled his shirt sleeves to his elbows, revealing his strong, tanned forearms, and a wayward longing swept through Callie. He began washing his hands, talking to her over his shoulder. "I want to see just how rusty my baking skills are."

She pulled her gaze from his arms, pulled her mind from the dangerous yearning. "Right here and now?"

"Yep. Are you still willing to assist?"

"That depends on what assisting requires," she said.

Quint grinned at her, that engaging heart-stopping grin, as the air between them crackled like heat lightning. His gaze slipped to her mouth, and her mouth tingled in response, and then a jackhammer pulsed through her veins, making her body ache for his touch. His kiss.

He leaned down as though he meant to oblige her mouth, but instead he whispered, "Damn it, Callee, I'm only human. If you don't want me to kiss you, stop looking at me like that, or I won't be responsible for what happens."

ACCLAIM FOR *DELECTABLE*

Delectable

Also by Adrianne Lee

Delicious
Delightful
Decadent

Delectable

Adrianne Lee

FOREVER

NEW YORK   BOSTON

Forever
Hachette Book Group
237 Park Avenue, New York, NY 10017
www.hachettebookgroup.com
www.twitter.com/foreverromance

Printed in the United States of America

Originally published as an ebook
First mass market edition: May 2014

10 9 8 7 6 5 4 3 2 1

OPM

Forever is an imprint of Grand Central Publishing.

The Forever name and logo are trademarks of Hachette Book Group, Inc.

The publisher is not responsible for websites (or their content) that are not owned by the publisher.

The Hachette Speakers Bureau provides a wide range of authors for speaking events. To find out more, go to www.hachettespeakersbureau.com or call (866) 376-6591.

*For Gail Fortune, who always believed I could
and proved it to me.*

Acknowledgments

THANK YOU:

Larry—for taking over the kitchen so that I can write.

Jami Davenport—Plot partner extraordinaire.

Critique partners—Orysia Earhart, Linda B Myers, Karen Papandrew

Karen Dunham—for Kalispell weather information, as well as suggestions for "seasonal" pies.

Gail Fortune—my fabulous agent.

Alex Logan—for making this crazy process so much easier.

Delectable

Prologue

$Quint$, *my boy, there isn't a problem so big that a man can't solve it with a piece of your mama's sweet cherry pie in one hand and a fishing rod in the other."* Quint McCoy heard his daddy's mantra as loud and clear as if Jimmy McCoy stood beside him.

But Jimmy would never stand beside him again. And the echo in Quint's ear was nothing more than a death knell damning him for not heeding this advice, for not freeing up one afternoon in the past year to spend fishing with his dad. Although his dad had kept asking.

A widow maker, the heart specialist called it. Fine one minute, gone the next.

The shock had hit like a lightning strike, knocking Quint to his knees, physically and emotionally. He'd held his weeping mother and his devastated wife, their tears wetting his shirtfront as he tried to console them, unable to console himself. No piece of pie would ease this loss.

More than half the population of Kalispell, Montana,

had turned out for the memorial service. Jimmy McCoy
was well-respected and deeply mourned. Not even that
consoled his son. As he stood next to the casket, Quint
felt guilt and grief seep into his spirit, into the soft tissues
of his brain, his heart, his soul, and streak them all black.
He stumbled through the funeral, through the celebration
of life party after, and through the weeks that followed.
He lost long stretches of time and couldn't say where or
how. He couldn't concentrate on work and started avoiding the real estate office, failing to return important calls.
At home, he operated on rote, barely speaking to or acknowledging his wife, Callee.

And then one day, anger overtook the numbing denial,
grabbing hold of Quint like a tangle of barbed wire, mean
and infectious. He lost all reason. Said hateful, hurtful
things. Blamed the real estate business he'd struggled so
hard to build. Blamed, also, his sense of obligation to
Callee and their fledgling marriage for keeping him from
fishing with his dad. He damned them both. Damned himself more.

Two of his friends intervened, talking him into an
afternoon of fishing on the local Stillwater River. The
moment his grip wrapped the fishing pole, Quint felt
the restriction around his chest loosen. He could breathe
without choking up or breaking down. From then on,
he went fishing every time grief and guilt overwhelmed
him—which was often and inopportune. Like on the night
of his second wedding anniversary. He completely forgot
the special occasion and the surprise Callee hinted at, and
took off on a two-week fishing trip with his buddies. He
sent her a text when he was on the road to Idaho.

But fishing wasn't a cure-all. It couldn't bring his father back, or permanently stave off his sorrow. Grief took an even tighter stranglehold. When he came home, Quint couldn't handle Callee's hurt and anger. Or their ensuing argument. At its apex, he shouted, "I can't take this shit anymore!"

Tears streamed down her face. "This shit? You mean our marriage?"

The tightness in his chest returned, clamping like a vise. He couldn't breathe, couldn't think. He threw his hands up in frustration and rage. "I don't know what I mean. Everything. All of it."

"Quint, please, talk to me. Share your feelings with me. I loved your dad, too." She sobbed, reaching for him. "We can work through this together. Please, let me help you."

He recoiled from her touch, stepping beyond her reach. He didn't deserve to be consoled. Or loved. "No, no. I can't stay here. I'm leaving."

"But... what about us? What about me? What do you want me to do?"

"I don't know. I don't care. Divorce me."

Chapter One

❧

I am one sorry son of a bitch, Quint McCoy thought. *A complete, total fuckup.* He didn't have a clue how to rectify the wrong he'd done. It had taken thirty days fishing in the wilds of Alaska, starting in Ketchikan, then deeper inland to the Unuk River, to bring him to his senses. To make him realize he couldn't run from the pain of losing his dad, or from the grief, or the guilt. He couldn't shove it all away. Or cut it out. It would always be inside him, wherever he was—as much a part of him as his black hair and his blue eyes.

Now that he was back in Montana, in the empty house he'd shared with Callee for two short years, he faced another raw truth. He'd bulldozed his life. Leveled every good thing about it. Nothing left for him but to move on and recoup. Somehow.

He grazed the electric razor over the last of the month-old beard, leaving his preferred rough skiff of whiskers on his chin, and slapped on cologne. After four weeks in a small cabin with three other guys, he appreciated the scent of a civilized male. He took note of new lines carved at his mouth and the corners of his eyes, lines that bespoke his misery. *Losing your dad, and then your wife, will do that to you.*

He wasn't proud of the man in the mirror. He didn't know if he ever would be again. He'd trashed his marriage to the only woman he'd ever loved, or probably ever would love. Treated her like the enemy. And worse. Her mother died when she was seven, leaving her to be raised by a taciturn grandmother. She'd grown up feeling unwanted and unloved. He'd made her feel that way all over again. He hated himself for that. If Callee never spoke to him again, he wouldn't blame her.

But then, he wasn't likely to have a chance to speak to her. She'd left his sorry ass, let their lawyers hash out the equitable property settlement, and moved to Seattle right after he told her to divorce him. It took twenty-one days for the paperwork to go through the legal system. By now, he was a free man. And he didn't like it one damned bit.

Quint glanced at the mirror once more, expecting to see *Dumb Shit* stamped on his forehead, but only noticed that he needed a haircut. He pulled on dark-wash jeans, a crisp blue dress shirt and tie, and his favorite Dan Post boots. His dirty clothes went into the duffle on the floor. A scan of the bathroom showed nothing was left behind. He swiped his towel over the sink and counter and stuffed it on top of his laundry, then a second quick perusal, and a nod of satisfaction. Nothing forgotten.

He plunked the tan Stetson onto his still-damp hair and grabbed the duffle. His boot heels thudded on the hardwood floors, echoing through the empty split-level as he strode the hallway, and then down the stairs to the front door.

As he reached the door, his cell phone rang. He snapped it up and looked at the readout. A fellow real estate agent, Dave Vernon. "Hey, Dave."

"Quint. Well, hang me for a hog. 'Bout time you answered your phone. You still in the land of igloos and Eskimos?"

"I wasn't that far north, Dave. But, no, I'm in town."

"Well, now, that is good news. Glad to hear it. How was the fishing?"

"Okay." If the trip had been about the fish, then the fishing was actually great, but it hadn't been about salmon twice as long as his arm. It had been about his inability to deal with the loss of his dad. His inability to stop setting fire to every aspect of his life.

"You still want me to sell your house?"

"That I do."

"Well, as you know, I had it sold...until you decided to skip town. The buyers got tired of waiting for you to return and bought something else."

"I'm sorry, Dave." Although Dave didn't convey it, Quint imagined he was pissed. Quint had cost him a sale. He'd been as irresponsible as a drunken teenager—without the excuse of adolescence. "I'm leaving the house now."

"All the furniture was moved out while you were gone."

"Yeah, I found the note about the storage unit and the key on the kitchen counter." He'd had to crash on the floor in his sleeping bag. "I just picked up the last of my personal items."

"Well, okay, that's good, actually." Relief ran through Dave's words. "I can put this back into the system immediately if you'll swing by and renew the listing agreement."

"Sure. I have to stop at the office first." Quint stepped outside into the overcast day. The end-of-May gloom suited his mood. "Give me an hour or so, and I'll head your way."

"I'm counting on it."

"See you around eleven." Quint stuffed the duffle into the back of his Cadillac SUV and gave the house one last glance before climbing behind the wheel and backing out of the driveway. The development was small, full of similar homes stuffed between Siberian larch and Scotch pine, the kind of place where newlyweds started their futures. *Started their families*. Like he and Callee had hoped to do when they'd moved here.

A heaviness as dense as the cloud cover settled on his heart. He kept his eyes on the road ahead and didn't look back. He didn't need to see the regrets in his rearview mirror; they were etched in his brain. As he drove north toward town on I-93, the vista vast in all directions, he wondered how it could all look so familiar, so unchanged, when he felt so altered.

But something about the crisp Montana air and the wide-open spaces gave him heart. In contrast, the wilds of Alaska—with giant trees pressing toward the river's edge and just a patch of sky overhead—had made him look inward, at acceptance. Here, he could look outward, at possibilities.

Like what, if anything, he might do to salvage his business, McCoy Realty. He knew he'd be lucky if he ever got another listing in this town, but by God, he meant to try. It had taken him three years to build his reputation and clientele list into one of the best in Flathead County, and three months to destroy it. He'd gone from Realtor of the Year two years running to a pariah. The only reason the office was still open was because he owned the building.

And his office manager, Andrea Lovette, hadn't given up on him. Although he'd given her enough reason. Was she at the office yet this morning? He dialed the number, but the female voice that came on the line was electronic. *"I'm sorry, the number you are trying to reach is no longer in service."*

Huh? Had he misdialed? Or had the phones been disconnected? He sighed. One step at a time. Instead of hitting redial, he pulled to the side of the road beneath a billboard and punched in the office number again. Slower this time. The response was the same. He disconnected. One more grizzly to kill.

He tried Andrea's cell phone. The call went straight to voice mail. As he waited to leave a message, his gaze roamed to the billboard. A gigantic image of his own face smiled down at him. An image taken a month before his dad died. Happy times, he'd thought then, not realizing he was already on the track to losing it all. Overworking, ignoring his wife, his mama. His dad. He shook his head. At least this was proof his business on Center Street still existed, sorry as it was. Right across from the Kalispell Center Mall. *Location, location, location.* If nothing else, he had *that* in spades. He supposed it was one positive to hang on to today.

He pulled back into traffic. He needed to confer with Andrea and figure out what steps to take to get the business back on its feet. Starting with getting the phone service reconnected. He called her cell phone again and left another message. Nothing would be easy. He didn't deserve easy.

"Quint, my boy, there isn't a problem so big a man can't solve it with a piece of your mama's sweet cherry pie in one hand and a fishing rod in the other."

Fishing wouldn't solve what ailed him, but a piece of his mama's sweet cherry pie might take the edge off this morning. The thought made his mouth water, but pie for breakfast? Aw, hell, why not? His spirits could use a lift.

His phone rang. He didn't recognize the number. Business as usual for a Realtor. "Quint McCoy."

"Quint," his mother said, warming his heart and his mood. She'd had that effect on him for as far back as he could remember.

"Mama, I was just thinking about you." He'd missed hearing her voice. "How's my best girl? I'm hoping she'll take pity on her poor, homeless son. Maybe do my laundry? I just left the house for the last time, and I'm feeling lower than a rattler's belly. I have some business that can't wait, but—"

"Uh, that's why I'm calling."

"How about I pick you up for lunch and you can tell me how the pie shop is coming?" She was remodeling the half of his building that he wasn't using into a take-out pie shop. It was set to open later that month. The plans he'd seen before leaving for Alaska included a kitchen in back and a display case and counter in front. Small and compact—like his mama. He smiled. "Yeah, that's what I'll do. I'll see you around one, then after lunch, you can give me a tour of your little shop—"

Call-waiting beeped. "Quint, will...please...I—"

He glanced at the phone's screen. A client. *Thank God for small blessings.* "Mama, I have to run. Say, you haven't seen Andrea, have you? She's not answering her cell phone, and I'm hoping to get together with her today. See what we can do to salvage my realty business."

"Well...as—" Call-waiting beeped.

"Look, I gotta take this call, Mama."

"Quint, about Andr—" Call-waiting cut off his mother's words again.

"See you at one," he said, and switched to the incoming call, realizing as he did that some small part of him kept wishing every incoming call would be one from Callee.

* * *

Callee McCoy pulled the small U-Haul truck into the parking spot at the Kalispell Center Mall, cut the engine, and listened to the motor tick-tick as it cooled. One more thing to do. Her hands gripped the steering wheel as though the vehicle careened downhill at uncontrollable speed and an ensuing crash could only be prevented if she hung on tight enough. But the crash had already occurred, rendering her marriage a pile of bent metal and smoking ash, rendering her shell-shocked at the velocity with which the devastation struck.

She felt as someone might who'd been hit by lightning twice—surprised, certain she was immune to any second such occurrence, given the first had been so devastating. Callee thought nothing could ever hurt as much as when her mother died. She'd been wrong. Losing Jimmy

McCoy, the only real father she'd ever known, had knocked the pins out from under her again. This time, however, everything should have been different. After all, she had Quint.

A bitter laugh spilled from her, and she gave herself a mental shake. It was all water under the bridge. She was moving on, sadder, but wiser, the Kalispell to-do list almost complete. After landing at Glacier Park International yesterday and renting this U-haul truck, she'd visited the storage unit she'd leased before leaving for Seattle and retrieved the belongings she'd negotiated in the equitable settlement part of the divorce. This morning, she'd met with her attorney, finally given him the go-ahead to file for the final decree, and signed the required paperwork. One loose thread left to tie, and then she was out of here. Montana would be a distant memory that she could look back on whenever she felt maudlin or needed a reminder of how good her new life was.

Live and learn, her mother used to say. Of course, she always said this after bundling Callee out into the night to somewhere her latest disaster of a romance couldn't find them. According to her grandmother, her mother was a tramp. She'd pounded this into Callee's head from the day she came to live with her, hoping, Callee supposed, to make sure that Callee didn't turn out the same. But the mother Callee remembered was a free spirit, always laughing and hugging and promising adventures.

When she was old enough to understand such things, she realized her mother had been acting out, rebelling against a too-strict upbringing by running wild, by living fast and hard as though she knew somehow it would all end too soon. Callee was the end product of both upbringings, as emotionally unequipped for a long-term relationship as a mother who had no idea who'd fathered Callee, and a bitter, taciturn grandmother. As proof, the first punch life threw landed squarely on Callee's chin and knocked her clean out of the ring.

The ring. She glanced at the third finger of her left hand, at the diamond and emerald ring that had belonged to Quint's grandmother. The family heirloom had a fragile, antique beauty, the platinum band filigreed. As much as she adored it, she couldn't keep it. She tugged it off, surprised at the sudden sense of disconnection it brought—as though she'd pulled something of herself loose. Silly. She should have removed it the moment Quint walked out on her.

But she hadn't had the courage to let him go then. Not then. Had she the courage now? Or was shaking Quint McCoy loose from her heart going to be as painful as shaking Montana from her red Dingo boots?

Callee tucked the ring into her coin purse next to a business card, trying to ignore the naked-finger sensation, but knowing it was responsible for her thoughts rolling back to the first time she met Quint. She was in Seattle, about to start cooking school, when she'd received a call that her grandmother had had a severe stroke. Callee flew back to Kalispell immediately, and it soon became apparent that she'd have to sell the house to cover the cost of a nursing home.

Quint represented the buyers. He'd come to present the offer, and one exchanged glance tilted Callee's world. Some might call it love at first sight.

A dinner date led to a kiss; a kiss led to an endless night of lovemaking. She lost her head, her heart, and everything she'd ever meant to be in that conflagration of sensuality. They were like a Johnny Cash/June Carter song—hotter than a pepper sprout, hotter than the flame on Cherries Jubilee, the sizzle and burn an irresistible blue blaze.

Just the memory of those erotic months could melt steel, but then the fire of excitement and sexual discovery calmed to a slow burn. She still craved Quint physically, sexually, but he was so intent on building his real estate business that he no longer had time for her. Somehow, she never got around to telling him that the classes she was about to start just before they met were at a cooking school. Callee feared he might laugh, given she could do little more in a kitchen than boil water. She'd never worked up the nerve to share her secret desire to become a chef or the secret fear that she was incapable of learning to cook.

But the adventurous part of her, which she'd inherited from her mother, was making her try. She'd re-enrolled in that same Seattle culinary college, and her first classes started next week. *Here's hoping the second time is the charm.*

She reached for the truck's door handle and hesitated. She had come to say the toughest good-bye of all…to Molly McCoy. Quint's mother had treated her like the daughter she'd never had and been the closest thing to a real mother since Callie lost her own. Staving off tears, Callee jumped down from the cab into the gloomy day and felt a sudden shiver, like a portent of something dreadful. Probably just her mood. She zipped her jacket and locked the U-Haul.

Her phone vibrated in her pocket, a text from her best

friend, Roxanne Nash. Roxy owned a Seattle waterfront bistro, and she'd opened her heart and her home when Callee arrived on her doorstep after leaving Quint. Roxy was always egging Callee on, making her try new things and face her phobia of learning how to cook.

Roxy wanted to know if everything was okay, if Callee was okay, and if she'd started the eleven-hour drive back to western Washington yet. She answered the text, then stepped to the curb at Center Street, her gaze skipping across the road to be caught by a new sign: Big Sky Pie. She knew Molly was renovating the largest part of Quint's office building into a pie shop, but her brows rose at exactly how much of a renovation had occurred.

She smiled, thinking of the treat that awaited Flathead County residents. No one made pies better than Molly McCoy. But it was the example Quint's mother was setting that filled Callee with pride and happiness. Molly had grieved the loss of Jimmy McCoy worse than anyone, yet she'd turned her sorrow into something positive and productive. Callee wanted that end result for herself.

She patted her purse to make sure the ring was still there and hastened across the street, admiring the exterior of the pie shop. Bay windows wore white awnings, and the exterior was painted a rich ruby red with white-and-tan trim and lettering, reminiscent of Molly's specialty, sweet cherry pie made with fresh Bing cherries from the orchards around Flathead Lake. The color scheme was one Callee had suggested when Molly first mentioned she might open a pie shop one day. Callee felt honored that her mother-in-law had remembered and taken the suggestion to heart.

She pasted a smile on her face and tapped on the door,

prepared to give Molly an "I love what you've done with the place" greeting. But she startled and then grinned at the woman in the doorway, Andrea Lovette, Quint's long-time office manager and Callee's friend.

Andrea lit up like a delighted child at the sight of a favorite toy. "Oh my God, Callee. I didn't know you were in town. Does Molly know?"

"Not yet, and I'm not staying." They exchanged a quick hug, and then Callee stepped back and looked at her friend. "I'd ask how you're doing, but you look fabulous."

"I look ragged. Two little boys will do that to you." Andrea laughed, her brown eyes sparkling as she shoved at her long, thick blond hair. She was taller than Callee, a fact made more pronounced by the skinny jeans and platform pumps she wore. "Since you're not staying, what brings you back to Kalispell?"

"Tying up some loose ends."

Andrea nodded, her lips pressed together. "Well, whatever the reason, I'm delighted to see you. And Molly will be, too. Besides, I hate being the only guinea pig."

Guinea pig? Callee found herself being pulled farther into the shop. "I don't know what you're talking about. Where's Molly?"

"In the kitchen with Rafe, her new assistant pastry chef. She's teaching him something, I think."

Muffled voices issued from the kitchen, one female speaking English and one male speaking Spanish. Callee smiled. "Do they even understand each other?"

"No clue, but Molly will be out in a minute. I'm sitting over there." Andrea pointed to a booth. "Go ahead. Sit. I'll bring you some coffee."

"Okay, but I can't stay long." Only long enough to give

Molly the ring and a hug good-bye. Callee settled into the booth and began to take in the décor. The interior reflected the colors used outside, but in reverse. The walls were tan, the crown molding and trim white, and the tablecloths and napkins a ripe red. This was all café, display cases, cash register, and an espresso/coffee and tea counter. Seating consisted of a row of four high-backed booths on one wall and round tables scattered throughout the space.

"Isn't it great?" Andrea handed her a cup of steaming coffee. "The kitchen consumes the largest portion of this building, an L-shaped chunk that isn't visible from this room."

"It's wonderful. Right down to the framed, poster-sized photos of juicy pies with sugar-coated crusts."

"Mouth-watering, huh?" Andrea took a sip of coffee.

"That's the idea, right?" Callee couldn't get over the size of the room. "I didn't know she was going to do a café. Last I heard, the pie shop would be take-out only."

"Yeah, well, the café was kind of last minute," Andrea said, quickly downing more coffee. "Molly told me the design was yours."

Callee shook her head. "Nope. Only the colors."

"All the same, I think you missed your calling, lady."

Callee smiled. "I missed a lot of things."

"So, how are you doing?" Andrea touched her hand.

The gesture made Callee feel less alone. Andrea had once been where she was now, figuring out how to be single again. The difference was that Andrea had had the burden of two little boys relying on her to get it right. Callee had only herself. *Thank God.* "I'm looking forward, not backward."

"I'm glad. I've been worried about you." Andrea offered a commiserating smile.

"I promise, I'll be okay, eventually." She smiled weakly.

"This whole thing is such a tragedy." Andrea shook her head, but never one to hold back how she was feeling, she added, "When Quint comes to his senses, he's going to be real damned sorry. I wish you'd stick around, Callee. I know he said and did some awful things, but that man loves you. Even if he can't see past his grief right now."

"If that's what he thinks love is, I want no part of it." It didn't matter if he did love her, or even if she still harbored tender feelings for him. He was, after all, her first true love, but she had never been a priority with him, and watching the love his parents had shared, she realized she deserved better than what Quint was giving. One day, maybe she'd find her Mr. Right. But Quint McCoy was not that man. "My U-Haul is parked right across the street. As soon as I have a minute with Molly, I'm on my way to Seattle. I've enrolled in college," she said, keeping the type of college to herself. If she ended up with her degree then she would share details with trusted friends, but for now, it was her secret. "Classes start next week."

"That's awesome. I'm so excited for you." Andrea's smile flashed, then quickly faded. "Uh, by the way, Molly just spoke to Quint. He's on his way here."

"What? I thought he was still in Alaska." The news tweaked Callee's nerves, and she gulped down a swallow of coffee, the hot liquid burning its way to her stomach.

Andrea was studying her. "He got back last night."

Callee set her mug aside, snatched hold of her purse, and scooted toward the end of the banquette. "It's been wonderful visiting with you, but right now, I need to see Molly and get out of here."

"Okay, Andrea, I hope you're hungry," Molly called, emerging from the kitchen. Quint's mother, a bubbly, middle-aged redhead with short spiky hair, was followed by a tall, handsome Latino in his early twenties, who carried a serving tray with fragrant goodies on dessert plates.

"Callee!" Molly squealed, foiling Callee's attempted escape. Molly wiped her hands on an apron spotted with flour, chocolate, and fruit juice and hugged Callee. "Oh my God, you're like a gift from Heaven."

Callee returned the hug, wishing she never had to let go, but she did, and since the memory of this moment would have to last her a long time, she held on a beat or two longer than she might have. Even though Molly would always welcome Callee into her home and her heart, Callee understood their relationship would never be the same once she left here today. Tears stung her eyes.

Molly stepped back, and Callee did a quick assessment. There was a smidge of flour in her choppy red hair and on her pert nose. The bedroom eyes she'd passed on to her son seemed weary, and the wide smile that lit up any room she entered seemed less brilliant. She was like a clock someone forgot to wind; not quite up to speed. Still missing her husband, Callee figured, still worrying about her son. At least the shop would joyfully fill a lot of lonely hours.

Callee glanced at the wall clock, wondering how soon before Quint arrived. She had to leave. Now. But Molly urged her back into the booth.

"I know why you're here."

How could she know that? Callee lowered her voice. "In that case, could I see you in private—?"

"You're going to stay and come work for me." Molly cut her off, hope erasing the worry lines near her mouth.

"What?" Callee's eyebrows rose. "Work for you doing what?"

"A pie shop can always use more than one pastry chef." She handed Andrea and Callee forks and napkins.

"A pastry chef?" Callee blushed, recalling the time Molly tried to teach her to bake a pie. Callee kept hearing her grandmother's voice, taunting, telling her that she was only fit for washing dishes and taking out garbage. Not for cooking or baking anything. The end result had been a crust that resembled lumpy clay, and although Molly had been kind, Callee couldn't stop cringing at the memory.

Callee gave Molly an indulgent smile. "You know perfectly well that my kitchen skills are limited to coffee and scrambled eggs. Period. Not pies."

"Oh, all right." Molly sighed. "But since you don't have anything against *eating* pies, you can help us figure out which of these three items belongs on the menu."

"I really need to go."

"I'm opening next week, and I need to tick this off my to-do list."

"I can't st—"

"Nonsense. It'll only take a few minutes." Molly slipped into her side of the booth, blocking her in. As stuck as gum in cat fur, her grandmother was fond of saying. Resigned, Callee turned her attention to the tray, which held three colorful pie slices. Her mouth watered. Her early morning breakfast had consisted of a grande latte. Eating something now meant one less stop along the road later on.

Andrea said, "If presentation means anything...wow."

Molly beamed. She handed Andrea a small green tart. "It's key lime."

Molly gave Callee a slice of chocolate pie and gestured for Callee to try it. "This is tar heel pie."

Callee tried a bite. "I've never heard of it."

"It's chocolate chips, coconut, and pecans. A word of caution. It's very rich and should probably only be eaten in tiny increments."

"Ooh, I like this," Andrea said. "A definite ten."

"This is to die for," Callee exclaimed, her sweet meter tilting off the charts. She shoved the slice toward Andrea. "Try it."

Molly pointed to the next item. "This last one is Daiquiri pie. Cream cheese, condensed milk, concentrated lemonade, and my own twist, ninety-proof rum."

Andrea and Callee dug in while Molly watched, waiting for their verdicts.

But Callee and Andrea could only moan in pleasure.

Molly glanced at Rafe. "So much for narrowing the menu."

He muttered something in Spanish that sounded like "a bucket of Tequila" and headed back to the kitchen.

Outside, tires crunched on the gravel parking lot. Inside, forks stopped halfway to mouths. The three women exchanged knowing looks. Molly scooted out of the booth, then stood frozen beside the table. "Quick, Callee, go see if it's Quint."

"Me? Why me? I don't want to see Quint." She would just mail the ring to Molly. Feeling none too composed,

Callee slipped from the booth. "Do you have a back door?"

"Please, Callee." Molly's face had gone a worrisome gray.

"What's going on?" Callee looked from Molly to Andrea.

Andrea winced. "A sort of intervention."

"Shock therapy," Molly said.

"What?" Callee had no clue what they were talking about, and she didn't want to know. She stole to the window and peered out through the blinds. The second she saw Quint, her heart began to thrum with a rhythm akin to a love song. He was sitting in his SUV, phone to ear. "It's him."

"It's for his own good," Molly muttered, as though to herself, as though her actions needed defending. "It's true what they say about tough love. It is harder on the giver than on the receiver. If I hadn't spoiled that boy to the edge of redemption..."

"What's he doing?" Andrea asked, still seated in the booth, sucking up Daiquiri pie like she was downing shots in a bar and ignoring her cell phone, which kept announcing a new voice mail.

Callee had a bad feeling. "He's putting his phone away."

"What's he doing now?" Molly asked, her face drained of color.

"Getting out of the car."

"Does he look angry?" Molly asked.

He looks heart-stopping delectable—like always
Damn. Callee hated that her pulse still skipped whenever she laid eyes on Quint, hated that every nerve in her body

seemed to quiver as he shoved back the Stetson revealing his incredible face. God, how she adored that face. His smile, his touch, the things he did to her body, the responses he elicited...just recalling left her breathless. *No. Stop it. You're over. He never put you first. Never.* "He's glancing up and down the street as though he can't understand why he isn't seeing what he expects to see."

"Like he's wondering if he's on the right street?" Andrea said, sounding...anxious?

And then Callee realized. *Shock therapy.* "You didn't tell him you were turning his office into the café portion of your pie shop?"

Molly gulped. All the answer Callee needed. Before she could ask what the hell Molly was thinking, a fist hit the door. All three women jumped. But no one moved to let him in.

Chapter Two

～⌒～

Quint felt like he'd driven down a familiar street right into the Twilight Zone. Rod Serling was probably talking into a television camera somewhere announcing, *"This was a day like any other day, or so Quint McCoy thought as he drove to his office. But it will be like no day he's ever known. The first day of the rest of his life. His nightmare life."*

He stepped out of his SUV. Checked the road sign. Center Street. Yep, right street. He gazed across the road at the Kalispell Center Mall with the Red Lion Hotel on one end. Yep, right location. He turned back to the spot where one perfectly located realty office should be and again encountered the impossible. McCoy Realty was gone. How could that be? Hadn't he just seen the proof of its existence five minutes earlier on a gigantic billboard?

He had. Quint lifted his Stetson and raked fingers through his hair. Then why the hell was his mama's pie shop—which was to have taken up only three-quarters of this building—now occupying the whole damned place? Who had managed this transformation in one month's time? Who had had the nerve to desecrate *his* office? Mama?

He didn't want to believe it, but who else could have done it? Someone had some serious explaining to do, and Andrea was still not answering her phone. Movement in the window caught his eye. Someone was inside. He rapped on the door. "Mama? Are you in there?"

He heard footsteps. Voices. But no one answered. He rapped harder. Identified himself. And finally the door cracked open. He resisted the urge to shove the door inward and knock whoever stood on the other side to the floor. Good thing. Since it turned out to be his mother. "Son, I…"

For the first time in his life, hearing her voice didn't warm his heart or ease his soul. He scowled. "What did you do?"

He saw movement from the corner of his eye and glanced up. A blonde was sitting in a booth where his conference room should be. "Andrea?"

"Quint," she mumbled, avoiding eye contact and stuffing pie into her mouth. Guilt in every bite.

"You're in on this, too?" Of course she was. Andrea would have to be. A flash of red near the window pulled his gaze in that direction. His eyes took in red boots, long, lean legs in curve-hugging denim, sleek waist, full, ripe breasts, and, finally, eyes so green a man would drown in their depths. Callee.

A jolt went through him, not unlike the one he'd felt the first moment his gaze connected with hers. He'd been a goner then. As hooked as a bull trout in a grizzly claw.

He pulled himself back to the present. Why was she here? "I thought you were in Seattle."

"I was."

"Did you come back to see me brought to my knees?"

A frown pulled her brows together. "What?"

"Quint, stop that right now." Molly stepped between them. "Callee had no hand in this."

As the words sank in, he knew them to be true. His temper flared too easily these days, before he could rein it in or think through what he was saying. Damn it. That was how he'd driven Callee away in the first place. "I'm sor—"

"You really don't know me at all, do you?" Callee cut him off, color like red cherries seeping into her cheeks. The urge to open his arms and embrace her swept over him unexpectedly, but she came at him like a hungry wildcat with its canines bared. Quint stood his ground. He would welcome her fury, the feel of her fists pounding the shit out of him. He deserved anything she wanted to unleash.

As she closed the gap, he noticed a smear of chocolate at the corner of her mouth. He stifled the urge to taste it. And then he caught a whiff of something sharper. Rum? It was only ten a.m. "Have you been drinking?"

Callee froze.

"Enough," his mama said, her face as burgundy as her hair. "We were getting close to launching the pie shop when I realized I needed more space. A café area. It isn't good enough to only sell take-out pies. If I want to build a strong business, I need to serve dessert here."

Her reasoning was sound. Solid. It was her acquisition he couldn't fathom. "So you took my office space?"

"It was the only space available."

"It wasn't available. It was my office." His voice rose with every word, his anger bouncing off the newly painted walls. The floor seemed to shift beneath his boots. Rod Serling was playing his eerie theme music and telling the television audience, *"Quint McCoy never saw it coming. Betrayal by a pastry chef who looks and sounds like his own mother, but can't really be his mother. Or can she?"*

"You closed the office and left town. It was just sitting here."

"But it's *my* building."

"Actually, it's not, son. It's mine."

"Well, yeah, but that's just a technicality. It was sitting empty before I turned it into something."

"And when you left it sitting empty, I turned it into something else."

He sank into a chair, realizing as he did that it wasn't *his* chair. His gaze fell to the floor. To the gleaming hardwood. He frowned. "Hey, where's my carpet?"

"Well, dear, when we took it out, we found this wonderful old oak planking—"

"But my desk? My trophy trout?" He glanced around the café, not seeing the beauty, but lost in the realization of all that was no longer here. A fear took hold of him...that he would never recover, never again find his emotional footing without something familiar to grasp onto. "Where are my files?"

"Safely stored in my garage, dear."

"In your garage?" Her unheated garage? Did she expect him to run a real estate office in an unheated garage? At his mother's house? The idea was so absurd that it

sobered him. Who was he kidding? He didn't have any
business. He hadn't had any for a month before he left
for Alaska. So where did he get off waltzing in here
this morning and expecting to resurrect that dead body?
Maybe he never could. Maybe he needed to lay it to rest
permanently. Move on. Find a different career. Somehow
that didn't seem right. He plowed his hand through his
hair. Was it too late for McCoy Realty? He didn't know,
but Andrea might. He shifted toward her. "How damaged
is the business? Our reputation?"

She shrugged. "You pissed off a lot of people."

He nodded. Yeah, that seemed to be the one talent he
excelled at these days.

"I—I thought you might want this." Andrea scooted
out of the booth and crossed to the cash register, a little
unsteady on her feet. She dug behind the counter and produced an old-fashioned Rolodex. Although Quint backed
up contacts electronically these days, this had belonged
to his father, and it had sat on his desk from the day he'd
opened the office.

She set it on the table beside him. Quint smelled rum
again. What the hell? Had Andrea been drinking, too?
Had the whole world gone crazy while he was in Alaska?
Grateful for something familiar in this storm of confusion, he caught hold of the Rolodex like a father finding a
child who'd been ripped from his arms during a tornado.
Or in this case, a son finding a piece of his father.

"Son, after you left, Andrea and I had a long chat. I
needed the space, and it seemed to me that it would be
best for you to restart your realty business at a new location. A fresh start, so to speak." She sat on the chair next
to him, laid her hand on his thigh, and spoke in a loving

voice. "That's what I'm trying to do. Jimmy would want me to. He would also want you to."

"Did you even think to talk it over with me before you tore my office apart"—he struggled to keep his temper under control—"before you stored it in your garage?"

He looked at Andrea again. "Why didn't you let me know this was happening?"

She gave him an exasperated look. "I tried. For a week. Every call went straight to voice mail. I left you messages and texts. You didn't respond."

His mother said, "No one could reach you, dear."

Guilt spiraled through Quint. He'd tossed his phone away shortly after he arrived at Ketchikan International. He didn't want to talk to anyone. He'd bought a new phone at the airport in Seattle yesterday. Once he'd activated it and saw the gazillion messages, he'd deleted them without reading texts or listening to voice mails. New phone, new start. He couldn't do anything about stuff that had occurred while he wasn't here. Which pretty much included this. But how did he reel in the anger and upset running through him?

His mother squeezed his knee. "Now that you're back, you can decide which of my other buildings suits you best and open your new realty office there."

"But this is the best location in Kalispell."

"Exactly. And for a pie shop, location is everything."

Location, location, location. Quint winced. Kicked to the curb by his own words. Hell. Damn. Shit. Fuck. Humiliation spread through him like a virus. His joints ached, his muscles cramped, his stomach felt queasy. His mother had always been in his corner. Always. But where had he been when she dealt with the loss of his dad? Off feeling sorry for himself. His dad would be not only be ashamed of him, he'd be disappointed.

That realization hurt almost as much as losing Jimmy.

A buzzer sounded from somewhere inside the pie shop.

"Oh, dear, my cobblers!" Molly jumped up and dashed toward the kitchen.

Quint lurched to his feet, too.

Andrea stopped him. "Let her be, Quint. Talk to her later. When you've calmed down. She's always supported you. It's time you returned the favor."

She didn't give him a chance to say he'd just come to that realization as she hurried after Molly into the kitchen. He stood there like a man lost on a frozen tundra, squinting into a white expanse of nothingness, no idea which way led to safety. All directions seemed nothing more than bleak wasteland.

The sound of a throat being cleared reminded him he was not alone. Callee. *Shit.* He closed his eyes and groaned silently. Once again he'd been a complete dickhead to her. He swallowed what remained of his shredded ego and faced her. The look of commiseration and pity on her beautiful face stole his breath. He didn't deserve it. He would rather she took a hammer to his shins than be kind to him.

"I'm on my way to back to Seattle. I only stopped by here to leave this with your mother." She was holding her coin purse, her brows knitting. "But since you're here...and she's busy, well..."

Callee walked to him, handing him a business card and the ring he'd given her the day they wed. The ring seemed to sear his palm.

"I can't keep it. It was your grandmother's." Her gaze was strong, but the slight quaver in her voice belied her poise. "You should have it…to give…to your…next… someone else, one day."

His tongue seemed to swell and swallow his voice. He still wore his ring. A plain gold band with the date of their wedding and *Love, Callee* engraved on the inside. Did she want it back? Could he take it off? Even if it meant letting her go forever? He had to do the honorable thing. She deserved it after what he'd put her through. A chunk of his soul broke off as he said, "Do you want my ring back?"

"God, no." She shook her head hard. "Keep it. It's not a family heirloom. It has no sentimental value to me."

Ouch! He hadn't imagined words could slice through his heart with such force. The pain elicited an actual groan. "I know it's too late to go back, or even make up for all the things I said and did, but I am sorry, Callee. Truly sorry." Sorrier than he could ever say. "I hope one day you'll believe that and forgive me, and that, that maybe we might be frien—"

"Friends?" She cut him off, red flaring in her cheeks, her hands flying up like a shield to ward off an incoming missile. "I…I…no. No."

Hell, what did he expect her to say? *Dumb shit. Get your head out of your ass. She wants nothing to do with you.* He stared at the business card. "What's this for?"

She sighed, looked away, then back at him. "It's my attorney. Your attorney can contact him."

Quint frowned. His attorney and her attorney had already exchanged numbers and dealt with the dissolution of their marriage. Hadn't they? His attorney's calls were among those he hadn't taken after leaving for Alaska.

"I had my lawyer file for the divorce decree this morning."

A gasp sounded in the doorway behind them. Quint spun around to see his mother standing there. She clutched her chest and then dropped to the floor in a heap.

"Mama!" He ran to her. "Oh my God! Someone call 911! Mama!"

* * *

Callee stood outside of the Kalispell Regional Medical Center's emergency room, cell phone to ear, speaking to Roxanne Nash. "Roxy."

"Hey, best friend, are you finally on your way back here?" A sizzle and clang came through the line and brought an image of Roxy standing over a hot stove in the kitchen of the bistro, white chef coat smudged with a rainbow hue of sauces, a chef cap holding rein on her wild, red mane. Roxy said, "I hope so because I've pulled a major coup. Booked a huge, secret event that I can't tell anyone about. Well, not on the phone anyway."

Callee bit back tears, wishing with all her heart that Roxy was standing before her so she could throw herself into her friend's arms and weep. When Roxy had talked her into going to cooking school in Seattle a few years ago, it was with the end-goal of opening their own catering shop in Kalispell. Neither could have predicted the detours their lives would quickly take. Roxy soon met and married a rookie Seahawk and went on to get her chef degree. Callee had quit cooking school on the first day, returned to Kalispell, and met and fallen in love with a

Realtor. And now when she needed her best friend, they were miles apart.

But maybe in-person comfort would be too much too handle, considering she couldn't seem to hang onto her composure long enough to state her reason for calling. The words kept choking her. "Uh, th-that's w-why I'm calling."

"Oh, good. You filed. I'll have the wine ready when you arrive, and we can toast our mutual divorces." Roxy said something to someone in the restaurant kitchen and immediately started in again before Callee could form the words she sought. "Mine is a horror movie. Ty's attorneys are playing hardball, as though he didn't cheat on me in every city the Seahawks played. They're just mad we didn't do a prenup. If his attorneys think Ty and his new fiancée are walking away with the lion's share of our joint estate, they better think again. Washington is a community property state. Fifty/fifty. Half of what we own is mine. I'm not taking anything less."

"Roxy, please."

The stress in Callee's voice must finally have registered because Roxy went silent, then said, "Something's wrong. What is it?"

This time Roxy didn't jump to conclusions, but waited until Callee found her voice and the words to explain Molly's collapse at the pie shop. She ran through what she knew, which was mostly speculation. "The EMTs said heart attack, probably a blood clot. They've given her blood thinners and a clot buster and are trying to stabilize her so they can run tests to determine exactly what is going on and what can be done. If anything."

"Oh, hell, no." Roxy sounded as stunned as Callee felt. "Quint's dad died of a heart attack."

"Exactly." A widow maker. And now his widow might also be gone from the same cause. The tears Callee had been fighting slipped down her cheeks. She closed her eyes and remembered Molly lying on the kitchen floor. Unresponsive. Her skin gray, her lips blue. Awful thoughts crashed like bumper cars through her mind, filling her with guilt and fear. "She overheard me tell Quint I'd filed the divorce papers this morning. She grabbed her chest and collapsed. If she dies, it's my fault."

"I'll catch the first plane out."

Yes! "No. No. You can't. You have that special event."

"My staff can handle that."

That was a lie. Roxy was too anal to trust the handling of a huge event to anyone else. That she even suggested her staff could handle the big event was a testament to their friendship. Callee loved her for the offer. "Thank you. But for now, sit tight, okay? Just talking to you has already pulled me back from the ledge." She could lie, too, for a good cause. "I'll call you later when I have more information."

"Are you sure you don't want me there now?"

"Yes." No. She closed her eyes against the sacrifice and hung up before the truth came tumbling out. A squeal of tires brought her head up. An ambulance pulled in, lights flashing, everyone moving at a manic pace. She stood riveted, watching as a patient was wheeled into the emergency entrance. A woman about to give birth. Her husband trailed by, helpless in the wake of the professionals. He glanced at Callee and said, "It's our first."

The random encounter shook her, bringing home all the lost possibilities. She prayed Molly would not be lost as well. Callee walked away from the emergency room entrance, a deep sadness settling over her. If she and Quint were in a better place, a good place, they could lean on each other, but he'd rejected her comfort when his father died, and she couldn't, wouldn't risk that rejection and hurt again.

She dialed the pie shop. Andrea was still there, dealing with an appliance delivery that was days late. "Oh, God, Callee, I'm afraid to ask. How is Molly?"

"She's still alive," Callee said, fighting back more tears.

Andrea inhaled sharply, then said in a shaky voice, "W-what's the diagnosis?"

"Don't know yet. They're doing an angiogram right now." Callee's voice was none too steady. "You know, where they run dye through your veins to see if there are blockages? If they find any narrowed veins, they'll insert stents right away. If it's more serious—" She broke off and swallowed hard. There were so many ways it could be more serious. "One option is bypass surgery."

"That's good, right?" Andrea sounded like someone grasping at straws, seeking hope in an otherwise hopeless situation. "Stents or bypass surgery. That means she has options."

"Yes." Maybe. Callee didn't tell her there might be nothing they could do if the damage to Molly's heart was too massive. Why worry Andrea further without knowing for certain what they were dealing with?

"Okay. The delivery guy is supposed to be on his way, or I'd be there with you guys."

"I know." She asked Andrea to make a couple of phone calls and to lock up when she left, but to leave a key for Quint somewhere.

"I'll stick the key in the decorative mailbox out front," Andrea said.

Callee made a mental note to tell Quint. "I have to go. Quint may have heard something by now."

"Poor Quint. He's had a pretty tough morning."

That might get tougher, Callee thought, guilt heavy on her heart. Fresh tears burned her eyes and thickened her throat. "I'll call you as soon as I have an update."

"Okay. Oh, tell Quint that Dave Vernon called. I guess they had a meeting or something. Anyway, I told him what was going on and that Quint would reschedule when he could." Her voice sounded full of tears. "He understands and sends prayers for Molly."

"I'll tell him." Callee doubted that scheduled meetings had even crossed Quint's mind after he'd shown up at the pie shop. Still, she understood Andrea's need to be useful in a situation where they'd all been rendered helpless. If not blameless. She tucked her phone into her pocket and strode to the waiting area.

The expectant father was at the registration counter looking in need of support from a friend or family member. She could use some of that herself, but she had no one to offer it, certainly not Quint.

She figured she'd find him pacing like a caged animal. Instead, he sat on a sofa in a corner, shoulders slumped, gaze on the floor, exactly as she'd left him. His Stetson was abandoned on a nearby coffee table, his hair mussed, but it was his expression that broke her heart. And threatened her resolve. He wore the mask of a lost man; it had been a day of losses for him, and she prayed losing his mother wouldn't be the topper.

God, don't let me have killed Molly.

Was he thinking of the night his father died? Trying to console his mother, who had collapsed against him, while he barely managed to stay on his feet? If his mother died, he'd be all alone. No more family. She was used to not having family to fall back on. No one to be there offering her support or to cheer on her triumphs. But Quint was not. She swiped away fresh tears. He wouldn't want her pity, but she had never felt more like taking him into her arms and holding him close until the fear eased from his soul, from his eyes.

She slipped onto the sofa beside him. Despite herself, she was unable to keep from touching his arm, the tiniest offer of commiseration, as she asked in a low voice, "Anyone tell you anything yet?"

"Nope." He shook his head. "The longer the angiogram takes, the better the news will be. If this can be fixed with a stent."

The pain in his voice so matched what she was feeling, she ached. She had no comforting words, no hackneyed platitudes, no cheery encouragement. Only a belly full of fear. Death had visited her too often. She moved her hand to his, and he grasped hold like a man clutching a raft in high waves, an anchor in a scary sea of uncertainty.

Every minute seemed to pass like an hour, but when Callee looked up to see a nurse coming toward them, she realized too little time had passed for Molly's heart issue to be resolved with a stent. Although she tried to brace for whatever bad news the doctor would deliver, she was unsteady on her feet. Quint continued to hang onto her hand as they were led into a small private office with chairs, a desk, and a large laptop to meet with the cardiologist.

Dr. Kyle Flynn was around fifty, trim and fit, with

steel-gray hair. He greeted them with a nod of the head, but addressed them formally as Mr. and Ms. McCoy.

Quint released Callee's hand and swept his hair back, then wiped his palms on his jeans and reached to shake Dr. Flynn's hand.

Callee sank onto one of the chairs, feeling sick. She admired Quint's effort to put on a brave face, knowing inside he was also terrified of whatever this compact man in green surgical scrubs would say. The doctor's serious expression did nothing to ease her worry.

Quint blurted, "How's my mother?"

"We've stabilized her." Dr. Flynn motioned Quint to the seat beside Callee. The tense set of Quint's shoulders seemed to loosen, and he fumbled for the chair, sitting hard, as though the news that his mother was still alive had zapped whatever inner strength had kept him going until now.

His mother was alive.

Callee still held her breath. She knew stabilized meant Molly wasn't okay, just okay for now. And there had been no stent, or he would have said. She tried not to let her imagination run wild with awful scenarios as she concentrated on what the doctor was showing them on the laptop screen.

Dr. Flynn explained that the set of six videos were images of Molly's heart. He clicked on one, and it filled the monitor. The veins showed white against the dark walls of the heart, pulsating on the screen. The doctor pointed out a narrowed section in an otherwise normal vein. "This is one of the problem areas. Due to a blood clot, she suffered a cardio infarction."

"Layman terms, Doc, please," Quint said, his voice ragged and deep.

Dr. Flynn explained that Molly had had a serious, nearly fatal heart attack. Bottom line: she needed a triple bypass, but was too weak at the moment. The surgery had to be held off until she was strong enough to withstand the procedure. That could be as little as a couple of days or even a week or two.

Quint went as white as the veins on the monitor. "Has she done much damage to her heart?"

"Actually, not as much as I originally feared. If she tolerates the surgery and recovers as expected, the damaged areas of her heart will likely regenerate with time."

"What if she has another attack before the procedure?" Callee asked, afraid she already knew the answer.

"We'll do everything within our power to prevent that, Ms. McCoy," Dr. Flynn assured her. "She will have to stay here, in ICU, until I feel she's ready for surgery."

Callee released a tightly held breath and felt the tension in her muscles begin to ease. Molly wasn't out of the woods, but she was in the best possible hands, and she had a chance. She could beat this and come out of it strong and well. Callee grasped onto that hope, small as it was. Happy tears blurred her vision of the doctor, but she could see that his expression was still extremely serious.

"Can we see her now?" Quint asked.

"First, I need to warn you that she is very fragile," Dr. Flynn said. "I am limiting visitors and visiting times. She must have no tension or anxiety. I cannot stress that strongly enough."

Quint nodded, guilt written in the worry lines around his mouth and eyes. "I promise you, I won't cause her an ounce of worry, but she might need to hear that from me."

"I won't either, Doctor," Callee said. Poor Molly. She

had to have been worried sick about her son returning to Kalispell to discover she'd confiscated his office, scared that by doing so she might push him farther over the edge. *Then, I showed up and made matters worse, losing my temper and going after Quint, the final straw that caused her collapse.*

When Quint walked out on Callee, his mother had tried to convince her that Quint didn't really want a divorce; that it was grief talking. But eventually, surely, Molly had to have realized and accepted the inevitable—especially when Callee moved to Seattle. Hadn't she?

Callee chewed a fingernail, thinking back on Molly's reaction to finding her in the pie shop. Excited. Hopeful. She shook her head as she started to realize what must have gone through Molly's mind. Quint's mother believed in fairy tales, believed that Callee and Quint would have the same long, happy relationship she and Jimmy had shared. Apparently, she'd mistaken Callee's sudden appearance in Kalispell as a homecoming, instead of a last good-bye.

"Tell her anything that keeps her calm," the doctor reiterated as he stood. He snapped his fingers as though just remembering something important. "Oh, by the way, she keeps insisting on speaking to someone named Kallie. Right away. If you could arrange for that person to come to the hospital as soon as possible, it would be a help."

"That's me." Callee rose unsteadily.

"I didn't realize. I don't believe I've ever heard your given name, Ms. McCoy, but that expedites matters for sure." The doctor smiled. "You may both follow me. Please, keep your stay brief, one person at a time, and remember, her situation is extremely precarious. Anything you can do to ease her mind will help her toward recovery."

Callee trailed beside Quint, wondering why Molly was anxious to see her. Did she think she could talk Callee out of getting the divorce? If she tried, then what would Callee say?

Tell her anything that keeps her calm.

Quint went in to see and speak with Molly first. Callee paced the hall, waiting her turn, playing scenarios through her mind, working out responses to possible questions or pleas that her mother-in-law might make. But no amount of mind-play prepared her for Molly's request.

As Callee entered the ICU cubicle, she was immediately wrapped in a perfume of medicinal smells and assaulted by the beeps and buzzes of monitoring machines. Her gaze bounced off the equipment and centered on Molly, so small and pale against the hospital sheets, plugs and wires poking from her. It was as though her internal dimmer switch had been activated.

Callee approached the bed on wobbly feet, afraid any movement might sever the thin thread connecting her mother-in-law to life. She loved this woman so much. She forced a smile and tentatively touched Molly's hand. "You gave us quite a scare, Mama, but the doctor says you're going to be just fine—as long as you do what you're told and rest."

"Callee, I can't stay here. That daft doctor won't listen to me. Neither will Quint. But I have to get back to the pie shop. Ads go out tomorrow announcing the grand opening next week. The shop must open as advertised."

Callee glanced toward the windows that looked into the ICU corridor. Quint stood there, peering in, his expression anxious, as though she wouldn't remember to reassure his mother no matter what. Callee returned her gaze to Molly. "Don't worry about the grand opening. Between Andrea, Rafe, and Quint, the shop will open as scheduled."

Redness seeped into Molly's face, and the steady beep-beep of the machine increased, alarming Callee. Molly said, "You don't understand. None of you. Andrea has no experience running a pie shop. Neither does my son. And Rafe? He's just an assistant. I'm not sure if he can bake anything but meat pies. That won't do."

The machines beeped a little louder, a little faster. Callee strove to calm her mother-in-law. "Molly, please, don't fret. Quint won't let you down."

But would he? Was that what worried Molly? If so, how was Callee supposed to ease her mind?

Molly snatched Callee's wrist, her grasp like a too-tight bracelet. "Don't go."

"But the doctor said I can only stay for a—"

"Don't go to Seattle," Molly interrupted. "I need you to stay and take my place at the shop until I'm back on my feet."

"Take your place?" Callee gaped. The request was insane on so many levels—including Molly being laid up for weeks after surgery. Maybe months. But mostly it was insane because she hadn't even gone to cooking school yet, and Molly knew she couldn't bake a pie to save her soul. "I can't bake pies."

"You're the only one with restaurant experience."

"As a hostess, not as a pastry chef." After Quint and she married, Callee had worked at Twangy's Bar and Grill as a hostess and was doing the same at Roxy's seaside bistro in Seattle. She hadn't ever worked in the kitchen of either restaurant, although Roxy had been encouraging her to give it a try. Molly's request roused her grandmother's criticizing words, stirring Callee's old fears and self-doubts. Maybe she should reconsider and give up the idea of becoming a chef. "Molly, I'm sorry, but—"

Molly cut her off. "Please, Callee, I need you to do this."

No. This was ludicrous. She couldn't stay in Kalispell or fill in for Molly. She couldn't quit culinary college either. The tuition was non-refundable; classes started next week. Somehow though, all that she managed to blurt out was, "B-but I can't make pies."

"I don't believe that." The beep-beep started escalating with every word.

"But—" *Beep, beep, beep, beep, beep.* Oh, God. Guilt and fear crashed in on Callee. Molly meant to win this crazy, unreasonable argument even if it killed her. Dr. Flynn's words rang loud inside her head: *Another attack could be fatal.* Her own promise to do whatever it took to ease Molly's mind followed suit. Promise her anything. Promise it *now*.

Before Callee could consider the repercussions, she said, "Okay. I'll do it, but you have to promise to stop fretting."

The beeps began to slow. *Beep...beep...beep.*

"I promise," Molly said. With that, she sank back on the pillows and closed her eyes, a smile wavering on her pale lips. The beeps began to level off.

She watched Molly's face relax. A moment later, the monitor attached to her heart settled into a steady rhythm—while Callee's heart began to beat off the charts. *What the hell did I just promise?*

Chapter Three

Whatever you said did the trick." Quint smiled at Callee as they made their way out of the hospital and into the parking area. Heavy clouds still blocked the sun, and the late afternoon was cooling fast. "She calmed right down."

The expression Callee made belonged to someone eating sour pickles. "She asked me to take her place at Big Sky Pie until she's on her feet."

"What?" He stopped in his tracks, disbelief spreading through him. Mama expected him to work with Callee, to see, every day, the hurt in her eyes, the unspoken accusations? How the hell was he supposed to do that?

He got that otherworldly feeling again and could almost hear Rod Serling cue the woo-woo music and tell the audience, *"Quint McCoy thought the worst outcome of his visit to the Twilight Zone was his realty office morphing into a pie shop café. Until his mother collapsed. Until his mother set it up for him to work with a woman he'd emotionally betrayed. No, friend Quint, the worse has yet to be revealed."*

"Look, I swear I didn't know she was going to do that."

"Ha. Neither did I," Callee said, the sucking-on-lemons look back on her face.

Quint scratched his head. "I can't understand what Mama was thinking. She must have known you'd turn her down flat."

"I told her I would do it."

"What? That's ridiculous. You're on your way back to Seattle."

Callee sighed and shifted from one red boot to the other. "I would have told her I'd paint stripes on the moon to keep her from having another heart attack."

He reached out and grabbed Callee by the upper arms, moving her out of the way of a car that was backing out of a parking spot. She tensed, then seemed to realize he'd only meant to save her from harm, and stepped closer to him. Her perfume wound into his nose, filled his senses, and stirred memories he'd avoided, longings he'd been too numb to miss. Those memories traced erotic fingers through his brain, and the yearnings awoke with a jolt. Blood rushed to his groin. He wanted to pull her closer, so close nothing separated them, not even clothes.

He released her and stepped back, fighting the inappropriate signs of his desire, but couldn't keep a huskiness from his voice. "If it's any consolation, I did the same thing. I told her I'd get Big Sky Pie up and running. What do I know about running a pie shop and café? I'm a Realtor, for God's sake."

"So, what are you going to do?"

"Mama said Andrea and Rafe aren't qualified enough

to help me out, but I know she's wrong about Lovette," Quint said. "Andrea can operate the business end even if her experience isn't in the food industry. Not only is she a fast learner, she has a finger on the pulse of the consumer. She'll be an asset. Too bad she's not a pastry chef."

Callee smiled. "Yeah, her idea of home-cooking is anything that can be microwaved. Say...if your mom is wrong about Andrea, maybe she's wrong about Rafe, too."

Quint frowned and shoved his Stetson back from his brow. "I don't know. Mama said Rafe has no experience with actual pies. He does something more akin to beef or chicken pasties. Whatever the hell those are. She planned on teaching him, but right now, the shop needs more than a pastry chef in training."

Callee hugged her purse to her chest like a kid clinging to a favorite toy while the security of the world fell away. Her expression was stoic. "Don't look at me. I can't make a pie either."

"Yeah, I know," Quint said, thinking over his options. Callee, however, did have a couple of years of restaurant experience under her belt. She hadn't run the kitchen at Twangy's Bar and Grill, but she'd complained often enough about how her employer was running it. She knew what made a good café employee. But would she be willing to help him out? She was on her way to Seattle when Mama collapsed and might still be planning to head out as soon as he dropped her off at the pie shop. "I don't suppose I can convince you to stay in town a couple of more days?"

She seemed as small and vulnerable in that moment as a trapped kitten with hungry wolves blocking every escape route. She closed her eyes and groaned. "I, er, I have an obligation that I can't put off next week."

Next week. Not tomorrow or for a few more days. "Well, you did tell Mama you'd be staying awhile."

She swallowed, looking away. He could tell she was torn. She loved his mother. He knew how fiercely she could love. The thought tore at his heart, punishment for screwing up the best thing in his life. Wanting her to stay and help him was selfish. They started walking, but back-up lights on another car had Quint reaching for her again, keeping her safe. The instinct to protect this woman was so strong, how could he have lost her? Why the hell had he told her to divorce him? And speaking of that... "I thought the divorce documents were filed before I left for Alaska?"

"No... I... I asked my attorney to hold off on filing... to give me some time to... I don't know... But, it's filed now, so don't fret—in twenty-one days you'll have your freedom."

Whether he wanted it or not. Why had she waited until now to file? "I guess I thought since our lawyers had hammered out the equitable settlement and neither of us was contesting anything that it was a done deal. I guess I haven't been thinking very clearly for a while now."

There were so many responses she might have given to this admission, but she said nothing. She didn't have to; her expression said it all.

He asked, "Are you going to leave before Mama has the surgery?"

The color left her face. She sputtered, "I—I—"

Callee started walking to his SUV, her wavy chestnut hair swishing with every step, her hips swaying, and those little red boots tap-tapping on the pavement. His heart began a tap-tapping of its own, his mouth watered, and heat pooled in his groin for the second time in five minutes. He was as entranced as a salmon watching a silver flasher. "Mama would want you here."

"I know," she said over her shoulder.

I want you here. Acknowledging that to himself caused an ache in his chest and a deep loneliness. His dad was gone. A million fishing trips wouldn't bring him back. He had lost Callee. He might lose Mama, too. Guilt and heartache had done their best to tear him to shreds. Only he could stop his downward spiral. He needed to do something positive. Right some of the wrong he'd done. To his mother. To Callee. If she'd let him.

He unlocked the SUV and held the passenger door open for her.

As she scooted onto the seat, she still wouldn't look at him. "I've made all the promises I'm making for one day."

Did that mean she was going or staying? He didn't know. He hurried to the driver's side, hoping she meant to stay. He climbed into the SUV, his mind churning through possible ways to convince her to hang around until after his mother had surgery, but then he realized Callee was eyeing his belongings in the back. And she had an obligation next week. Truth came slamming in. No matter how long he delayed her departure, no matter how he tried to tell himself it wasn't happening, their marriage was over. His own damned fault.

Callee wasn't staying in Kalispell. She had a future mapped out in Seattle.

Their gazes collided, and a wall of emotions seemed to

rise between them. They drove to Center Street in silence, as close as two people could be in an SUV with bucket seats, as far apart as two people could be with their eyes set on different paths.

As he pulled up in front of Big Sky Pie, Quint felt the same jarring chest-hit he'd felt this morning at first sight of that sign on his building. Okay, technically Mama's building. He parked and, for the first time, considered the pie shop from a professional point of view. From a Realtor's perspective. "It has great curb appeal, doesn't it? The colors are eye-catching, and the façade seems to say 'come on in'."

"It did turn out nicely," Callee said, looking pleased that he liked the color scheme. "Though I'd seen the original blueprints before I left town and knew what to expect, it's not the same as seeing it in person, is it?"

"Yeah, especially when it's bigger than you'd expected it to be."

Callee bit her lip. "I didn't know there would be a café either."

"It was a surprise. You know, I never gave much thought to Mama as a woman with ambitions and goals as I was growing up, or even when I was fully grown, really. She was just…my mama." Memories assailed him, bringing a smile. "But all through my childhood and teen years, there was an endless stream of bake sales and blue ribbon prizes for her pies. At county fairs and church socials. I suspect she has always wanted to take her pie baking to the next level."

Callee nodded. "Probably, but she always put you and your dad before everything else."

The wistful note in her voice touched Quint's heart. He

knew Callee was right about Mama and now, he realized, the time had come for him to put Mama before everything else. And he would. He glanced at Callee. The streetlights had activated. Light shone on her head, highlighting the russet tones in her hair. He stifled the urge to reach across the console and shove his fingers into the thick tresses, to feel the silken texture. *Think about something else, Quint*

"Did I ever tell you this building started out as a bakery?"

Callee shifted toward him. "No. You didn't."

He gazed into her emerald eyes, realizing there were a lot of things he hadn't told her. Things he'd thought they'd have a lifetime together to share. "You knew Dad used to buy up old buildings around town, like this one, when the businesses went defunct."

She nodded. "Which one of the others are you going to use for your new realty office?"

He shrugged and laughed low in his throat. "I haven't even thought about that."

"So, tell me about this building then."

He rubbed his chin, pulling up the memory. "I think the original owner ran a lucrative bread business out of here until bread was mass-produced and sold in grocery stores."

She unhooked her seat belt. "Funny how so many folks would rather buy fresh baked bread again."

"And pies?" Quint asked, not knowing, but hoping that was the case.

"Yes, and pies."

"Well, that's a relief. At least I'll be peddling a trending commodity. If I can find a pastry chef, that is . . ."

"Why don't you worry about that tomorrow?" She stepped out of the SUV, a peachy scent trailing in her wake. "I think you've had enough to deal with for one day. We all have."

He glanced at the shop again. A dim light shone from behind the closed blinds. The business was closed for the night. The employees had gone home. "You're right. I don't need to deal with this tonight. Tomorrow is soon enough. I should probably go in and make sure everything is locked up tight. Mama had me take her key. She's been wearing it on a chain, like a necklace."

Callee smiled. "Your dad told me once that she was always losing keys."

"That's a fact." He chuckled as he got out of the SUV and slammed the door. "I haven't eaten anything since breakfast. Neither have you. You want to grab a pizza and a beer at Moose's Saloon?"

"No." She shook her head. "I have to go."

"Are you leaving for Seattle, then?"

"Not tonight." She glanced away from him. "I can't leave until I know Molly's going to be all right, but I do need to make some calls—"

"Oh, crap." He hit his forehead with the heel of his hand, dislodging the Stetson. He caught it by the brim and held it to his side. "I better hightail it to Mama's and phone her friends to let them know what's going on."

"No need," Callee said. "I had Andrea call one of Molly's lunch bunch and ask her to phone everyone they felt should be notified."

"Thank you," he said, relieved that he didn't need to handle that on top of everything else. "Then I guess I'll grab a bite and head back to the hospital. Not too late to change your mind and join me."

"Why don't you get some rest, Quint? The doctor will

call you if there's any change in Molly's condition. They aren't going to let you hang out there all night, and you won't be able to rest on those waiting room chairs."

He felt certain he would get little sleep no matter where he landed. In the end, he decided Callee was right. If he was going to tackle opening a pie shop, he needed to come at it with a fresh perspective. He couldn't go home. No furniture. No bed. Last night on the hard floor had been enough. He could crash at Mama's, but knew he'd be better off across the street at the Red Lion. Less to distract him. Like his office piled in the unheated garage. Like, everywhere he looked, memories of his dad. Of Mama.

He secured a hotel room, called the hospital to make sure Molly was still sleeping, and then strode down the block to Moose's. He shoved into the noisy saloon, slid onto a bar stool, and ordered a beer and pizza. He sat alone, eating, drinking, trying to make sense of the craziest day of his life.

* * *

If you want to make sense of your life, Callee thought, struggling to crack open her eyes, *don't drink a bottle of wine by yourself*. She pushed out of bed, started the hotel coffeemaker, and dove into a long, hot shower. Her head still pounded afterward. She toweled off and dressed. Four aspirin later, hair dried and makeup in place, she stood at the window overlooking a steady stream of traffic on Front Street. Early morning rush hour and the onset of tourist season.

She should be one of those drivers heading west this

morning, on her way to Seattle, but once again fate had intervened and changed her plans. For now. She couldn't leave without knowing Molly would be okay, and she couldn't stay with classes starting next week.

What was she going to do?

She sipped coffee, thinking, realizing the only thing she wanted at the moment was to see Molly. Just to peek in on her. But if she showed up at the hospital this morning, Molly would wonder why she wasn't baking pies, or at least trying to bake pies, as promised. *Note to self: in the future, don't lie.* If she wanted information about her mother-in-law's condition, she had to go to the pie shop and ask Quint for an update. Not that he'd be there this early.

Callee sighed and downed the rest of her coffee. Damn it. She wasn't leaving Kalispell today, or tomorrow, or if she was honest, probably not until after Molly had surgery. She just couldn't. She pushed the cup aside and listened to her stomach growl. She needed food and espresso. The Red Lion offered limited services, a complimentary breakfast buffet and 24/7 food services via one of the fast food places in the mall. She felt like something else.

An idea struck. There was a perfectly incredible kitchen right across the street that no one was using today. It was a chance to test out her skills on a real chef's stove and be at the shop when Quint showed up. Smiling, she grabbed her purse, headed to the pie shop, and found the key Andrea had placed in the decorative mailbox.

The night lights were still on as she let herself in. The small bell over the door sounded a hollow welcome, but even in the semidark, the café held a warm ambiance.

Callee had no doubt this business would be a success once its owner returned. She made straight for the espresso machine and started it as well as the regular coffeepot, the strong, familiar aromas boosting her morale.

At the doorway to the kitchen, she paused, waylaid by a nightmare flash of Molly sprawled on the floor. Pulse thudding, she searched for the light switch. In the sudden flare of light, the shadows disappeared, revealing a kitchen that was every chef's fantasy work room. The décor was what she'd seen described in magazines as modern French Country: cream-colored cabinets, granite and marble countertops, and a slew of high-end, stainless-steel appliances. It was bright and inviting, and Callee felt another twitch of joy that Molly had used her suggestions for the décor in this room.

She strode to the back wall and raised the blinds on windows that overlooked the employee parking lot. The day promised blue skies and sunshine. Callee hoped it was an omen of good things to come across the board, hoped that she and Quint could set their differences aside long enough to keep this pie shop on track for its opening. But she couldn't help but worry that Quint might decide right in the middle of it that he'd rather go fishing than follow through.

She sighed and realized the air, while chilled, smelled like the inside of a cookie jar. Spicy with a hint of flour and chocolate and cinnamon. Exactly like Molly's home kitchen always smelled. This memory brought a smile. Callee nudged the thermostat higher and removed her coat. She found an apron, grabbed a frying pan, and set it on the burner of the gas stoves and then turned on the overhead fan. She pulled eggs, cream, and butter from the gigantic Sub-Zero side-by-side refrigerator. Maybe one day she'd command a kitchen like this, handle the appliances with expertise, and even develop some original recipes.

She activated a burner on the gas range. It started with a gentle swoosh. She leveled the flame and dropped a dollop of butter into the pan. It began to melt and sizzle. She cracked the eggs onto the butter, then added cream and spices and scrambled her breakfast. Simple. But so tasty.

"Umm, something smells mighty good." A man's voice. Right behind her. She hadn't heard anyone come in. The noise of the overhead fan and the distraction of her thoughts, she supposed. She spun around, her only weapon a spatula. Quint stood inches from her, his pulse-stopping grin and bedroom eyes causing her heart to swoon. *Get a grip, Callee. You're done with this guy. He's done with you.*

"I thought I was at Mama's for a second."

"How is Molly this morning?" Her voice came out in a squawk as she noticed his damp hair, tousled as though from a shower.

"She's still weak, but they said she had a good night and is staying calm."

Callee nodded and bit back tears of relief at the good news while trying to ignore the lure of his aftershave. "Thank God."

"I know." He moved to stand beside her.

Callee caught the scent of soap and something earthy that spoke to intimate parts of her female anatomy, a silent, sensuous voice that made her blush.

Her emotions were so conflicted that she wanted to smack him for scaring her, and smack herself for wanting him. What was the matter with her? Was she going to feel this ache for him the rest of her life? Somehow, she found her voice. "Have you eaten?"

"Grabbed something at the hotel." He gestured toward the mall.

Surprise shot through her. He was booked at the Red Lion, too? She'd assumed he'd gone home or would stay at his mother's, looking after the place. The idea of him sleeping somewhere near her room rattled her. She tried not to show it and carried her food out to the café.

Quint followed. "Want some coffee?"

"Please." She settled into the booth, glancing over at him as he filled two mugs from the regular coffee pot, realizing in that moment how much she had missed seeing him do something as simple as this. "Why didn't you stay at your mother's last night?"

Quint shrugged and said in a quiet voice, "Couldn't face it."

She placed a napkin on her lap as she thought about his response. Given Molly's precarious hold on life, she might not have been able to stay at her house, either. She picked up her fork and began eating, trying to imagine what it would have been like to grow up with stable parents, who lived in the same house for as far back as you could remember, parents who loved you unconditionally, and then to face that house after losing one of them. Especially when he might lose his mama, too.

No. Molly was not going to die. She shoved the awful thought away, trying to hang onto the positive. "I'm just grateful Molly is hanging in there."

Quint slid onto the bench seat opposite Callee and pushed her mug toward her, their fingers bumping, the contact jolting. His gaze seemed to caress her. "Mama needed lots of reassurance this morning that you were filling in for her here."

"That's because, even though she wants to deny it, she knows I can't cook anything more than this." Yet. Callee took a pointed bite of eggs and smiled. Oh, my, this was exactly the taste she'd been going for, buttery, smooth, just the right mix of spices. It was her go-to dish, the one thing she made well, and it never failed to offer her comfort when things in her life were going awry. Like being forced into close contact with the man who didn't want her, and a man she didn't want to want, but still did. This torture needed to end. "Speaking of pastry chefs, have you found one yet?"

He gave her a lopsided grin and said in a teasing voice, "Isn't that why you're here?"

"I was hungry." She put another forkful of eggs into her mouth.

"They serve a perfectly fine breakfast at the hotel."

"I did a swing through of the breakfast room. Wasn't impressed."

"But…it comes with the price of the room." He sounded perplexed.

She glanced up from her plate, saw he was serious, and frowned. "Is that the way all guys look at food? If you can get it for a bargain, you'll settle for pretty much anything?"

He thought about it and shrugged. "Most of the time, sure."

She finished the last of her scrambled eggs, her mouth awash in buttery deliciousness. Men were unfathomable. "Women are more particular."

"Oh, yeah. How so?" He watched her as he drank, a devilish glint in his blue eyes.

She'd walked right into that one, she thought, shaking her head. She wasn't about to answer such a loaded question, not with her hormones responding to that dangerous, challenging look on his face. She just smiled and carried her dishes into the kitchen to the sink.

Quint followed, emitting a whistle of appreciation. For half a second, she thought it was for her and blushed. Then he said, "Boy, this kitchen must be a chef's wet dream."

Callee laughed. "Roxy has a kitchen similar to this one, and she raves about it in pretty much that term."

"Roxy would." He chuckled and hitched a hip against the island, watching as she washed her dishes. She could feel his gaze on her backside like steam from a boiling pot. Elusive, yet tactile. And memories of a certain Sunday morning bounced into her mind. She'd been doing dishes then, too. Quint had moved up behind her, started kissing her neck, rubbing his hands down her hips, up to her breasts, across her belly and lower. He pulled her to him, his body hot and hard with need, and they made love at the sink, a fast, furious, erotic few moments.

That was the last thing she needed or wanted to think about. Callee scrubbed the frying pan with a fury, as if that would cleanse the clinging bits of desire and lingering sensuous impressions from her mind. Maybe it wasn't such a great idea being alone with Quint in the pie shop. There was something too intimate about it, something that made her want to forget all the bad things that had gone down between them. Forgetting those things would be a bad mistake.

He said, "So, are you here to fix breakfast, or have you decided to stick around for a while and help me find a pastry chef?"

"I can't leave without making sure Molly is strong enough for surgery, but I do need to be in Seattle by next week. I—" Callee broke off, swearing. "I totally forgot about the U-Haul truck sitting across the street in the mall parking lot. It's due in Seattle in four days or I have to pay another three hundred and fifty bucks."

Before she could pull out her phone to call the rental truck company, Quint said, "I'll cover any extra costs, hotel and rental truck, if you'll help me find a pastry chef."

The Red Lion layover was cutting into her carefully budgeted funds, and his offer to pay for the extra rental on the truck and the hotel room cheered her. "Thank you, Quint, I accept."

She spun toward him to offer a smile of appreciation and caught him staring at her with such longing it stole her breath. How was she supposed to do this if he kept arousing feelings she'd worked so hard to set aside?

"Great." He grinned, and her heart skipped.

She turned back to her dishes. What did he want from her? Forgiveness? Reconciliation? To be friends, he'd said. The hell with that. There was a mountain of hurt and heartache and shattered trust separating them. She'd help him find a pastry chef for Molly, but she couldn't give in to any residual feelings she harbored for Quint.

He said, "I don't know where to start looking for a pastry chef, but I'm thinking you do."

Callee dried her hands on a dish towel, pushed her hair back from her brow with her forearm and stared into those sexy blue eyes. He didn't know that she was starting cooking school, so where had he gotten the idea that she had some inside track on finding pastry chefs? "Why would I know how to find a pastry chef more than you?"

"You have restaurant experience. And contacts, right?" He said this as though it contained all the logic one needed to follow his thought process.

"I was a hostess at Twangy's Bar and Grill, and trust me, there were no pastry chefs among the kitchen staff."

"Oh. Well, what about in Seattle? Maybe Roxy knows someone?"

"She might. Someone who lives and works in Seattle, but probably not anyone who lives in Kalispell. You don't have time to hire someone out of state, not if you intend to meet your mother's opening deadline of next week."

"Good point." He rubbed his chin and frowned. "The only experience I've had hiring anyone was through a temp agency. Remember? That's how I found Andrea. But I'm not sure temp agencies handle out of work pastry chefs."

Callee brightened. "Hey, at least it's a place to start. Maybe they can give us some leads."

He nodded. "Would you mind making another pot of this delicious coffee? I have a feeling it's going to be a long morning."

She had a feeling he was right.

* * *

"It's just wrong," Andrea said, arriving ten seconds later and looking scattered and very upset. Close to tears.

"What's wrong?" Callee was in the end booth with a

pen and her leatherbound journal, searching the Web on her iPhone for employment agencies.

"Is Molly okay or what?"

"Mama's holding her own." Quint sat near the bay windows.

"Well. Then." Andrea huffed, her cheeks red, her eyes glittery. "Wouldn't you think the hospital could tell me that? But no...I'm not family. And they wouldn't let me see her, either. And I couldn't reach you because your call waiting isn't working or something. And I...I...I got so scared."

"She's good, Lovette, I swear." Quint shoved out of his chair and pulled her into a bear hug. "She's still a little weak, but stronger than yesterday. Honest."

The thought of how precarious Molly's health remained spilled over Callee. She'd put her mind to the task of looking for prospective pastry chefs, shoving the worry aside for a while this morning, but Andrea's distress brought it rushing back. She thought about joining them, turning the hug into a group thing, but then gave herself a mental shake. Fretting didn't help Molly. Getting this pie shop on its feet was all she'd asked, and Callee wanted to make that happen, if she could. She went back to her Internet search.

But she couldn't concentrate, and her gaze drifted back to Quint, his soft side exposed in the tenderness he was showing Andrea. This was the Quint she missed, the Quint she'd loved, the Quint she still wanted. No. Damn it. How could she still yearn for a man who'd treated her so badly?

She looked away, stared at her phone, and tried to focus on the website she'd brought up. It wasn't Quint she wanted. It was a sexy romp in the hay with a gorgeous, randy cowboy that would cure what ailed her. Unbidden memories of Quint's glistening, naked body, his fiery touches, and his deep sighs sent a sensuous shiver through her. Okay, maybe Quint was the gorgeous, randy cowboy she ached for, but who could blame her?

In bed, Quint McCoy was everything a woman could want...and more. Just look at him. His fine ass in those tight blue jeans, that blue shirt hugging every muscle in his amazing back, that lock of ebony hair curling over his collar...Callee gulped espresso, fanning herself with her phone. Maybe she should switch to iced coffee.

Quint broke the embrace and spoke quietly, updating Andrea on Molly's condition in fuller detail, explaining the doctor's restriction on visitors. "They aren't letting me in for more than a minute at a time either. But I'll make sure she knows you came by to check on her."

Andrea wiped away her tears, blew her nose in a tissue, and fluffed her blond hair higher. She straightened her curve-hugging sweater and gave them both a sheepish grin. "I just love that woman so much. You know?"

The question needed no response. They all felt the same and knew it. Andrea helped herself to coffee, then sat on the edge of one of the tables, glancing from Quint to Callee. She seemed braced for bad news as she pinned Quint with a serious expression. "So, what's going to happen to Big Sky Pie? Are you shutting it down?"

A dropped eggshell would have sounded like a cannon in the silence that followed, Callee thought. She wondered at Quint's momentary hesitation and jumped in to answer, "We're looking for a pastry chef."

"Oh?"

"Yeah," Quint said. "I promised Mama I'd keep her planned opening for next week, but I'm not sure that's realistic, given my inexperience with running a café and take-out counter. Long answer short, I'll do my best to launch this place. Somehow."

Andrea said, "I'll be here to help."

Callee tapped her pen on the journal, and asked, even though she knew better, "I don't suppose you've learned to bake pies since I moved to Seattle?"

Andrea glared at her. "The only thing I can bake are no-bake cookies. But, hey, where's Rafe?"

"We haven't seen or heard from him," Quint said.

"That's strange," Andrea said, glancing at the clock. "He's usually very punctual. Always here by the time I show up."

Quint frowned. "Then he should have been here by now, right?"

Andrea nodded, but looked as though she were think-ing about something. "You know, he was pretty shaken up when Molly grabbed her chest and collapsed. He mut-tered something in Spanish that sounded like *Madre de's ass*, whatever that means, and ran out the back door."

"Well, hell. What's Rafe's number?" Relief eased Quint's tense expression. "Mama says he doesn't know how to make pies yet, but he's better than nothing."

Callee sipped her coffee, wondering if that were true. Molly had led her to believe Rafe was only doing grunt work—like pitting cherries, peeling apples, washing dishes, and cleaning up. "Andrea, did you see him making pies?"

"No."

"Still," Quint said, obviously not letting anyone rain

on his parade, "I want to see for myself what he can and can't do."

"He doesn't speak much English." Andrea made a face of uncertainty. "I don't speak Spanish. Do either of you?"

"Not enough to make conversation." Callee stood and crossed her arms. "Quint, you took Spanish in high school. Do you recall any of it?"

"Some," Quint said, but judging by his frown, she doubted what he remembered would suffice. They might need an interpreter. She sensed another disaster in the making and wanted to scream. If something didn't start going right soon, she would never get out of this town.

Andrea started for the kitchen. "Rafe's phone number is in the office. I'll go call him."

"Good." Callee turned to Quint. "I've found a couple of employment agencies online, but I can't tell from their websites whether or not they handle restaurant help. I'm going to call." Callee settled back into the booth with a fresh cup of coffee and determination.

"Okay. I have Mama's personal phone book. I think I'll contact some of her friends and see if any of them can give me some leads." Quint sat back down at the table where he'd left his phone, whistling softly. "Maybe by the end of the day we'll have secured a new pastry chef."

"Ask for an assistant pastry chef while you're at it." Andrea stood in the doorway to the kitchen, cringing like a messenger about to be shot for delivering bad news.

Quint stared at her as though he couldn't decide if she were joking or serious. He chuckled. "Not funny, Lovette."

Andrea made a face and sighed. "Not joking, McCoy."

His expression went stormy. "What do you mean? Where's Rafe?"

"Good question. The phone number he gave us is disconnected."

Quint swore. "Where does he live? I'll go get him and drag his butt in here if I have to."

Andrea winced. "I looked up the address on his employment application just now, and it's an empty parking lot."

Chapter Four

$\sim$

Quint felt like a man buried beneath a pile of bricks, and every now and then, someone passed by and loaded on a few dozen more. *Not down one pastry chef, but two* Not to mention his real estate business in the toilet.

What the hell was he going to do? This was another complete fuckup. He went outside to the front parking lot. He needed to cool off. Get a grip on his emotions. Figure out what to do next. He'd been running on shock and fear, his brains scrambled like the hotel eggs he'd eaten earlier. How did a guy handle so much shit hitting the fan at the same damned time?

His phone rang. For one fleeting moment, he hoped it was one of his fishing buddies giving him an excuse to run to his storage unit for his rod and reel. But sanity returned the next moment. No more running away to fish. No more delaying responsibilities and problems. Face them down. Deal with them.

Fortunately, it wasn't a fishing buddy. It was Dave the Realtor. "Not a good time, Dave."

"I understand, man. I heard about your mama. How's she doing today?"

"Better. But like I said, this is not a good time."

"Well...of course...I could call later, but, you see, the thing is, I might have someone who wants your house. They're only in town through today though. Moving here from Texas. I've shown them a bunch of stuff already, but what they're describing sounds like your place. And they're prequalified and want a quick closing. All-cash deal."

Quint felt the weight of a few more bricks cracking his rib cage.

"What do you say? All I need is your signature on the listing renewal."

Quint stared at his boots, at a small pile of pebbles near the tip of one Dan Post. He kicked the pile and watched it scatter. It was like his life...his hold on everything he knew scattering away from him. His sigh sounded like a scream of agony inside his head.

"Okay. I'll be here at the..." He'd started to say office, but his gaze flew to the sign. Big Sky Pie. Damn. He glanced up and down the street, then back at the sign. He struggled for control. Of something. Anything.

"Quint, you still there?"

"Yeah." His gaze steadied on the pie shop. He was going to need to be here for a few weeks. At least. And he also needed to do something about resurrecting his real estate business. Since cloning himself was out, it seemed like he had but one other option. He sighed. "I'm where my office used to be."

"Oh, I just heard your mama turned that into a pie shop. Man, I'll bet that was a surprise, huh?"

Quint didn't answer. Dave made a gulping noise, then blundered on. "I'll swing by in a few for your John Hancock."

Quint hung up, his mind back on the problem at hand. He'd stayed locked in a time warp while everything and everyone he cared about moved on without him. He understood now that he had to face his father's loss by dealing with his regrets and guilt, by taking back control of his life, starting with small things, small decisions.

He entered the pie shop. Andrea and Callee sat in the end booth discussing whether or not Rafe might be an illegal alien.

Quint had been feeling like an alien in his own country, in his own skin, but that was about to change. He strode up to the booth and braced his palms on the table. "Ladies, I have a plan." The call about the house seemed to have cleared his head. It was time to start killing grizzlies. "I'm going to commandeer this booth to temporarily run my real estate business. Once Big Sky Pie is operating efficiently, I'll choose another location for my new office. For now, though, I intend to use this booth to meet clients and potentials, make calls, et cetera. That way, I'll be on hand to manage this place."

"You're going to try and run two businesses at the same time?" Callee shook her head. "Don't you think you should concentrate on this one for now?"

"What choice do I have?" Quint didn't expect an answer. He knew what he had to do. "Right, Lovette?"

Andrea got up and went for more coffee. Once she'd

filled her cup, she released a huge breath and faced Quint, her cheeks a guilty pink. "Uh, I'm not sure I work for McCoy Realty any longer."

"What are you talking about?" Quint couldn't believe she'd say that, let alone think it. "Of course you still work for McCoy Realty. Just because we lost the office space doesn't mean—"

"It's not that simple," Andrea said, setting her mug on the checkout counter. "When your mother took over this building, it was with the understanding that you'd be back in two weeks, and we could relocate the real estate office into one of her other buildings."

"Why didn't you just choose one of them then?" Quint strode to the coffeepot to refill his mug. She knew what would suit their purposes better, almost more than he did. "I would have been good with whatever you chose."

"Oh, no. Don't put this on me." Two red spots sprouted on Andrea's cheeks, and her eyes narrowed. "It's not my fault you didn't know about this. You weren't answering my calls or my texts."

"I'm not blaming you for losing the office." Or for the lack of business. That was all on his head. "But I will resurrect McCoy Realty at a new location. And you will always have a job with me."

Andrea shoved her hair behind one ear. "I appreciate that, but meanwhile, what was I supposed to do?"

She had Quint there.

Before he said anything, she hurried on. "Molly said evicting the realty office, and you not returning immediately to relocate, shouldn't leave me caught between a rock and a hard place. She offered me a job as assistant manager for Big Sky Pie—with the proviso that I could choose which of you I wanted to be my boss once you'd returned."

Quint was taken aback. *Damn, did I do something to piss Mama off?* She had not only robbed his prime location, she'd jacked his office manager as well. But actually, Andrea did more than manage his office; she *was* his office. She knew everything about his everything where real estate was concerned. She was irreplaceable.

Quint shrugged in an "isn't it obvious who you should work for" gesture. "Well, I'm back."

"What is that supposed to mean?" Callee asked, butting into the conversation. The question felt like a challenge.

Quint clenched his jaw, afraid he might say something he'd regret, and God knew there was a lot he already regretted. He spoke to Andrea. "It means you still have your job with me. After all, this pie shop isn't even up and running yet. Seems to me your choice is simple."

Andrea and Callee exchanged one of those female glances that usually ended up being bad news for him. His mouth went a little dry. He glanced from one to the other. "What?"

"Technically," Callee said, exiting the booth and bracing her backside against its table, arms folded. "Neither business is 'up and running' at this point."

"But, at least, the pie shop is almost ready to launch." Andrea huffed. "Those other buildings need work."

"Yeah," Callee added. "So, even if you selected one of them this afternoon, Quint, it would still be a while before you could do any real business there."

"Thank you for pointing out the obvious." His voice came out in a low growl.

Callee gave him a "someone had to do it" look.

Quint turned his attention to Andrea. "Does this mean you'd rather work for Mama, Lovette?"

"I'm not sure," Andrea said. She bit her lower lip, something she often did when she hated to tell him something. "I'm weighing the pros and cons."

God, he had to make her see reason. He could not lose the one true asset his realty business had. "If it's more money you're after, you could always get your Realtor's license. That would put you on a whole new tier of income, and hey, you could even close deals if I'm out of town for some reason."

"Some reason like...fishing?" Callee's tone was icy.

Quint spun around and met her gaze. Her stony look threw him off balance, stirring his own anger. "I can go fishing if and when I want to."

"And you seem to always want to." Callee shifted into a defensive stance, legs spread, spine stiff.

Quint stifled his temper. This was not an argument he could defend and win. He brought the subject back to Andrea. "This isn't about fishing. It's about Lovette."

"Yes, it is," Callee said. "She has two little boys. She can't be running all over the place, all hours of the day and night and on weekends. Selling real estate isn't a nine-to-five job."

Where had she gotten that idea? Of course...from him. She must believe that the crazy hours he'd put into building the real estate office were hours all Realtors had. That just was not true. "Lovette can schedule her showings around her home life."

"Like you did?" Callee snapped.

He blanched. He'd chosen to be available on nights

and weekends, but knew better than to say that out loud. She might think he'd chosen to not spend time with her. Not true. Damn it all. He'd been securing a solid future for them. He thought that she knew that and was okay with the sacrifices required.

Instead, though, she must have felt she was second or even third on his priority list. Guilt and anger tangled in his gut. He grappled with his temper, but heard his annoyance as he said, "Why don't we let Lovette decide what she wants to do?"

"Because she—"

"Whoa! Time. Out." Andrea cut Callee off, her tone suggesting a ref who'd blown a whistle at a football game and was about to penalize both teams. "I think one or both of you should update me on what is going on with this pie shop."

"I told you," Quint said, taking a deep breath and reining in his ire. "I'm keeping it open."

She glanced at Callee, eyes narrowed. "But why are you here? I mean, I get that you're still in Kalispell because of Molly, but why are you *here*?" She spread her arms, indicating the pie shop.

Callee's cheeks glowed bright red. "I, er, I made a sort of promise to Molly."

"To help Quint open the pie shop?" Andrea gave a shake of her head, clearly perplexed by the idea that Molly would make such a request.

"Oh, it's even worse than that. I promised her that I'd take her place as the head pastry chef until she is well enough to return."

Andrea's eyes widened, and she burst out laughing. "I'm sorry, but you? Make pies? Molly did not ask you to take her place. This is a joke, right?"

"I wish." Callee explained what had happened, how upset Molly had gotten. "I would have promised her to jump hoops down Front Street to get her to calm down."

"So, until Molly is out of the woods and you find a pastry chef, the two of you are supposed to coexist in this pie shop?"

"Yes," Callee said, lifting her chin as if to say "it's no big deal" and cutting her liquid green eyes to Quint as though expecting him to concur. Was that what she wanted? He wasn't sure. He'd once been able to read her expressions, but she seemed to have developed a shield against him.

He added a weak "That's the plan."

"Good luck with that," Andrea muttered.

"We can do it." Quint felt a sudden need to assure them, but he needed the assurance more than anyone. He'd thought he and Callee were doing fine today until she blew up about his fishing and then butted into his attempts to hang onto his employee.

"The trick will be to find a pastry chef quickly," Callee said. "Then I'll be out of Quint's hair."

Quint didn't like the sound of that. He didn't want Callee out of his hair...even if she was touchy as hell about some things. "And once Mama's had the bypass surgery and is recovering, she'll understand that Callee can't put her plans on hold indefinitely."

"Well, just in case none of that happens..." Andrea sounded like a teacher addressing a couple of naïve Pollyannas. "I suggest you two lay down a few ground rules, since bickering isn't good for business."

With that, Andrea turned toward the kitchen.

Quint called after her, "Lovette, we didn't settle who you're working for—"

She stopped and faced him. "McCoy, Callee made some valid points. I need to work hours that are compatible with being a single mom. My boys come first. Before real estate sales or pie sales."

"What does that mean?"

"It means that for now, I work for you *and* Molly. I'll do what is required for both businesses... within reason."

Quint knew a fair compromise when he heard it. She was right. Her kids deserved the best their mama could give them. The same as he'd had. He nodded. "Okay, I can accept that."

For now.

"Whether I end up taking the job here or with you in the realty office," she said, "will depend on how this venture turns out. But as long as I have a job and don't have to move in with my mom, I'm good. Do you have any idea how humiliating that would be?"

An image of his office stored in his mother's unheated garage flashed before his eyes. Quint shuddered. He totally understood. "As humiliating as having your mother turn your office into a pie shop?"

"Yeah, that," Andrea said. "Callee, have you phoned any of those employment agencies yet?"

"The number for one was disconnected, and the line was busy for the other. Must be a small agency."

Andrea said, "I'm going into Molly's office. I'll tackle some realty business calls. Let the loyal few know that we're still operating and where and that we're moving into something bigger and better very soon."

"Ask them if they know any pastry chefs while you're at it," he said. "And thank you."

"Meanwhile"—Andrea cast a serious gaze at both of them—"you two might want to work on those ground rules."

Quint felt Callee's gaze on him and knew she was still angry, but he didn't know what to say. And he didn't want to argue anymore either. "I don't know about you, but I could sure use a piece of Mama's sweet cherry pie about now."

Callee mumbled something under her breath, gathering her phone and heading toward the kitchen. "I need some air. Don't follow me."

What? Quint watched her retreating backside, torn between following and admiring the view. The view won out. What had he said? Why would wanting a piece of pie piss her off? Women. He didn't understand them at all. Moments like this, he really could have used his dad's counsel.

He sank onto the bench seat of the end booth. His gaze fell to the table, to Callee's journal. He touched the edge of it, the smooth leather soft against his fingertip. He'd seen her jotting in it often enough during their marriage, but he'd never read it, nor asked her what she wrote. He figured that was private or she would have shared it with him. The urge for pie hit even harder.

Gravel crunching out front announced a car pulling up. He went to the window. Dave the Realtor. He hurried toward the door hoping neither woman had heard the car and would come to investigate. He didn't want Callee to find out about the listing renewal or the possible buyers. He didn't want to get her hopes up that she'd be getting some extra cash soon, in case it didn't happen.

He was only gone a minute. Two at most. He came back into the pie shop to find Callee near the counter. She moved toward the window. "Who was that?"

Guilt tripped through him. He blocked her view. If she'd seen Dave's sky blue Cadillac, she would have known who it was without asking. "Someone asking about Mama."

It wasn't a lie. Dave had asked about his mother.

"I tried the employment agency again. Still busy." She walked toward him. "Do you have your list?"

"List?"

"Of ground rules...?" She seemed about to lose her temper again. She had her arms crossed over her chest, a sign that she was closed off to him. But all it did was draw his attention to her breasts. Try as he might to quell images of her naked, he felt his grip on self-control slipping southward, hunger pooling in his groin. Every rule he might have come up with sank into a black chasm of lust. He thought about grabbing her. Kissing her.

"Andrea is right. We need to maintain some civility or I can't work here."

Her threat to leave cooled his jets like a sudden hailstorm. He motioned to the booth where she'd left her journal. "You want to write these down?"

"I don't think so. My list is short." She ticked the points with her fingers. "No sexual innuendoes. No touching. No kissing. Break these rules, and I'm gone."

It was like she'd read his mind. Picked up on his lustful thoughts. But now that she'd said no kissing, all he could think about was kissing her. He stared at her lush red lips, craving a taste. "Is that all?"

"Don't make this any more difficult than it is. Okay?"

She was all lady warrior. Her expression screamed she'd taken down more powerful enemies than him. Instead of warding him off, her fierceness reignited the fire in his blood.

"What are your rules?" she asked, impatience causing a scowl.

He made a face and raked her curves with a smoldering gaze. *No sexy clothes. No dating other men. No divorce.* "Present a united front when dealing with employees."

Her chin came up, and her gaze locked with his. "Even when I think you're wrong?"

"Yep." He tilted his head and grinned. "You're here temporarily, but I'm the boss. I can't run this pie shop effectively without my employees' respect."

She considered that and then nodded. "Fair enough. Anything else?"

"No." *Nothing I can say out loud without starting World War III.* "I'd shake on it, but I'm not supposed to touch you."

"And don't forget it."

He changed the subject. "Why don't you try that employment agency again?"

"Good idea." She sank into the booth with a fresh cup of coffee, flipped through the journal at her notes, and dialed. Apparently someone had answered. He heard her explain why she was calling, mumble, "Okay, I see, and thank you." Then she hung up, shaking her head. "No luck there. They deal mostly in office staff or medical professionals."

He felt discouraged, not sure what to do. "I don't know where else to look."

She tapped the pencil on the phone. "We could always do it the old-fashioned/new-fashioned way. Advertise in newspapers and on the Internet."

"Great idea." He sank into the booth and snatched a piece of paper and pencil and made some notes. "I'll have Andrea place ads in the *Flathead Beacon, Daily Inter Lake*, and any online place that seems appropriate."

"If she'll come up with the ad, I'll hunt down some websites."

Discouragement crept away. He and Callee made a great team. Why hadn't he appreciated that when they *were* a team? "Will you sit in on the question-and-answer part of the interviews for the potential hires, then take charge during the kitchen testing?" He set the pencil aside and glanced at her green eyes. He loved the color, a deep emerald with flecks of gray. "You'll know if someone really is what their résumé claims. I won't."

"I don't know about that, but sure. Of course. Absolutely." She stretched and yawned. Her breasts thrust upward against her soft red sweater. He noticed, admired, and remembered how soft, yet firm those breasts were, then forced his gaze higher and caught her eyeing him with disapproval. He shrugged. "Your rules didn't include *No Looking*."

Callee's mouth tightened and her cheeks reddened. "The sooner we get Molly a pastry chef, the sooner I can leave for Seattle."

Quint's good feeling vanished.

Callee gave a toss of her chestnut hair, scenting the air with an aroma reminiscent of ripe peaches, and he wondered if he would ever be able to eat another peach without thinking of her. He distracted himself by asking, "How is Roxanne?"

"Busy. She really needs me there." Callee sighed. "She has some big event she's landed, and I'd love to help her pull it off."

He thought about the house, about it being the final thread that connected them, about the very real possibility that it was sold. It wouldn't be soon enough for her. It would be too soon for him. "What if we start calling everyone we know who can bake, and everyone they know who can bake? And hope for the best."

Quint ripped the page with his notes for the ad from her journal, took the paper to Andrea, and was back in a couple of minutes. He returned to the table near the bay windows and started to dial one of his mother's friends.

Call-waiting interrupted. It was Mama's cardiologist. He answered, listened, and gasped. "On my way."

Chapter Five

W hat is it?" Callee cut short the call she'd been making and scooted out of the booth.

"Mama. She's worse." Quint's face was ashen. "Gotta get to the hospital."

"Not without me." She grabbed her purse, heart in her throat as she hurried after him.

Quint stopped at the door. He seemed glad she wanted to go with him...for all of a second, then he shook his head. "No. You better not. The doctor said it was something to do with Big Sky Pie. That she's having a bunch of anxiety about it."

"Did she have another heart attack?" Callee feared his answer and couldn't keep from touching his chest as though she hadn't decreed a "No Touch" rule. His heart thudded beneath her palm.

"No." His hand covered hers, clung to it, needing to know he wasn't facing whatever was to come alone. "But the doctor is concerned some new anxiety she's having will bring on another attack."

"Then let's go."

He shook his head, dropped her hand, and stepped back. "If her stress is about the pie shop, I don't think seeing all of us rushing to the hospital is going to calm her down. She's more likely to immediately imagine she's in trouble and then she will be. The idea is to relieve her anxiety. I need to assure her that you and Andrea are taking care of pie shop business."

"Okay," Callee relented, accepting the situation. She wouldn't risk upsetting Molly. "Then go, but text me as soon as you can. Okay?"

"I will." With that, Quint hurried out the front door, the jangle of the bell jarring Callee's last nerve. She should get back on the phone and make more calls, but she couldn't deal with another false lead at the moment, not with her stomach in knots. What she wanted was to walk to her hotel room, check out, and hit the road for Seattle, putting her own stress behind her. As if that would help. *What if Molly had another heart attack as I was running away? What if Quint couldn't reach me? What if I couldn't get back in time?*

What if Molly dies? Callee felt cold to the bone. She strode into the kitchen and out the back door, gulping in fresh air like it was a scarce commodity. Sunshine did nothing to warm the chill at her core. She walked off the relentless nerves, pacing the small parking area until she could breathe without shaking, until the iciness began to subside and her unshed tears receded.

Panicking about Molly wasn't helping anything.

Finding a pastry chef for the pie shop would, though.

Callee went back inside, and as she approached the office she heard Andrea talking. "Yes. Everything is going as planned. He should be there soon." A pause, and then she continued. "A minor brouhaha, but I'm hopeful. So you take care of yourself—" She broke off as if she realized Callee was just outside the doorway. "Gotta run."

Frowning, Callee peered around the corner. "Who were you talking to?"

"Um, my mom." Andrea sat at a small desk, amid a sea of sticky notes and invoices, staring at a laptop computer. "The boys had an argument this morning, and I wanted to give her a heads-up in case they started in again while she's sitting for them tonight."

"Oh." That hadn't sounded like what Callee had overheard, but it was none of her business. She glanced around the cubbyhole office and decided there should be a sign on the wall: MAXIMUM CAPACITY = 2 PEOPLE. One seated, one standing. The space was more like a high-ceilinged walk-in closet than an office. Every inch was jam-packed. Wall shelves held office supplies and recipe books, as well as an all-in-one printer/fax/copier. "You going out tonight?"

"Oooh, yeah. Mommy has a playdate scheduled with one sexy cowboy." Andrea's gaze remained on the computer, on whatever she was doing, but Callee heard the smile in her voice. "My long dry spell is just about over, and let me tell you, I am more than ready for some adult male attention."

Boy, could Callee relate. "Hot guy, huh?"

"Burn the house down." Andrea laughed, then she shoved her thick, blond hair behind one ear and glanced at Callee. "Okay, the ads are placed, and I've been trying to clear up some of the other paperwork. Any leads from the cold calls yet?"

"I haven't made but one," Callee said.

"Why not?" Andrea frowned. "Say, what's going on? You look ill."

"Molly's doctor called Quint. She's upset about something."

Andrea frowned. "Then why didn't you go with him?"

Callee explained. "Quint wants us here, manning the fort. He'll phone if that changes. For now, he's gone to reassure her and do whatever he can to get her to stop fretting over this shop. She won't believe we have things under control if we all show up. You know how she is."

Andrea sank back onto the chair. "Too clever by half."

"Absolutely." Callee gestured toward the laptop. "Any e-mail responses to the ads yet?"

"It's too early for that. I'm thinking folks will look later today, after work or tonight."

"Probably so."

A knock on the back door startled both women. Andrea said, "Hey, maybe that's someone answering the ad now."

Her little joke broke the tension gripping Callee. She smiled at her friend. "Hah. Or maybe it's Rafe."

"You wish."

The knocking grew louder, and Callee's phone began to vibrate, too. As they strode into the kitchen, Callee read the text from Quint. "Quint just arrived at the hospital."

"Good." Andrea headed to the door.

Through the windows that overlooked the back parking area, Callee spied a big-busted woman with bigger brunette hair peering in. "Are you expecting a delivery?"

"No. It's Sharla Tucker," Andrea said. "She's the new Chamber of Commerce events coordinator. Wonder what she wants?"

Callee replied to Quint's text, only half listening to Andrea say something about commerce. "Could she be here over something to do with the pie shop's city business license?"

"No." Andrea crossed to the door. "City business licenses aren't required in Montana. We have a state license, and we're approved by the Flathead County Health Department. Besides, Sharla only handles events."

Events? Callee glanced up as Andrea opened the door and greeted their visitor. "Good afternoon, Sharla."

"Andrea," Sharla said, flashing a woman-on-a-mission smile. Her clothes were also flashy—a leopard print blouse, gold pencil skirt, and scuffed, squat-heeled pumps. Her shoulder bag was the size of a mini-suitcase. She had big features—big eyes, big nose, big mouth—to go with her big bust and big hair. Somehow, it all worked together. She was striking. Except for the shoes, which seemed to hint that this was a person who took care of the big picture but not the telling details.

Sharla said, "May I come in?"

"We aren't officially open yet," Callee said, offering her a smile.

"Well, goodness, I know that. Just the same..." She shoved past both women and into the kitchen like a blast of wind that would blow wherever it chose. She stopped just inside the door and gasped in appreciation. "Oh my, this is so lovely. Last time I was here, they were still installing the cabinets. None of this was done. I must say, I would love a mini-version of this in my own kitchen—if

I liked to cook, which I do not—but it would so impress for special events, wouldn't it?"

"It is incredible," Callee agreed.

"Sharla, I don't know if you and Callee have met yet." Andrea stepped in and offered introductions. "Callee is Quint's wife."

Only for twenty more days, Callee thought. Although in fact, she was already no longer Quint's wife. They weren't living together, or sleeping together; they'd split their mutual belongings into individual possessions, and she'd returned his ring. "It's nice to meet you, Sharla."

Andrea said, "What brings you here today?"

"Well, goodness, I heard about Molly," Sharla said. "Guess the whole town has. How is she doing?"

"Better." *God, let that be so.* By now, Quint would be exuding his two-hundred-kilowatt McCoy charm and, hopefully, calming his mother with the same power as a giant Valium. "Thank you for asking."

"Oh, my, that's wonderful news."

"It is," Andrea chimed in, her smile looking forced.

Callee glanced at her phone, hoping for another text. Nothing. It was too soon. *The man needed time to work his magic.* Callee started to suggest they all go into the café and discuss whatever Sharla wanted over cups of coffee, but she reconsidered. What if something involving Molly required rushing to the hospital? Instead, she went to the Sub Zero and pulled out a couple of bottles of water, setting them on the counter. "Anyone?"

"No, thank you." Sharla stepped to the center island and plopped her gigantic handbag down. Andrea retrieved one of the water bottles, opened it, and took a swig.

"Did you get that text yet?" Andrea asked Callee.

Callee opened her own bottle of water and shook her head. "Not yet."

"Well, goodness, you're obviously busy. I should stop wasting your time and get down to business." Sharla glanced from one to the other. They were standing around the work island as if it were a conference table.

"What business?" Andrea asked.

Sharla touched her big hair. "This year I've initiated a new event to show appreciation for our local Kalispell businesses in the form of a buffet luncheon. Several of the local restaurants and bakeries are providing the food. It's a great opportunity for social networking with other members of the community and to get your company noticed among your peers. Word of mouth and all. An especially good chance for a fledgling business."

Callee listened, intrigued, seeing possibilities. She suspected that advertising like this would have wider-reaching potential than even Sharla realized. The Chamber of Commerce's new events coordinator deserved kudos for coming up with the idea. Callee took a drink of water. The event signified what she loved about being a Montanan. The state was more than the beautiful mountains, the vast prairies, and the wide rivers; it was the people with hearts as big as the sky, always friendly, always supporting one another. A piece of her soul would always live here, no matter where she lived.

Andrea gave a shake of her head and light danced off her earring, catching Callee's attention, and prompting her to ask, "Are you asking Big Sky Pie to participate?"

"Well, goodness, no," Sharla said. "You're already committed to the event."

"We are?" Callee looked at Andrea for confirmation.

She gave a slight shake of her head and a clueless shrug. "Must have been something Molly did without telling me."

"Okay." If Molly wanted to have the pie shop in this event, then who was Callee to say otherwise? She nodded with enthusiasm. "Then sure, we're in. Oh, when exactly is this event?"

"Not for three weeks."

Plenty of time to secure a pastry chef...or two, Callee was certain. It felt great having something going right for a change.

"We're holding the luncheon in the mall," Sharla said. "Hoping to kill two birds with one stone. This economy has been tough on retail, and a few of the small businesses have folded. It would be great if this event attracts new renters."

Yep, definitely a community that pulled together. Callee nodded. "I'm glad you stopped in to let us know about it. Quint will appreciate the heads-up."

Providing he doesn't get distracted with a big real estate deal or the opening of fishing season. Worry nibbled through the good feeling. He wouldn't do that, would he? But she knew he might. He'd proven that to her again and again.

Sharla shoved a slip of paper in her direction, explaining the buffet positioning for each participant in the luncheon event.

Callee listened with half an ear. Her mind was back on Quint. On Molly. She realized Sharla was looking at her, awaiting a response. She enthused as though she'd actually been paying attention. "It looks good."

"Oh, but the big event is not why I'm here." Sharla stuffed the papers back into her enormous handbag.

"Oh?" Andrea and Callee said in unison.

"No. I'm here about the pre-event."

"What exactly is that?" Andrea lifted her hair from her neck, then let it fall back to her shoulders. It was a nervous gesture Callee had seen whenever she was anxious about something. The something at the moment was probably how Molly was doing. Why didn't Quint text?

Callee set her water bottle on the counter, trying to keep her mind off Molly and on what Sharla was saying. This was all she could do for Quint's mother at the moment. So, concentrate.

"Well, goodness," Sharla said, "It's a tasting event. Dinner, actually. At the mayor's ranch. Participants will bring the dishes they would like to provide for the big event. Chamber members, their spouses, and of course, the business owners and their spouses will imbibe and decide which dishes they'd like served at the luncheon."

Callee's phone vibrated. A text from Quint. Finally. *All's well.* Relief slid through her. She tried to signal Andrea.

But Andrea was eyeing Sharla like a shark eyes a baby seal. "If they don't like certain dishes, will those businesses be eliminated from the big event?"

Sharla gave a slight nod, as though she feared Andrea might take a bite out of her if she didn't give the correct response. "Well, goodness, that depends on whether or not there are negative reviews. And just how negative the reviews are."

"When is this pre-event?" Callee asked, buoyed by the text and anxious to share the good news with Andrea.

"In two days."

"Two days?" Callee's happy feeling withered like berries in the boiling sun. Without a pastry chef, this deadline was impossible, and yet, if they passed on the pre-event, they would be disqualified from the main event. Damn. What would Quint want her to do? What would Molly do?

"Yes, two days. Well, goodness, you can see why I scooted on over here as soon as I heard about Molly's health issue." She took a big breath, puffing up her big chest, and Callee swore it puffed her big hair a bit bigger also. "Ladies, do I need to find a replacement for Big Sky Pie?"

"Replacement?" Andrea said. "Who do you have in mind?"

But Callee didn't care who Sharla had in mind. After weighing the pros and cons, she realized she needed to err on the side that was best for the pie shop. This was too good of an opportunity for Big Sky Pie to pass up. You couldn't buy this kind of publicity. And it was being offered for free.

Callee ignored the tiny voice in her head shouting, *But you haven't found a pastry chef!* She'd think about that later. "We have no intention of bowing out, Sharla. Molly set up contingencies for emergencies. Count Big Sky Pie in."

Andrea's mouth dropped open. Callee ignored her.

Sharla made a delighted squeal. "Well, goodness, that is a relief. Then I will see you and that sexy hubby of yours on Thursday night—with a variety of five or six pies, right?"

"Right." Wait. What? Sharla expected to see her and

Quint? Together? Callee's stomach flip-flopped. It was one thing to work with him in the pie shop for Molly's sake, but quite another to attend a dinner together. What if people knew about their divorce and asked embarrassing questions?

Chapter Six

Once Sharla was backing out of the parking lot, Andrea dug her fingers through her hair and gave Callee a what-were-you-thinking look. "Woman, you better hope someone answers that ad immediately, can start right away, and is every bit the pie maker that Molly is. Oh my God, how is Molly? Have you heard from Quint yet?"

"He texted about five minutes ago. He got her calmed down."

"Yes!" Andrea threw her head back as a breath whooshed from her. A second later, she was frowning at Callee again. "But who'll calm *him* down when he hears you've committed the pie shop to both events, and one of them in two days?"

Would he be upset? Or would the two-day deadline be the kind of challenge he loved? Or, what if it was one task too many on top of the stress of his mother's heart attack? "Five or six pies isn't that much."

"Says she who can't even bake *one* pie." Andrea scrubbed her face, then offered a sympathetic smile.

Callee grimaced. Two days. Five or six pies. No pastry chef. Maybe she shouldn't have agreed to the pre-event, but she wanted desperately for Molly to see her dream of owning a successful pie shop become a reality. Somehow that was more important right now than even reaching her own goals.

To that end, she spent the afternoon calling and texting friends, fishing for leads to a pastry chef, and coming up empty. Quint had been at the hospital going on four hours. He'd texted to let her know that Molly was calm, but that he was going to stay and sit with her for a while. Callee was glad to see he had his priorities right for a change. She stood, stretched, and went to see what Andrea was doing.

"Any luck?" Andrea asked. She stood at the sink, cleaning out her coffee cup, but before Callee could respond, Andrea's cell phone rang. She answered, offered a few short responses, then said, "Okay. On my way."

Callee's first thought was Molly. Her heart clutched. "Was that Quint?"

"No. The boys' after-school sitter. Much as I'd like to stay and watch you wear a groove in the floor around the island, Logan is running a temperature. Wouldn't you know it? And me with the first sexy dinner date in a month. I need to pick up the boys right away and explain to Mom why they won't be spending the night. Then break my date." She heaved a sigh. "You have no idea how much I was looking forward to that dinner. *Especially dessert.*"

"I'm so sorry." Callee stopped pacing and gave her a

commiserating grin. "I'm long overdue for a little man-dessert myself."

Andrea nodded, as she pulled on her coat. "More than me, I figure."

"You have no idea, my friend." Callee took another swallow of cold water, as if that could douse the need that coursed through her veins for some serious male atten-tion. The kind Quint used to supply. The thought sent a thrill spiraling through her. "I don't suppose you can stay a few minutes more? Just until Quint returns."

Callee would rather not be alone with him, and not because he might be upset about the pre-event. Andrea offered another sympathetic smile. Callee was starting to hate those. "No. Logan needs me. When you're a mom, you'll understand."

Callee had once thought she and Quint would have kids, had even imagined a little boy with her eyes and Quint's smile, a little girl with his hair and her nose, but that was another dream gone. And now she was just grate-ful no child would be hurt in the divorce. "If I ever do have children, I hope I come close to being as terrific a mother as you."

"You'll be a great mom," Andrea said, patting her hand.

Considering her two role models, Callee hoped she landed somewhere in the middle. A warm, fun-loving, yet compassionate mother with an income that offered both herself and her child financial and physical security.

Andrea gathered the last of her things. "I'm sure Lo-gan will be fine in the morning. Kids often catch twenty-four-hour bugs. And maybe we'll have good news on the pastry chef front by then."

"From your lips to God's ears," Callee agreed, motioning her toward the door. "You better get home. I'll see you tomorrow."

After Andrea left, she locked the back door and lowered the blinds, readying the shop to close for the night. She was tired and hungry and looking forward to climbing into a hot bath and ordering whatever passed for room service, but a key in the front lock had the thought fleeing and her anxiety returning. The bell tingled, the door closed, and familiar footsteps approached.

Callee braced herself against the island, the hard surface offering physical support. Emotionally, she was on her own. She reminded herself that everything she'd done was for the pie shop. For Molly. Quint came into the kitchen, hair rumpled, eyes weary, but a wide grin on his incredible face.

"I take it that smile means your mother is doing better?"

"Definitely, better."

The taut muscles in her shoulders eased, and she realized everything that was going on with Molly, with the pie shop, and with Quint was also taking a toll on her. She noticed tiny lines around his eyes and wondered if he'd slept any better than she had last night. The last two days had been brutal, coming back to town, filing for the divorce, Molly's collapse. Two days. Damn. She had to tell him.

"Ah, Sharla Tucker was here earlier."

"Was she?"

Callee's mouth dried. She wiped damp palms on her jeans, watching his face as she said, "Apparently, your mother agreed to an event at the mall."

"Yeah, I know." He set his car keys on the counter behind him. "It was what had her so upset today."

Callee said a silent prayer. *He already knows about the luncheon. Thank you, Molly.*

"Mama was fit to be tied that she'd forgotten to tell Andrea about some of the upcoming events she's agreed to participate in." He shook his head and smiled. "You know how Mama is about obligations."

"What did you tell her?"

"That we would handle that and any other event she's booked. That calmed her right down."

"I'm glad. The event should be great for the shop's launch."

"I didn't tell Mama we'd honor the obligations." A sheepish grin warmed his eyes. "I said we'd *handle* the obligations. Not actually a lie. Tomorrow, Andrea can check the calendar for any commitments Mama's made, then phone and bow out of all of them or postpone them until we hire a pastry chef and an assistant pastry chef."

Hah. That's what you think. "If, and when, your mama discovers you've done that, there will be hell to pay. And you know it."

That wiped the smirk from his face.

She felt suddenly much better about agreeing to the pre-event, about not letting Quint get away with sloughing off jobs Molly wanted him to handle. "Besides, it's too late."

"What do you mean it's too late?"

"You weren't here, and Sharla was so persuasive that I didn't know what to do, so I made the decision based on what would be best for the shop in the long run. I told her we were definitely planning on keeping our commitment to the Chamber events."

"What?" He gaped, his mouth working faster than she could answer. "How? Why? What were you thinking?"

"There was no other choice. Sharla was going to replace Big Sky Pie." Callee stood straighter, shoulders squared, and looked him in the eye. *Just depersonalize your defense Don't use the pronoun "I." Just state the facts.* "This is an amazing, not-to-be-passed-up opportunity. It will introduce the pie shop to a huge audience on a level that an ad on television or the Internet or the newspapers can't do. This isn't just a mouthwatering photo op; it is an actual tasting event."

Her argument seemed to fall on deaf ears. His scowl grew more fierce, and his voice dropped into its lowest register. "Did you forget I don't have a pastry chef? Or even an assistant pastry chef?"

"That could change tomorrow."

"And if it doesn't?" He swore, then stormed outside, slamming the door. She heard his boots on the pavement, caught a few more curse words, then nothing. A minute passed. Two. Three. Four. He returned. His coloring was back to normal, his expression reasonable. His gaze settled on the wall clock.

He hadn't made up his mind, but he was in full-on thinker mode. She could see the wheels in his businessman's brain start churning as he considered every angle of the problem, weighed pros and cons, pluses and minuses. Finally he said, "Okay, okay. No need to panic. It is a great, no, *super* opportunity, and the event isn't for another three weeks. I will definitely have found someone before then."

Three weeks? Uh-oh. Callee grimaced. "You don't have that long."

He stopped grinning. "Why not?"

"Well, I guess Molly forgot to mention the pre-event."

"What pre-event?"

Callee explained about dinner at the mayor's ranch and that they were expected to show up with a variety of five or six pies for the guests to sample. "Apparently, everyone will be voting on the dishes served at the dinner, and the ones with the highest votes will be what is presented at the luncheon."

"Okay..." He waited for her to go on.

Her throat was dry. She reached for her water. "It takes place on Thursday night. *This* Thursday night."

"So that's why Mama tried to talk me into telling—" He broke off as though catching himself about to reveal a secret. He shook his head, running his hand through his hair, obviously seeking some solutions. "That's impossible. There's not enough time. Damn. Okay, don't panic. If we don't find a pastry chef by tomorrow night, I guess I'll just buy some pies."

She wanted to throttle him. "Oh my god, you are such a man."

That seemed to galvanize him. His gaze narrowed and grew dangerous and hot. "You used to like that about me, Callee."

She froze. Where had that come from? He'd dumped her—didn't want her—so why say something that suggested otherwise?

He exhaled loudly. "You should be applauding my resourcefulness."

"Where do you plan to get these pies? At Rosauer's, or Albertson's, or one of the bakeries in town?"

"Why not?"

She shook her head. "Like someone won't recognize you there and wonder why Molly McCoy's son is buying pies from anywhere other than his mother's new shop?"

His expression turned contrite. "Well, at least it's a plan of action. What brilliant ideas have you got to offer?"

"Not that we try to pass off store-bought pies as something original from Big Sky Pie."

"Why not? Who the hell will really know the difference by the time they get to dessert?"

"What?"

He went to the fridge and dug around until he found a carton of milk and drank straight from it.

Callee rolled her eyes. It was one thing for him to do that at home, but not in his place of business. She handed him a paper towel and a look of disapproval. He seemed to ignore the latter.

He wiped his mouth and put the milk away. "The mayor has the best bar in town. By the time dessert is served, everyone will be too tipsy to notice if the pies aren't up to Mama's usual standards."

Callee just glared at him. "Someone will notice."

"Who?"

"I don't know who, but Murphy's Law tells me it will happen and then what?"

"Okay, then I'll pick up some premade crusts, and you can make the fillings using Mama's recipes."

Her hands landed on her hips. She didn't try to keep the disgust she felt from her voice. "Premade crust? Have you tasted that stuff?"

"It can't be that bad or so many people wouldn't use it. Besides, no one eats crust."

Callee's mouth dropped open. She'd seen him down

his mother's piecrust like it was the best part of the pie—it was that delicious, that flaky. "You're representing your mother's business. Her *pie* business. What do you think will happen if she gets wind of you taking store-bought pies or crusts to the mayor's dinner party and pawning them off as something from her pie shop?"

He blanched. "Shit."

"Exactly." Callee needed to reel him in, to get his feet back on the ground and his head out of the quick-fix clouds. "Quint, you said yourself this is too good of an advertising opportunity to pass up. Think about what you'd be advertising."

He put his head in his hands and groaned. Mr. Easy Solution couldn't find one that worked. Would he do as she feared? Bail on his promise and run off to some river or lake and fish? Let his mother down completely?

He lifted his head and caught her staring at him. She blinked and glanced away. There didn't seem to be anything else to say. She should just grab her purse and head back to the hotel. "Maybe someone will answer one of the ads in the morning, someone who can bake a mean piecrust."

He didn't answer. He seemed to be mentally weighing something serious. She couldn't even guess what it might be. He said, "Didn't I see a few different kinds of pies in the fridge just now?"

"Those were samples your mother presented to Andrea and me yesterday." Just prior to her collapse. "She's thinking of putting them on the menu. They're fabulous. The recipes must be here somewhere. Andrea probably knows where."

He pulled the pies out of the Sub-Zero, placed them on

the island, and removed the protective covers. Callee set two plates and two forks on the counter, along with a pie server. She slid a sliver of each pie onto the plates and offered one to Quint. He thanked her and dug in.

"Since this will be the community's first introduction to Big Sky Pie, whatever is brought to the pre-event can make or break this shop's launch," Callee said around a bite of tar heel pie. "Whichever pies you decide to take to the mayor's dinner will need to look as good as they taste."

"They're pies," Quint said dismissively and stabbed a piece of key lime tart with his fork. "Everyone knows Mama's in the hospital. I figure they'll forgive presentation being less than perfect as long as the pies are delicious. And I gotta say, these are. Damn. Mama outdid herself."

"She always does. That's what people expect from her pies. Something they can't get anywhere else." She hated harping on the subject, but she had to make him understand whatever they took to these events represented his mother. "That means presentation and taste are equally important."

He nodded as though she was finally getting through to him. Good. The success or failure of the pie shop launch depended on him, and Molly was counting on him not to fail. So was she.

He snapped his fingers. "Oh, hey, I know where Mama's recipes are. I forgot she mentioned that today."

Callee munched a piece of Daiquiri pie, the smell of rum still as potent as it had been the day before, the flavor still as scrumptious. It melted in her mouth, along with a sigh of appreciation. She hated to spoil the moment with a negative thought, but she couldn't keep it to herself. "You realize if no one answers the ads by tomorrow night, that will leave us just one night to figure out how to get these pies done?"

"Us?"

Callee blushed. Had she actually said us? She had. "Don't take that wrong. I'm not volunteering to make pies." She chuckled. "That would be like you volunteering to make pies."

"What?" His fork froze halfway to his mouth. He looked as if she'd poked him. "Why did you say that?"

"I was kidding." Had he lost his sense of humor along with his dad? Or was he just slow-witted from worry and exhaustion?

"I knew that." He laughed, then ate more pie with the expression of a man mulling serious thoughts. "Do you think anyone has responded to the ads yet?"

She shrugged. "No one had before Andrea left, but that was over an hour ago."

He glanced at the clock, then pushed back from the pies. "Well, the average workday is over; most folks should be home by now. I'll go check if anyone is scouring the Internet for work in a pie shop."

While he went into the office, Callee returned the pies to the refrigerator and then carried their dishes and silverware to the sink. Quint returned as she was putting them into the dishwasher. She glanced up, hopeful. "Anything?"

"Nope." He walked toward her, plowing his hand through his hair. She wanted to suggest a haircut, but she used to cut his hair. He caught her gaze on his hair and grinned. "We probably won't hear from anyone until tomorrow."

She wished she shared his confidence, but Kalispell wasn't a big city like Seattle, or Spokane, or Billings. How many out-of-work pastry chefs could there be in the Flathead County unemployment pool? She didn't like the odds. "I know I'm repeating myself, but what if no one applies in time?"

He looked away and seemed to be staring at the pattern in the marble countertop, his brows knit. "If push comes to shove, would you be willing to fill in as an assistant pastry chef? All that involves is some prep work for the pie fillings and clean-up and stuff."

"As long as you don't try to cajole me into making dough."

"No. Believe me. I'd rather buy the premade." Quint grinned his teasing grin.

"Me too," she laughed, but Callee noticed whatever he'd been mentally weighing seemed to be getting heavier.

He made a tiny groan deep in his throat. He had the look of a pained man about to make a soul-shattering confession to his priest. "I, ah, I, oh God. I know someone who can make piecrusts almost as good as Mama."

Callee's eyes widened. "You know someone?"

He looked away, like he already regretted telling her.

Her temper sprang from its cage, and she fought the impulse to slug him. "You know someone? You had me on the phone frantically calling anyone and everyone and all the while you 'know someone'?"

"Maybe."

"Which is it?" Her voice came out in a low growl. "Maybe or definitely?"

"Definitely."

"Who?" His uneasy expression gave Callee pause.

Was this person a girlfriend? Her bad mood worsened. "Just tell me who it is."

He hesitated, and the distress in his eyes deepened to that of a tortured animal. "If I tell you, and you tell another living soul, I will have to hunt you down and kill you."

Huh? This was not the response she expected. She didn't understand. "Why? Is it a secret or something?"

"It is. And I need your promise that you won't share what I'm about to say with anyone. Not even Roxanne. Or Lovette. Okay?"

Was he kidding? Callee's patience thinned. "Who is it?"

"Promise me first that this stays between you and me."

Callee wanted to laugh at his cloak-and-dagger manner, but she could tell he was dead serious. She made a Scouts Honor sign, followed by her hand on her heart. "I promise. I won't tell anyone. Ever. Not even Roxanne. Or Andrea."

"Especially Andrea."

She glared at him. "Who is it?"

"Me."

Chapter Seven

⁓

Y ou?" Callee chuckled, her temper swallowed in a chasm of disbelief. She'd never seen Quint do anything in the kitchen except help himself to coffee or a meal someone else had prepared. "Since when?"

"Since I was a kid. I used to watch Mama making dough, and one day she let me help. It was like shaping clay. I had a knack for it. She showed me how to hone the skill. I got pretty darned good at it, if I do say so myself."

Callee felt gob-smacked. Molly had begged her to fill in at the pie shop as a pastry chef when she knew damn well Callee couldn't bake a pie, when she knew damn well her son could? What the hell? "Why is this the first I'm learning of this secret talent?"

He glanced away. "It's embarrassing."

"Seriously?" Did he even know the definition of embarrassing? Her temper flared anew. Telling your friends that your husband would rather fish than celebrate your wedding anniversary together was embarrassing. Telling your friends that your husband didn't want you anymore...that was embarrassing. But being able to bake a pie like his mother? That was a God-given talent that he should shout from the rooftops. She did not understand why this was a secret. "Is it that you think real men don't bake pies?"

"Well...yeah."

Her hands went to her hips. "There are a lot of famous male pastry chefs, I'll have you know."

"That's not the point." He mumbled, discomfort stark in his eyes.

Something in that look cut through her fury and raised a slew of insecurities about her own baking skills. Mrs. O'Reilly's home economics class flashed into her mind, and she groaned inwardly. She'd been full of junior high expectations, thinking to prove her grandmother wrong about her kitchen skills, and she'd learned to scramble eggs, make coffee, and could even bake a potato. And then came the pie class. Callee chose to make a peach pie, which had resulted in a lumpy crust and a soupy filling. Although Roxy had dried her tears and tried to console her, Mrs. O'Reilly's appalled expression lodged in Callee's head and reinforced every cooking criticism her grandmother ever laid on her. Callee had transferred classes and never learned to cook.

She sensed now that something similar had occurred to Quint, something that had left him with an indelible emotional wound. "What happened?"

"Nothing." He tried to shrug it off. "It was just, you know, junior high, and I began playing sports. No more time to bake pies. That's all."

She wouldn't feel this strong sense of empathy if that was all. She shook her head "No...there's more..."

He sighed. "I made the mistake of mentioning at basketball practice one day that I was helping Mama bake pies for the church bake sale. It was a charity event. The proceeds were going to sponsor a couple of needy families for Christmas dinner and presents."

As he remembered a smile appeared, and Callee realized he'd liked doing something for a family less fortunate than his. She pictured him as that teenage boy torn between being macho with his pals and doing something that many would consider unmanly. "It was a commendable cause."

"Yep. But I should have kept it to myself."

She sensed where this was headed. She knew firsthand exactly how cruel kids could be to one another. Having her grandmother as her only parent in grade school had brought out the bully in some of her classmates, but her mother had taught her that what others thought about her didn't matter as much as what she thought about herself. *Nobody can hurt you unless you let them.* Those words saw Callee through a lot of her grandmother's negative rhetoric. Just not all of it. "So your teammates started teasing you?"

He nodded. "They were brutal. Name-calling went on for weeks."

"And you never baked another pie..."

"Nope."

Callee couldn't speak. She'd never baked another pie either, until Molly tried to teach her, and that had been another disaster, but Quint had something she didn't. A talent. And he'd been wasting that talent.

Quint cleared his throat. "Long story short, I can probably be a temporary pastry chef if we can't find anyone else before tomorrow night. My skills are pretty rusty, but maybe it's like riding a bike. Once you know how, you never forget."

"I guess." Callee wouldn't know as she'd never had a bike. And her mind wouldn't stop reeling back to the question she needed answered. "Is that what your mother was trying to get you to tell me? That you could bake pies? If so, why did she insist I fill in for her when you were the obvious choice?"

He met her gaze, and she could see the reason made him squirm. "After what I've put her through since Dad died, I don't think she trusts me to follow through."

Any more than I do, Callee thought, having worried about exactly that. But that didn't excuse Molly or Quint for not telling her that Quint could bake pies. "So, in other words, your mother wanted me to be your babysitter?"

His neck turned the color of ketchup. "Hell no. But I wouldn't be surprised if she hoped we might…you know."

Callee didn't know for a few seconds, and then she recalled the odd phone conversation she'd overheard Andrea having and suddenly even that made sense. "She's playing matchmaker? Hoping we'll kiss and make up?"

He looked as though he didn't think that was such a bad idea, and something inside her leaped with joy, while something else screamed at her to run as far and as fast as she could. "Give me one good reason why I shouldn't walk out that door, check out of the hotel, and start for Seattle right this minute."

Quint swore. "Please don't do that. I need you."

Callee just looked at him. "I needed you once, too, but that didn't seem to matter to you."

"I was an ass." His face was awash in sincerity, his voice husky. "I would give anything to go back and do things differently."

She didn't believe him. Couldn't risk believing him. She shook her head, fighting tears, feeling betrayed by him and by Molly.

"I promised to keep my distance. I swear I will honor that." He crossed his heart. "Besides…can you really walk away with Mama as ill as she is?"

That was the question, and she'd already answered it. Even if Molly hadn't tricked her into staying and working at the pie shop with Quint, she was going to stay until Molly had surgery.

"Callee, I really do need your help to find a pastry chef. I don't want to bake pies for a living. I'm not comfortable with anyone else knowing I can bake a pie."

Callee walked to the sink, her mind churning. He'd kept this old skeleton in his closet as though it were a murder he'd committed, not even comfortable enough to confess the secret sin to his wife. Quint's reluctance to broadcast his ability to bake pies might seem preposterous to some, but Callee had a different perspective on it. The only one who knew she was going to give cooking school another try was Roxy, and if she failed this time, no one else needed to know. If and when Quint wanted to share his "secret" skill with the world, he would reveal it, not her.

She made up her mind. She would stay, would help Quint, but only because Molly needed her to. She faced him. "Maybe we should make a list of what pies you want to make for the pre-event, dig out the recipes, and make sure we have all the ingredients."

"Thank you." His sexy grin threatened to melt her resolve, but he made no move to grab her and hug her like he used to do whenever she gave him good news, although she felt as if he wanted to.

He said, "One pie I'm including is Mama's sweet cherry pie. It's her specialty and the mayor's favorite. Folks will expect it. The mayor will expect it."

Cherry pie? In May? "Quint, Flathead cherries aren't in season yet."

"The cherries are in the freezer. This is a twist on Mama's original recipe. She calls it Frozen Sweet Bing Cherry Pie. The recipe is in the office, she said, in her favorite cookbook." He walked into the office and returned a minute later with the recipe on a loose sheet of paper. "Found it."

Callee was amazed. Given the gazillion cookbooks in that office, she would've had no idea which was Molly's favorite. "What pies besides the Bing cherry are you considering?"

"Let's just concentrate on one pie for now." He spread the cherry pie recipe on the work island along with a recipe for dough. He crossed to the sink and rolled his shirtsleeves to his elbows, revealing his strong, tanned forearms, and a wayward longing swept through her. He began washing his hands, talking to her over his shoulder. "I want to see just how rusty my crust-making skills are."

She pulled her gaze from his arms, pulled her mind from the dangerous yearning. He was going to bake a pie. This she had to see. "Right here and now?"

"Yep. Are you still willing to assist?"

"That depends on what assisting requires," she said, suddenly reluctant, the old insecurities ready to attack her. She joined him at the sink and washed her own hands, savoring the tiny bump of their shoulders, the fleeting graze of fingers and hands beneath the rush of water. The sensations, as intimate as new lovers discovering each other, reminded her of the beginning of their romance—before reality set in and differences reared their ugly heads. Before his father died.

She turned off the tap, wishing she could shed all sensuous longings for this man. She couldn't change what didn't work between them. But she so missed the feel of his warm, inviting skin, and although she didn't want to think about that, she couldn't seem to stop. There was something oddly seductive about being alone with him in this kitchen.

He grabbed a towel and dried his hands, also seeming a bit ill at ease. Maybe it was that he was about to try making his first piecrust in years. Or maybe he, too, felt the tantalizing hum in the air. He tossed the towel to her. She caught it and dried her hands as he turned away, and her gaze snagged on his amazing backside. *Damn. Stop it. Look somewhere else. Think about something else.* Where the hell had she put that chilled water? There. She crossed the room, grabbed the bottle, and downed a gulp. Quint was peering into the freezer.

She kept her eyes on the back of his head, not daring to look lower. Safe territory. Except that lock of ebony hair curling over his collar captivated her. He needed a haircut. Bad. Her fingertips itched for a pair of scissors as a memory of one particular haircut flashed into her mind, rocking her back in time.

The bathroom in their master bedroom. The air, steamy with the aromas of peach shampoo, spicy bath gel, and unbridled sex. She was replete with a delicious feeling coursing through her veins and passion for this man who was her husband, filling her heart to the edge of overflowing—a magical sensation only intimate lovers experience.

Quint had sat on her makeup stool, a towel wrapping his lean waist. She bent forward over his back, teasing her fingers through the hair on his chest, tracing it down his flat belly to where it disappeared into the towel. He grinned at her reflection in the mirror and reached behind him, playfully slipping his hand inside her robe and between her legs. Her body responded to his every touch, every stroke, need coiling deep in her core.

Laughing, she kept threatening to take a chunk of hair out of the back of his head if he didn't stop. But she didn't want him to stop. And he didn't. Soon the scissors were slipping from her hands, the robe falling to the floor, his towel gone. Her blood began to sizzle at the high-def memory.

Oh my God. Stop. She cleared her throat, but her voice croaked when she asked, "What do you need me to do?"

A good assistant always deferred to the chef. *Just like a willing lover.*

He grabbed a package of frozen and pitted dark red cherries from the freezer and emptied it into a huge glass bowl. "At room temp, this should thaw in an hour, hour and a half."

"Okay," she said, determined not to stare at him or to have any more erotic memories as he bent and began to dig in the refrigerator. She spun toward the cupboard that faced the Sub-Zero and, for the first time, noticed a built-in CD player. She considered turning it on, but Quint interrupted the thought.

"Aha. There's the butter." He placed two sticks of un- salted butter on the work island. "Do you know where Mama keeps the flour, salt, and sugar?"

"Oh, you know what?" She crossed to the linen cup- board and withdrew two chef coats, one small and one that must have been Rafe's. "Before we go any further, I suggest we put these on. Baking pies can get messy."

Quint grinned at her, that engaging heart-stopping grin, as she helped him adjust the coat over his broad shoulders. The air between them crackled like heat light- ning. His gaze slipped to her mouth, and her mouth tin- gled in response, and then a jackhammer pulsed through her veins, making her body ache for his touch. His kiss.

He leaned down as though he meant to oblige her mouth, but instead he whispered, "Damn it, Callee, I'm only human. If you don't want me to kiss you, stop look- ing at me like that, or I won't be responsible for what happens."

She straightened, heat suffusing her cheeks. Had she lost her mind, mooning over him like a lovesick school- girl? Feeling sorry that he hadn't ignored her stupid rules and ravished her on the center island? She swigged water from her bottle to cool her jets.

He busied himself cutting the two sticks of butter into cubes and placing them on a dish.

She fumbled the buttons closed on her chef coat, her hands still shaky, her body still trembling. Part of her wanted to dwell only on the good things in their marriage, but it hadn't been all bliss. Too many times he'd let her down, let her know other things and other people were more important. She did a quick read-through of the crust recipe. "Should I get out a food processor?"

"Sure." He placed the dish of cubed butter into the freezer. "Mama always says the secret to flaky piecrust is ice-cold butter. It should stay in here around thirty minutes. Overnight is even better, but we don't have that kind of time."

She avoided eye contact, still grappling with her poise. It occurred to her that if there were responses to their ads, then they would be doing interviews tomorrow. And those interviews would include having the applicants make piecrust. "While you're working on the dough, I'll cube more butter for use tomorrow."

"Or you could watch and learn." His voice held a teasing smile.

"Professionals have tried to teach me and failed." Her chest felt tight, her palms damp. "Even Molly tried to teach me."

"Don't fret. I won't make you participate…if you don't want to."

Relieved, she set about slicing the butter while Quint took a couple of trips to the pantry, bringing flour, sugar, and salt to the work counter. Then he went through the drawers and cupboards, locating a rolling pin, pie plate, and measuring cups and spoons.

Callee watched him measure two and a half cups of flour into the food processor, add a teaspoon of salt, and a teaspoon of sugar. He set the food processor dial to pulse, mixing the dry ingredients. Then he filled a measuring cup with ice water and placed it next to a tablespoon. He glanced at the clock. Twenty minutes had passed since he'd placed the butter into the freezer.

"I'll get it," she said, putting the freshly cubed butter into the freezer and taking the one Quint had prepared to him. He added the cubes to the processor. He hit the pulse button. Seven times the whirling started and stopped. She looked at the mixture in the processor. "Is the butter supposed to look like small pearls?"

"It is. Next I add ice water one tablespoon at a time, pulsing until the mixture just begins to mesh."

He pulsed and tested.

She moved closer, totally focused on his technique.

He demonstrated. "If you pinch some of the crumbly dough between your thumb and forefinger, like this, and it holds together, it's ready. Otherwise, add a touch more water and pulse again. Too much water equals tough crust."

Teeth-crunching tough, like her piecrust. In her defense, though, the school hadn't had food processors. She'd made her crust by hand, and she had no feel for kneading.

Quint dumped the mealy mixture onto the marble surface of the island. "The marble keeps the dough cool and the butter from melting."

Callee watched Quint work the dough with the heels of his hands, pushing it into the marble countertop.

He looked at her and grinned. "You want to try it?"

She shook her head, not about to jinx this process. "No, thanks."

The gentle movements of his big hands coaxing the floury mix into something solid fascinated her. Why was this so easy for him and so difficult for her? If only she'd known that he could bake pies, she might have found the courage to tell him about her dream of becoming a chef. Too late now. But when things between them were good, it would've been like discovering you and your best friend shared a secret passion for Lady Gaga music. Not something you'd ever discussed, but then one day the happy secret came out and enriched your friendship...or your marriage. Divorce, she was starting to understand, wasn't a decision reached in the heat of the moment. It was a breaking down of communications that accumulated over time.

Quint, she realized, had stopped kneading. She asked, "How do you know when the consistency is right?"

He shrugged, gently shaping the dough into two disks. "I don't know really. It's something I can feel, but the trick is to not over-knead." He sprinkled some flour around the disks, and then he wrapped each in wax paper and placed them into the Sub-zero. "These need to refrigerate a good hour. Like the butter cubes, it's better to prepare the dough a day or so before using, but tonight an hour will have to do."

Callee checked on the cherries. "These are thawing nicely."

"Great." He began tugging off his chef coat. "Why don't you clean up the flour and, if the cherries are thawed before I get back, then go ahead and mix the filling?"

Mix the filling? Her eyes widened. He said, "Is that a problem?"

"Of course not. I can follow a recipe." This wasn't brain surgery, after all. Just because her peach pie filling had turned out runny didn't mean this filling would. "Where are you going? To the hospital?"

"Not yet." He brushed flour from his jeans. "I thought I'd run after some chow. Anything special you want?"

"Whatever. You choose." The pie samples seemed hours ago. She was hungry, too.

* * *

Without Quint, the pie shop seemed eerily quiet. She didn't like being alone. She'd felt so displaced since leaving Quint; nowhere seemed like home and now, with Molly almost dying, the sting of loneliness ached worse than ever. She phoned Roxy and they chatted for half an hour before Roxy had to run. Feeling the loneliness again, Callee glanced at the CD player. There was already a disk inserted. She switched it on. Loud Latin music spilled from the speakers, startling her. She hit the volume knob, easing the sound to a pleasant level. She wouldn't have thought Molly was into this kind of music, but maybe the CD belonged to Rafe. The strings and horns were upbeat. She couldn't understand the words, but had no doubt this album was one of love songs.

She hummed along as she cleaned the work counter. She spread out the infamous cherry pie recipe and began reading. It was handwritten in a crisp printed script. The title was not Frozen Sweet Cherry Pie as touted, but rather Great Grandma McCoy's Secret Recipe for Frozen Sweet Cherry Pie. A small ruby red juice stain painted one corner. A strange sensation came over Callee. She was holding onto a piece of Quint's family history, passed from one generation to the next, long before he was born, long before his parents married. No telling when the stain had come into being.

She couldn't imagine having a connection to generations past, not even one based on something so simple as a recipe. Her family history was a mystery. She would never know who her birth father was, her mother hadn't seemed to know any stories of their ancestry, and her grandmother shunned the subject as though it were a scandal. Callee was left accepting that nothing lasted forever. Not even family. But she was holding proof to the contrary.

She rubbed absently at the stain. The concept of ancestors connected to her through something as simple as an old recipe felt as alien as a walk on the moon might.

She shook off this musing and concentrated on what she was doing. The recipe had been updated through the years. Not surprising, really, since there were more varieties of flour, sugar, and other ingredients than when the original recipe was created. Not to mention a more health-conscious America. And there were wonderful gadgets that made baking much less time-consuming, like food processors and cherry pitters.

Callee gathered the ingredients listed on the recipe. She measured the called-for amounts of sugar, cornstarch, salt, lemon juice, almond extract, and a dash of cinnamon, then poured everything onto the cherries as directed and gently tossed until blended. The aroma brought a memory of the first time she'd met Quint's parents. Molly had insisted he bring her home for Sunday dinner. The kitchen had smelled of ripe cherries and pot roast. She'd been so nervous and wanted them to like her so badly that she'd knocked over the gravy bowl, ruining the white tablecloth.

Molly and Jimmy McCoy laughed and told her not to worry about it. That kind of thing happened all the time in the McCoy household. She'd loved them instantly and taken them into her heart as they'd done with her. She missed Quint's dad so much that grief could still sneak up on her when least expected. He had been the only real dad she'd ever known, and their time together had been so very short. A tear rolled down her cheek. She hugged herself, trying to touch that sad spot that felt like a hole in her middle. She was blessed to have known him, blessed to have happy memories of being loved unconditionally despite her shortcomings.

She was just washing up when Quint returned.

Delicious smells trailed in with him, issuing from the red-and-white bags he carried. Her spirits lifted with one look at the logo. "You went to Thai Palace?"

"I did."

"I haven't been there in forever." Not since the last time they were there together. Thai was her favorite, not his. But about twice a month, he indulged her preference. "I've been craving it. Thank you."

He grinned, pleased with himself. "Glad to accommodate, ma'am. But that's not all. I also picked up a bottle of your favorite vino."

He set the bottle on the countertop and started searching drawers for an opener. Alarm bells went off in her head. Wine? Quint didn't care for wine. He only drank it when beer wasn't available. Why was he being so good to her? Maybe she shouldn't question his motives, but just enjoy his thoughtful gesture.

They ate at one of the round tables in the café. Dessert plates served as dinnerware. Coffee cups as wine glasses. She used the complimentary chopsticks. He couldn't get the hang of them and preferred traditional silverware. Their conversation stayed neutral: the weather and Molly.

She swallowed the last of a spring roll, followed it with a sip of wine, and said, "I have the pie filling ready."

"Great." Quint scraped back his chair and stood. "The dough should be ready, too."

This was the part she wanted to see, Callee thought, gathering their dishes. Her blood tingled in anticipation, and she had a sudden and surprising realization. The idea of watching Quint roll pie dough into a crust that was a work of art actually excited her. Turned her on. She found it sexy as hell. Romantic, even.

Given this new insight about herself, she had better watch her step.

She carried their plates and silverware to the sink. He followed with the wine bottle and their cups. Quint removed one of the disks from the Sub-Zero. "It needs to sit at room temp for roughly ten minutes, until it softens enough to make rolling easier."

He glanced at the wall clock, then offered her more wine. She declined, carrying her cup to the sink. She didn't tell him she'd polished off a whole bottle by herself the night before, but she wasn't about to overindulge two nights in a row. Or to let wine release her inhibitions worse than the sexy memory and her new insight already had.

She donned her chef coat and offered him his. He put it on. Hers had specks of cherry juice in a connect-the-dots pattern that might be a star. His was still pristine. Not even any butter grease.

He refilled his cup with wine, then set the bottle on a back counter. He placed the marble rolling pin and pie plate on the island. Callee read over the crust recipe again. "Are you going to use parchment paper?"

He eyed her with a "I thought you didn't know how to bake a pie" expression. She laughed. "It's mentioned here on the recipe."

"Mama started using it a few years ago. She says the parchment paper allows for minimal handling of the dough—less handling, lighter crust. Do you know where she keeps it?"

"No, but it must be in one of these drawers or cupboards." She searched while Quint floured the rolling pin.

Callee found it in an upper cupboard. She ripped off two large sheets of parchment paper and brought them to Quint, slipping them onto the counter. She stood so close to him their arms grazed. She flinched, but didn't move away. She watched him sprinkle flour lightly on the sheet, then place a disk of dough in the center of the paper.

He began to pound the dough with the rolling pin, explaining, "This is called 'rapping.' Do this until the dough is about six inches in diameter, like this, then lightly dust flour around the mound, cover with the second sheet of parchment, and roll to a size an inch or so larger than your pie pan."

"You really haven't forgotten," she said, impressed. He made it look so easy. Was it that easy? Could she really learn to do this?

"Are you thinking maybe you could do this?" He gazed down at her, bemused, his smile disarming.

"No," Callee lied, startled that he'd read her mind and ignoring the warm shimmers racing across her skin. "I can't..."

"You can, Callee. I believe in you." His eyes darkened with something that heated the shimmers to a dangerous level. "Let me teach you..."

He stepped back, silently urging her to take his place. She shook her head. "No, thanks."

"Ah, come on," he pressed. "Give it a try..."

"I've tried and been shown—"

"Not by me."

Callee's gaze fixed on the mound within the parchment paper, her throat dry, her palms damp. It was dough. It couldn't get the best of her...if she didn't let it. Reluctantly, she moved to where Quint had stood. He said over her shoulder, "Now, grasp hold of the handles of the rolling pin."

She wiped her hands on the chef coat and then gripped the handles of the marble rolling pin. They felt like ice against her palms, while Quint's breath felt like a summer breeze on the back of her neck. He said, "Okay, now start at the center and roll toward the edge, keeping the pressure even."

She started, then inexplicably froze. His hands came down on hers as he leaned over her, their bodies spooned. Her heart began to race. His cheek touched hers, his mouth near her ear, his voice husky. "Keep the pressure even. Like this. That's right."

He leaned into her and away from her with each extended roll, his body heat like a comforter she wanted to snuggle. She didn't mean to nuzzle his head, but she did, and the next thing she knew...

"Oh, God, Callee," Quint groaned, spinning her into his arms, his mouth finding hers, his body meeting hers. A fiery rain of irresistible sensations washed through her, burning away her resistance.

She kissed him with all the need she'd suppressed for months and months and tore at his chef's coat as he tore at hers, their lips locked in an ever-deepening reunion. His hands were in her hair, hers were in his. He tasted of red wine and Thai food and smelled even better. Her sweater vanished, followed by her bra, and his shirt, his belt, his jeans. He pulled her naked torso to his, eliciting a gasp of pure pleasure at the ached-for feel of his body. Her nipples were rock hard against his chest, his arousal against her thighs.

She didn't remember kicking off her boots, or her jeans, or her panties. Every breath, every touch, raised her higher and higher toward the heavens, and she didn't want it to ever stop.

Quint swept the parchment paper, piecrust, flour, and rolling pin from the island. The ensuing crash brought Callee to her senses with a bang. Dear God, what was she doing? She shoved against Quint's shoulders, tore her lips from his, and pushed him away, panting. "No. No. I don't want this."

"Could've fooled me." His words came out in a breathless rasp.

Callee gathered her clothes, tugging them on, humiliation and embarrassment scorching her insides. She glanced at the mess on the floor. It was just like their marriage. It had started out as something wonderful and ended up thrown away. She left him standing there, naked, aroused, and making no attempt to cover himself. He looked perplexed and angry and sexier than any of her memories.

Chapter Eight

~~~

Carrie Underwood broke into Callee's dream, belting out a song about a kickass female fixing her cheating beau. *The ringtone on my cell phone.* Callee pried open her eyes, glancing at the bedside clock. The numbers swam. It was either six after nine or nine after six. She fumbled for the phone, pulled it close, and read the screen. Andrea. She hesitated and debated whether to answer. Probably Logan was still sick, and she was calling to say she wouldn't be at Big Sky Pie today.

Well, neither will I.

She let the call go to voice mail. Still not sure of the time, she checked the phone's readout. Eight after nine. She groaned into her pillow. Half the morning gone. She never slept this late. *That's what you get for staying up past four.* Too little sleep and too much stress came with the twin bonus of too many disturbing dreams. The one she'd been having when the phone rang seemed lodged in her brain, like a tune she hated but couldn't get out of her head.

Think of something else.

She kicked off the covers and went to the bathroom, slipped out of her sleep shirt and into the shower. She shut her eyes, focusing on the sensation of hot water beating on her scalp, clearing her mind of everything else, but the moment she began rubbing soapy hands over her body, Callee recalled Quint's hands caressing her here, there, and everywhere. A short scream burst from her. Damn it all. Why couldn't she stop the lingering sensations of his touch?

She was still asking herself that question twenty minutes later when she carried a cup of coffee to the table by the window and sat to apply makeup. *Maybe if you'd stop dreaming about him . . .* The dregs of last night's pity party still littered the table top. She scooped the three mini Jack Daniel's bottles and the Diet Coke can into the wastebasket. Bending over amplified the banging in her head. Damn. She never drank more than an occasional, social glass or two of wine, but in the last couple of days, she'd set a new, personal-best record—not something she was proud of. If this kept up, she'd be an alcoholic by month's end.

Groaning, she sat and downed more coffee, her gaze snagging on her journal. The burgundy leather cover held lined and tabbed pages, along with a couple of recipes she'd never had the nerve to attempt and most of her private thoughts. It lay open to the pages she'd written last night, a pen resting in the center groove.

After leaving Quint in the pie shop, she arrived here shaken to the core and headed straight for the courtesy bar. She'd taken the Jack and Diet Coke to the bathroom and indulged in a long bubble bath, scrubbing her skin until it glowed red. But nothing helped. She could still feel him on her, smell him, taste him. The scene in the kitchen kept rolling through her mind like some movie of the week on a marathon replay.

She'd poured another whiskey, then another. Nothing soothed her frazzled nerves or calmed her tortured soul. When she could stand it no longer, she phoned Roxy. She confessed all and cried and laughed and vented. Roxy listened and commiserated and suggested Callee might be in the land of "go-backs."

Go-backs, Roxy explained, are the last gasp of lingering emotions parting couples often confuse with true love. They "go back" together, thinking all will be good this time, only to discover it's the same old bad.

"Do you think that's what I have?" Callee asked.

"One way to know for sure," Roxy said. "Make a list of all the reasons not to go back to Quint. If after reviewing your list, you would still leave him, then at least you'll have new armor against his sexiness."

Callee took the advice, jotting every major and minor grievance she could conjure up. Just writing it down in black and white made her feel better, sleepy even. The result: she slept, dreamed of Quint, and woke up mad at him.

Callee yawned, drank more coffee, and dug in her makeup bag for something to cover the dark circles under her eyes. Carrie Underwood started singing again, a siren wail to Callee's hangover-sensitive ears.

Andrea. Oh, shoot, she hadn't listened to her earlier message. She let her leave another one, then keyed up voice mail. Andrea sounded anxious. "Callee, Quint asked me to phone and let you know that we had some responses to the ads. I've set up interview appointments for today. Starting at ten. I hope you get this message before then and phone me back. You are coming in today, right? Call me."

Callee set the phone down. Her emotions were all over the place. She would give her eyeteeth to leave Kalispell this morning and not have to face Quint or the scene of their debacle. But she knew if the situation were reversed, if she were the one in the ICU, that Molly would do whatever Callee needed. Callee couldn't walk out on Molly, no matter what. And maybe someone who was a master or mistress of pies would be among the applicants.

She dressed, avoiding the red Dingos. She chose Crocs, baggy jeans, and a flannel shirt layered over a t-shirt. She tied her hair into a ponytail. The effect was anything but irresistible, suiting her mood and her purposes.

As she headed across the mall's busy parking lot, she wondered if Quint would already be at the pie shop. Had he cleaned up the mess in the kitchen or had Andrea come in this morning and found it? Would there be questions she didn't want to deal with from her friend? The thought gave her pause. She veered back into the mall to pick up a couple of lattes and a variety of muffins. A little sugar for her mood and something solid for her acidy stomach.

Andrea greeted Callee, the latte, and the muffins with a delighted squeal. "Oh, thank God. I was afraid you didn't get my messages."

"I overslept," Callee said. "I brought you a skinny caramel macchiato."

"Yum." Andrea helped herself to a poppy seed muffin,

eyeing her. Callee knew she looked like shit. She braced for questions but when none came she offered no explanations. Andrea offered her a muffin. "I suspect you could use one of these."

It was blueberry, Callee's favorite. Was there anything better than a friend who knew when to pry and when to hold off? Who knew when you were more in need of comforting than a solution or advice? She grinned. "I should have married you."

They laughed, and Andrea shook her head. "If only I liked women that way, life would probably be easier."

"Same here." The muffin felt like a sponge in Callee's stomach, soaking up the acid and easing away the tummy ache. "How is Logan?"

"He's great. No fever. Good appetite."

They each finished their muffin, left the box on the table near the coffee for Quint and the applicants, and went into the kitchen to set up for the interviews. Callee was relieved to see all signs of last night's fiasco were gone. The floor was spotless. She sniffed the air. Was that the mouthwatering scent of baked cherry pie?

Andrea came up behind her. "So you smell it, too."

"What?" Callee struggled to hold onto her composure, not an easy task given her still-pounding headache.

"Cherry pie," Andrea said. "It was even stronger when I first arrived this morning."

"I thought it was just me." Callee tried not to look guilty as she scrambled for some sort of plausible explanation. "Is there a pie in the refrigerator?"

"Nope. I thought there were a couple of slices of Molly's cherry pie left over from the other day, but there aren't any in the fridge now."

"Well, there you go," Callee said, wondering if Quint had dumped out the ingredients for the pie or actually made the pie. From the smell of the kitchen, she was guessing he'd baked it and taken the pie away. She didn't like lying to Andrea, but she'd promised to keep Quint's secret. "He probably found that last slice and heated it for his breakfast this morning."

Andrea frowned, looking thoughtful, but nothing more plausible seemed to occur to her. She shrugged. "Yeah, that's probably it. So, speaking of Quint, how did it go with him after I left yesterday?"

Callee wanted to drop through the floor at the images that spun into her mind. Especially the images of Quint, naked and aroused. Her cheeks heated. She mumbled, "What did Quint say about it?"

"Nothing. I haven't seen him. He asked me to stand in for him during the interviews today. Said he was going to the hospital to check on Molly and meet with her doctor to discuss the surgery. Afterward, he was going to hole up in his hotel room and tackle his voice mail and other real estate business."

The news untied the knot in Callee's stomach. She didn't have to see or deal with Quint today. Yes! There was a God. She did a mental happy dance, but since Molly was still in ICU waiting for a bypass, her relief lasted about five seconds. "I hope this means she's improving."

"I told him to text me as soon as he could with an update." Andrea tilted her head, studying Callee. "So quit hedging and tell me what Quint said about the pre-event."

Callee recounted his reactions, his reluctant acceptance of it being good for the pie shop, and his enthusiasm for the affair once he was on board with the whole promotional aspect. As she spoke, her anxiety over the pre-event escalated into full-on dread. Yesterday, the thought of attending the dinner with Quint made her uncomfortable. After last night, the thought sent shivers through her, and not the feel-good kind. "I need a favor."

"What sort of favor?"

Callee went to the fridge to see what ingredients were available for pie filling. There was no bowl of cherries inside. No second disk of dough. No cherry pie. "You remember when Sharla Tucker said she'd see me and my, er, hubby at the pre-event?"

"Yeah."

She took some cherries from the freezer to thaw. "Well, I, er, would you please take my place?"

Andrea hesitated, and Callee rushed on, "I don't want to walk into a dinner with my almost-ex and have those attendees who know about our divorce jumping to wrong conclusions or asking impertinent questions."

"Oh, ouch." Andrea pushed her blond hair behind one ear. "That would not be fun. Is Quint okay with me taking your place?"

"Why wouldn't he be? You work for the pie shop, after all."

Andrea seemed to be considering this argument, but her hesitation showed she still had reservations. Callee said, "Look, I know it's late notice. I'll sit with the boys. So, no excuses about not having a sitter. Will you do it?"

Andrea nodded. "As long as it's okay with Quint, then, sure."

"Good." She doubted Quint would object…after last night. In fact, he would probably be glad to avoid her as much as possible. "Then it's settled."

Andrea looked at the clock. "Our first interviewee is five minutes late. That does not bode well for her reliability."

"How many applicants are scheduled?"

"Five, so far."

"Five? I thought we'd be lucky to have one response." Callee was shocked and glad, but maybe she shouldn't get too excited until she saw some résumés. "How qualified are these applicants?"

"You're the one with restaurant experience." Andrea shrugged and slid some printouts across the counter. "You tell me."

Callee took the sheets and began reading the one for the applicant who was late, noticing the referrals all had the same last name, which was the applicant's last name. Suspicious. But there was one good thing that caught her eye. "Hey, this one's been to cooking school. In Spokane. That's promising."

"Except for the tardy part." Andrea indicated her disapproval with a raised brow. "I've put them in the order of their appointments, and I've scheduled them at two-hour intervals. Does that give you enough time to check out their baking skills?"

Quint was supposed to be here to judge that, and although she was glad not to have to deal with him today, she also resented him leaving something this important to her and Andrea, given neither of them had his baking expertise. But apparently he had more important things to do today—*like avoiding me*—than interviewing possible pastry chefs.

She forgave his visit to see to his mother and the appointment with her cardiologist to discuss her surgery, but that wouldn't take all day. And he meant to blow off all of the interviews. Typical Quint. Never there when it mattered. Probably going fishing this afternoon.

"Earth to Callee?" Andrea said, pulling Callee out of her dark musings. "Do you think this is enough time between interviews?"

Callee shrugged. "I have no idea, but better too much time than not enough. And I want you sitting in on the interviews. You're the one who will be working with this person, not me. So your opinion is equally as important as mine in Quint's decision of who to hire."

"If any of them."

"Let's think positive."

Andrea gave a begrudging, yet hopeful laugh. "Agreed."

"I'm thinking we'll have each one make a pie. The pies can bake while we're interviewing the next applicant, and later, Quint can judge all the pies against each other for appearance and taste."

"Oh, I like that idea. So what's the interview strategy?"

"Did Quint give you any idea what we should include in the questions?" Callee didn't know if he cared more about long-range goals, or urine testing, or what salary the applicants expected.

"Nope. We're on our own."

Callee tried to tamp down her irritation as they discussed a plan of action while setting flour, sugar, salt, and food processors on the center island. As Andrea gathered measuring cups and spoons, Callee searched the drawers for a rolling pin. Bottom drawer. As she bent to grasp it, her foot crunched something solid. A small wedge of marble on the concrete. It wasn't the same color as the countertop or as the rolling pin she held.

She carried the wedge of marble to the waste container and discovered the chipped rolling pin, the parchment paper, and the food containers from the Thai Palace. She moved a couple of the items, but found no disks of dough. There was, however, one curious thing. A chopstick coated with flour and bits of dough.

She closed the lid, went to the sink to wash her hands, and caught another whiff of baked cherry pie. She wished she could have seen and even tasted Quint's pie, a pie she'd helped make.

"It's a shame to cut into the applicants' pies," Andrea said. "Since we're desperate for pies for the pre-event."

"Any pies that go to the mayor's dinner will be representing Molly and Big Sky Pie. Not just any pies will do." Callee dried her hands. "In an effort to not waste the pie-filling ingredients, if I detect someone really doesn't know how to make a decent crust, then I won't continue to that next step. Okay?"

"Sounds good." Andrea joined Callee at the sink and handed her a coffee cup. "This needs to be washed. It was shoved back behind a food processor. Smells like wine…"

Callee took the cup and rinsed it out, hoping Andrea didn't notice her cheeks were as red as the dregs of merlot. She opened the dishwasher and spied the big bowl on the bottom rack. Everywhere she turned, there were reminders of last night, reminders of Quint. Of her reaction to him. And of the humiliation she'd dealt herself. And him.

A knock on the front door pulled her back to the moment.

"Twenty minutes late," Andrea said, shaking her head. "She better have a darned good reason."

"Do you want to conduct the first half of the interview? Or do you want me to do it?" Callee snatched the résumés and her journal and followed Andrea to the café.

"Let's both handle this one."

* * *

Quint walked into the second-floor office of Adz R Taz, an advertising firm located two blocks off Front Street, about six blocks from Big Sky Pie. This was another building his dad had purchased back in the day. The space consisted of a large, open loft-style area, and two smaller rooms. It served as Nick Taziano's living and working quarters.

Large picture windows showcased posters that advertised the many services offered at this one-man operation, and an eclectic variety of the owner's amazing photographs hung on the brick walls. Near the back wall, there was a desk with a huge Mac desktop, a laptop, an all-in-one printer, and a couple of digital cameras. A round consulting table stood by the windows overlooking the street. Albums and brochures rested within easy reach.

Nick sat there with Wade Reynolds, a local cherry grower, bullshitting over mugs of coffee. Quint stopped for a second to stare at them, realizing this was the first time since he'd returned from Alaska that something he expected to see was actually as it should be. As though he'd finally cut loose from the Twilight Zone. Why did that seem so amazing and feel so good?

"You two missed a hell of a fishing trip," Quint said, striding to the table. He set the pie box down between his friends.

"Welcome home, stranger." Wade offered up a big grin and a handshake. "How're they hanging?"

"'Bout time you got back to civilization," Nick said. "Help yourself to some brew. Fresh pot."

Quint grimaced and asked Wade, "Is it the usual mud and acid?"

"Do bears still shit in the woods?" Wade laughed.

Nick cocked his head. "It's just the way you like it, McCoy."

"Don't let me interrupt your conversation."

As they resumed their discussion of camera equipment, Quint filled a mug for himself. Left it black. He joined them at the table, listening with half an ear. Cameras held no interest for him, but if a man wanted to commiserate about a female, these were his go-to guys. They might give him lip, but neither would seriously bust his chops about being an idiot over Callee. They'd both had their own trials in the romance department.

Women seemed to consider Nick the icon for tall, dark, and handsome—with his olive skin and classic Italian features—but Callee had once said it was his dimples that drew the softer sex to him. Whatever. Nick excelled in advertising, and his business was starting to take off, but when it came to romance, his conquests were more convenience than commitment.

Wade, on the other hand, never seemed to notice the endless stream of women tripping over themselves for his attention. At six four, he stood out in a crowd. His hair was brown, his eyes aqua. He had the body of a carpenter, but the conservative nature of a preacher's son. Woman liked the shy type, and that was Wade in spades.

But Callee said the real appeal was that he was a widower; apparently that made him ripe for plucking.

Wade was too busy trying to keep his failing cherry orchard from going under while raising his preteen daughter for any serious romantic involvement. But Callee had told Quint that someone would come along one day and sweep him off his feet.

Quint caught Nick staring at the pie box like it was a rattler about to strike, then his dark gaze steadied on Quint. "So, how're you doing with the pie shop renovation on your realty office?"

Quint grimaced. "About like you'd expect."

"As soon as I found out about it, I tried to call and tell you, man, but every call went straight to your voice mail," Nick said.

"I appreciate the effort. You and everyone tried to reach me. My own damn fault. I didn't want to be contacted."

Nick offered him a sympathetic head shake, then grew serious. "How's your mother doing?"

"She needs a triple bypass." Quint drank his coffee. He'd taken the pie to the hospital to show her, said he and Callee made it together, and that had brought a smile. She was in pretty good spirits, and even he could tell she was quite a bit stronger than yesterday. "I talked to her doctor today, and the surgery is scheduled for the day after tomorrow."

"Hell of a homecoming all around," Wade said.

"For sure," Nick agreed. "But she's going to be okay, right?"

"Doctor said her chances of making it through the surgery and an eventual full recovery are good." Quint decided not to share the negative percentages the cardiologist mentioned. The ones that scared him. Not everyone with hearts as bad as his mother's survived the surgery. He shoved the negative thought back and brought the pie box forward. Both men watched like a captive audience. A papery crackle sounded as he opened the lid, releasing a delicious sugary cherry scent into the air. "So, gentlemen, who wants pie?"

"Pie? Before ten a.m.?" Wade scowled disapprovingly. But Quint wasn't going to let his "rules are rules" attitude keep Wade from indulging in a good time or good food.

"Loosen up, Reynolds," Quint said, grabbing another swig of his coffee. "It's one of Mama's pies."

Not really a lie. Just sort of a fudge.

Nick sniffed. "Is that sweet cherry pie?

Quint nodded. "Her specialty."

Wade still hesitated, but Quint could see the aroma had him interested. "She make this before she had the heart attack?"

Uh, um, uh. How did he answer that without lying? He settled for another nod. He was growing uncomfortable with how comfortable he was becoming at evading the truth. In his line of work, lying came easy to a lot of folks. Dave the Realtor was fond of saying, "Buyers are liars." In Quint's experience, sellers could also be liars. He didn't do business with liars if he could avoid it. If he wasn't careful, though, he might become one himself.

Nick went to a cupboard and returned with paper plates, plastic forks, and napkins.

Quint produced a knife and a pie server from the box and cut three portions.

"Pie for brunch…" Wade sounded like a man rehearsing for an upcoming visit to his church's confessional. It didn't stop him, however, from accepting the slice of pie.

"Sweet cherry pie," Quint said again, poking his fork into the pie, but not actually taking a bite. After Callee left him in the pie shop last night, he'd almost tossed the whole mess into the garbage. Instead, he'd dressed and returned to the hotel. He took a twenty-minute ice-cold shower. Afterward, he still ached for her. He took another icy shower. One thing kept repeating in his mind: even after the hell he'd put her through, Callee still wanted him. And somehow, he couldn't let her go without at least trying to win her back.

A shot of straight whiskey had calmed his frazzled nerves and returned his good sense. He couldn't leave the pie shop in a mess for Andrea to find in the morning. He went back and did something he hadn't done in years. Baked a pie. This pie.

"Are these Bing cherries from my orchard?" Wade licked sticky filling from the corner of his lower lip, a look of pure pleasure on his face.

"I believe so. Mama froze all those cherries she bought from you last summer."

Nick groaned his approval. "Damn. This is good pie."

The unsolicited compliment cheered Quint, giving him a much-needed ego boost. He almost blurted out, "Thank you." But caught himself in time.

As the men ate without talking, his mind spiraled back to the night before, to his return to the pie shop. One look at the mess on the kitchen floor brought back Callee's near capitulation in a knee-weakening rush. He stopped short of turning on his heel and walking out. Instead, as he set about cleaning up, he realized the heaviness in his heart was not anger, but disappointment.

He spied the recipe on the floor, bent and retrieved it. As his gaze settled on the old-time handwritten notations, it struck him that he was holding a piece of his family history, something once held by his great-grandmother, her mother, and his mother. A family of pie bakers. Like it or not, their blood ran in his veins; their traditions were his traditions; their skills were his skills. Baking pies was his heritage. He had a knack for it because he'd inherited that knack. Just like he'd inherited his dad's instincts for good real estate deals.

Quint wasn't secure enough to go public with the fact that he could bake a mean pie and risk setting himself up as the poster boy for laughingstock of the year. Once in his lifetime had been enough. But from here on out, he needed to stop denying it to himself.

"You give your mama my compliments when you see her," Nick said after gulping the last of his pie and rubbing the napkin across his mouth.

Quint said he would, secretly pleased that his pie rivaled Mama's in taste and texture. He supposed, if all else went to hell, he could always find work as a pastry chef.

Oh, please God, don't let that happen.

Wade ate more slowly and still had a few bites to go. He poked the edge of the pie with his plastic fork. "This crust is interesting. Kind of looks like a pleated, mini–air filter."

Nick grabbed a camera and took a picture of what remained of the pie, zeroing in on the crust in a second shot. "Do you know how your mom does that?"

Quint wasn't sure Mama had ever done this. It was an

idea that struck him last night as he was tossing out the remains of the Thai Palace debris. "By using a chopstick to crimp the edge."

"That's pretty creative." Nick set aside the camera, shoved his paper plate to the center of the table, and leaned back in his chair, studying Quint. "So, how *was* the fishing in Alaska?"

"Fierce," Quint said, spreading his arms wide. "You should have seen the size of the salmon."

"I hated to miss it, but I couldn't pass up that job in Spokane. It ended up taking eight weeks." Nick smiled the smile of a man happy with the results of his efforts, a sign that the job had gone well. But something else flashed through his brown eyes that told Quint the trip had included some fun, too. Some fun Nick couldn't get out of his head. Curious, he started to ask, but Nick cut him off.

"The fishing might have been fierce, old buddy," Nick said, leaning toward him, "but you don't look like you caught what you were after."

"Yeah." Wade nodded, finishing off the last of his pie and patting his stomach with satisfaction. "You still look like a man with woman trouble."

Quint groaned, finished a bite of pie, and said, "You have no idea."

"What's going on?" Wade asked, his expression sympathetic.

"I just found out my divorce is not final, and I want to stop it from going through," Quint said.

"I thought you wanted the divorce," Wade said.

"I thought so, too," Quint said.

"Not me," Nick said, his photographer's vision seeming to capture Quint in some invisible lens that revealed more than the naked eye.

Quint arched a brow. "How'd you know?"

Nick gave a wry chuckle and shook his head. "Couldn't understand your breakup in the first place. Yeah, I get the grief messing with your head, but I figured you two would get through it together."

"I fucked up. I don't know how to undo it."

"Have you tried talking to her about it?" Wade said. "Maybe she feels the same."

"Maybe. Without going into details, I know she still wants me. But that's not the same as still wanting to be married to me."

"You should take her some of this pie," Wade suggested. "That might win her over. It's that good."

"Yeah, well, pie isn't her thing." If he could figure out what was her thing, maybe he could win her back, but he was clueless.

"Too bad she doesn't like to fish," Nick said.

She doesn't? Quint frowned. The truth was, he had no idea whether or not Callee liked to fish. It had never occurred to him to find out. He knew she resented his trips, and maybe he'd just assumed that meant she didn't like fishing, but in fact he didn't know. He'd never suggested she join him, or even asked if she'd like to go. What other important things had he never learned about his wife? The question settled like a thorn in the soft tissue of his mind.

"Well, I couldn't have gone fishing," Wade said, "even for a week. Not with Emily in school. But I could use some time on a river. Either of you jackoffs up for some fly-fishing on the Stillwater one day this week?"

Fishing? This week? On the Stillwater River...one of

his favorite fishing spots. Hell, yes! Quint felt the itch begin to take hold, like a virus deep inside that he couldn't ignore. He was definitely up for it.

Then he remembered. "I'd have to wait until after Mama's surgery, and until I know she's going to be okay." Quint put the pie back into the box, along with the knife and pie server. "Let's say three or four days from now?"

"Count me in." Nick gathered all the dirty plates, forks, and napkins and tossed them into a waste can.

Quint stood, readying to leave. Nick leaned against his work desk. "What are you going to do about your real estate office?"

"Coming here has given me an idea. I might remodel one of the other buildings that Mama owns. In fact, remodeling and selling some of those old places, or renting them out, might turn out to be a profitable venture. If I can find a good contractor," Quint joked, looking pointedly at Wade. "If you ever decide to go back to being a builder, Reynolds, I'll be your first client."

But Wade's expression went cloudy. "Sadly, McCoy, that might not be as farfetched a possibility as you think."

Quint said, "Ah, sorry to hear that, man. This damned economy."

"Give us a call when you're free to hit the Stillwater," Wade said.

"Will do." Outside, Quint texted Andrea to let her know that his mother was strong enough for surgery and that it was scheduled. He felt buoyed by the whole morning. His pie was great, applicants were trying out for the pastry chef job, and he had a fishing trip to look forward to. Things were finally looking up.

Chapter Nine

⁓

The first applicant, Jane Wilson, reminded Callee of a Kewpie doll: strawberry blond hair, flushed cheeks, big blue eyes, cupid lips.

"I'm sorry." Jane stood just inside the door, twisting her hands, casting anxious glances from Andrea to Callee. She began to gasp. "I, I, I didn't mean to be late. S-should—I—just—l-l-leave?"

Oh, God, she was crying. Callee hurried toward her with a tissue. "Don't cry. You weren't that late."

"Humph," Andrea said in a stage whisper.

Jane turned as if to make a run for it. Andrea beat her to the door, cutting off the escape route. Callee silently applauded. With only five applicants, late or not, they couldn't afford to send anyone packing without interviewing them.

Jane snuffled and sniffled and blew into the tissue, struggling for composure. "I-I-I don't know what's wrong with—with—with me. I never cry."

Callee was too tired to deal with weepers or drama today. "You're here, and that's what counts. Why don't you take a seat?"

"Okay. I'm sorry." Jane daubed at her face, blew her nose again, and began to glance around the café for the first time since her arrival. "Gee, this is such an inviting space. Lovely colors and textures."

As Jane went to the table and began peeling off her coat, Callee sized up this potential pastry chef. An inch shorter than her own five-seven, Jane was as curvy as her résumé was thin. She wore a French braid with peek-a-boo bangs, black leggings beneath a lime sweater, and black Crocs on her small feet. Callee wiggled her own toes, comfy in the same footwear, the choice of most chefs. Washable and great for long hours in the kitchen. That Jane had come prepared to work earned her a mark in the plus column, making up for her lateness. "Would you like some coffee, Ms. Wilson?"

"Please, call me Jane, and no, thank you." Jane folded her hands in her lap.

Andrea settled into a booth to observe the interview as Callee poured herself a mug. The caffeine jolt in the latte hadn't put a dent in her weariness. She stifled a yawn as she walked to the table and sat opposite Jane.

"What is that subtle aroma?" Jane sniffed the air like a dog catching a suspicious scent. "Bing cherry pie?"

Callee blinked, impressed that Jane recognized the type of cherry with one sniff. Another point in her favor. "It's the specialty of the house."

"Some people think Bing cherries are too sweet for pie, but not everyone is a fan of Montmorency cherries.

Too tart." She smiled, then blushed. "I'm sorry. I'm talking too much. I tend to chatter when I get nervous."

As well as cry?

"Nothing wrong with chattering about pies in a pie
shop." Callee placed her journal and Jane's résumé side
by side and realized she was almost as nervous as Jane.
She'd worked at Twangy's Bar and Grill and suspected
that was why Quint thought she would be good to do the
interviewing, but this was Molly's pie shop and having
the right staff on board at its opening was of major importance.

Earlier, Andrea and she had decided to judge the applicants on the three A's: attitude, appearance, and aptitude.
Later, they would discuss their personal impressions of
each interviewee. Callee had written Jane's name at the
top of a clean page, then beneath it ATT, APP, and APT.
She put a check mark beside APP. She asked, "When did
you finish cooking school?"

"Two weeks ago," Jane whispered as though it were
some dirty secret that would immediately terminate the
interview—as though she didn't have a chance in hell.
Yeah, like qualified pastry chefs were queued outside the
pie shop all the way to Glacier Park. Jane really was in
the right place at the right time. She just didn't know how
right.

Callee asked, "Is this your first job interview since
cooking school?"

Jane nodded. "Yes, but I promise, if you give me a
chance, you won't be sorry. I love making pies. Ask any-
body."

Callee let her ramble on for a minute, then said, "Tell
me about your references."

She listened as Jane explained why all the referrals shared her same last name, holding back a smile. Reserving judgment. Making notes in the journal. If enthusiasm counted as good attitude, this applicant deserved a check and a star beside ATT. "Do you have any long-range goals?"

"Oh, yes." Jane's small hands became animated. "For now, to work in a shop like this and gain experience and knowledge, and maybe one day, to own my own bakery."

Callee liked that Jane seemed excited. Eager. Ambitious. She added another mental "yes" in the plus column and put that check beside ATT. There was only one more hurdle to jump. "Well, then, let's see what you can do in the kitchen."

Callee rose, expecting Jane to follow suit, but Jane hesitated, her gaze darting around the room, seeking something. Did her complexion look slightly green? Or was it a reflection off her sweater? "Are you okay?"

"Bathroom?" Jane stumbled to her feet, hand over her mouth.

"There." Callee pointed. "Just this side of the kitchen door."

Jane ran. A moment later retching sounds issued from behind the closed bathroom door. Andrea joined Callee. "What the heck? Is she upchucking?"

Callee sighed. "I think her nerves have gotten the better of her. She wants this job so badly."

More retching sounds.

"Well, that's a lot of nerves," Andrea said.

Five minutes passed. Jane came out of the bathroom looking coconut white, tears flowing. "M-may I c-come back tomorrow afternoon?"

She didn't wait for a response, but tore out the door, leaving it ajar. Her car made a hasty retreat from the parking lot. Andrea closed the door, her puzzled expression echoing how Callee felt. Andrea said, "I hope this isn't an omen for all the interviews."

"I don't get it. It was going great. I mean really great. She seemed exactly right for the job. Then boom, she just got sick."

"Do you think she has that nasty flu that's going around?" Concern clouded Andrea's face. She disappeared and returned spraying disinfectant through the air. "Just in case her upset stomach wasn't nerves." She scrubbed the table top where Jane had sat and then went into the bathroom and disinfected it.

Callee followed. "It's too bad. I have a feeling she might know her stuff."

"Yeah, but without getting to test her..."

"She said she'd be back tomorrow afternoon," Callee said. "I mean, if none of the other applicants pan out, then I'd be willing to give her another shot."

"Well, she'll have to make a better impression than this one. Late. Distracted. The thinnest résumé I've ever seen."

"We all have to start someplace," Callee said, realizing she sounded protective about someone she didn't even know. Why? Maybe it was as simple as seeing what she wanted to be in Jane: a cooking school graduate. "Besides, it's kind of sweet. She lists her family as her references because she claims she's been baking pies since she was around six or seven." Like Quint. Maybe Jane had a knack for making pies, too. *Or maybe I want to find a pastry chef so badly I'm grasping at straws.*

"Bottom line is, Quint still needs a pastry chef."

Quint. Molly. Callee forgot about Jane. "Have you heard from Quint?"

"He texted a few minutes ago." Andrea updated her on Molly's condition and her scheduled surgery.

"That is such great news," Callee said, grinning. "I think we should both have another muffin to celebrate." And they did. Feeling relieved and even hopeful, Callee went back to the table. "I need to read these other résumés."

"And I'll check with the applicants, see if I can convince one of them to show up earlier." Andrea started toward the office. "It will shorten our day."

Before she reached the kitchen doorway, however, the second applicant arrived. An hour early. Francis Bronkowski's eagerness was as promising as her résumé. For starters, she was an actual pastry chef with thirty years' experience, the past ten spent in the local Albertson's bakery department. She came looking even more prepared to work than Jane Wilson had. In white chef pants, coat, and hat, she had iron gray hair slicked into a bun, wire-rimmed glasses on a button nose, and lipstick slipping into the crevices around her thin mouth. She resembled an aging Pillsbury Doughboy and smelled like a smoker.

"My specialty is cakes," Francis announced, as she sat opposite Callee, her chest puffed with pride. Andrea gave Callee a good-luck-with-this-one glance and headed toward the office, presumably to call the next applicant.

Callee was still frowning about Francis's specialty being cakes. How did that translate into creating the perfect pie, with the flakiest possible crust? And after watching

Quint prepare the dough last night, she had come to accept that nothing less would do from whoever he hired.

"While I don't doubt you make a great cake, that's not—"

"Oh, seriously." Francis cut off Callee's objection before she could make it. "A pie is just a cake with crust, right?"

"Not really…" A headache started at Callee's temples and began to spread. "A pie—"

"Is a pie. I do know the difference." Francis huffed. "We can sit here all day and argue semantics or you can let me show you I know my stuff. Where's the kitchen?"

Who was conducting this interview? Callee's temper stirred. Roxy had a couple of chefs working in her bistro as arrogant as this woman, and she was thinking of firing them. Callee resisted the urge to toss Francis out on her plump behind. She was too tired to expend the energy. Besides, what if she did know her stuff? "The kitchen is through here."

Francis glanced around, said nothing, but grunted approval…until she got to the marble countertop. "I prefer butcher block, but I suppose this'll have to do."

Callee wanted to tell her cold countertops equaled flakier crusts, but bit her tongue. The pie shop needed a pastry chef. The sooner one was found, the sooner she could leave Kalispell. Keep the goal in mind. Don't offend this woman.

Easier said than done. Callee's tongue began to ache from biting it as Francis's list of "prefers" kept growing. She preferred not to use a food processor. Preferred not to use parchment paper. Preferred to make dough the old fashioned, hands-on way. Preferred to handle the dough too much. Preferred to take a smoke break in the middle of the process. Preferred Montmorency cherries over Bing. Preferred to work at a snail's pace.

Andrea peeked out of the office. She'd obviously been eavesdropping, from the face she made at Callee. She glanced at the clock, probably worried this interview was about to run over into the next one. But Francis finished with five minutes to spare.

The end result: her cherry pie couldn't touch one of Molly's in appearance. Still, it did look edible. The tasting would tell. Callee placed the pie in the oven. "Thank you, Ms. Bronkowski. You're not the only person we're interviewing today. Quint McCoy, Molly's son, will be evaluating the pies later and making a decision over the next few days. We'll call you one way or the other. Thank you."

Francis left lighting up a cigarette and wearing a Poppin' Fresh grin, as if she thought she'd nailed the interview and the job was hers. Andrea shook her head. "Wow. Now there's someone who knows what she does and doesn't *prefer*."

"I'm pretty certain Molly would *prefer* a pastry chef who doesn't think pies are cakes with crust."

"And who doesn't stop in the middle for a smoke." The two burst out laughing.

"At least the pie smells good." Andrea sniffed with exaggeration.

"It should. It's Molly's recipe." Callee yawned and checked the time. "The next applicant should be here any minute."

But the next applicant didn't show up. Or call. Or answer his phone.

"Well, this jerk flunks all three A's," Andrea joked, ripping the résumé in half. "The guy's a donut hole."

The inane curse referenced the applicant's previous experience at a Dunkin' Donuts. Callee laughed, realizing she must really be beat if she thought that was funny. "Don't bother heading to Vegas with your comedy act just yet."

"Okay, then I'll head to the shredder." She came back with her wallet. "I'm hungry. Thought I'd scoot across the street for some takeout. Can I bring you back something?"

"A salad, please." Callee wanted to curl up and take a nap, but she added, "Any kind."

Early afternoon saw the next two applicants receive good marks for the first two A's and mediocre aptitude marks. Callee promised someone would call them once a decision was reached. She rested against the kitchen counter, the aroma of cherry pies filling her nose. An olfactory treat.

Andrea leaned her elbows on the island. "What do you think? Any serious contenders?"

"No. Not even so-so contenders." Callee sighed as exhaustion crept into her muscles, disappointment into her voice. No one used Quint's technique for making flaky dough. No one showed the kind of skill required for this position. "Unless these pies prove me wrong, the hunt continues."

"Then I better check for new responses to the ads."

In preparation for the next morning's applicants, Callee began cleaning the kitchen. She put away the ingredient bins and scrubbed the counters. She looked up as Andrea returned. "Please tell me someone else is on their way."

"Someone else is on their way," Andrea said, one hand behind her back.

"Honest?"

"Honest." Andrea wasn't smiling. "Just Quint."

Callee's stomach dipped. "No more applicants today?"

"Nope. But there will be a couple in the morning." She grinned and pulled her arm from behind her back. New résumés dangled from her fingers. "You want me to put these with the others in the café?"

The timer went off.

"Why don't you? I need to get this last pie out of the oven, then I'll be right there." She opened the oven door and peered inside. The pie was nicely browned and aromatic; the crust edges, however, appeared chunky and uneven. She turned off the timer, slipped on a hot-pad mitt, and placed the pie on a rack on the counter to cool. Thick, ruby red cherry filling bubbled through the slits in the crust. The temptation to dip a finger into that mouth-watering goo swept through her, but she resisted, figuring it would probably scorch her fingertips. She placed a green toothpick into the center of the pie. She'd used different-colored toothpicks to delineate which of the applicants had baked which pie.

Andrea was reading the newest résumés when she walked into the café.

"Anything promising?" Callee asked, stretching her stiff neck.

"Not that I can see. Looks like a repeat of today. Here, see what you think." She slid the two résumés across the table to Callee.

Callee sat and read. "Well, they've each had experience in bakeries, but again, not specifically with baking pies." Reality settled in, dimming her hope of rapidly finding a pastry chef. "Maybe Jane—"

The back door opened, and Callee startled.

"It's just me," Quint called. "I'll be right there."

Callee's stomach did something akin to a high spiraling dive that culminated in a belly flop. Every nerve filled with dread. She knew she had to face him sometime, but now that the moment had arrived, she couldn't deal with it. Or with him. "I'm going to the hotel. You can tell him what went on today."

"He'll want to read your notes," Andrea said, reaching for her journal.

Callee blanched and hugged the book to her chest, shaking her head. "Ah, this isn't just a notebook. It's my, ah, private journal." *That holds my deepest, darkest issues with Quint.*

Andrea gave an understanding smirk. "Then just leave the pages. Or stay and share them with him."

"No."

Andrea frowned, her lips pursing as a suspicious glint popped into her eyes. "What's going on?"

"Nothing. I'm just tired." Callee stood to leave and only then realized she didn't have her handbag. "Would you mind getting my purse for me? I left it in the office."

Andrea didn't move. She tucked her hair behind one ear, an intuitive expression wrinkling her brow. "Something happened between you two last night, didn't it? Something disturbing? Oh my God, something sexual? No, don't deny it. It's written on your face."

Callee's cheeks burned. "Could you just get my bag?"

Andrea pursed her lips and nodded. "I could."

Then why didn't she? Callee thought, wanting to shoo her toward the office.

Quint called out, "Could you two come help me judge these three pies?"

Resistance stole through Callee. Why hadn't she left when she knew he was headed over here? Did she actually want to see him? No. Not after last night.

"Oh, yeah," Andrea said. "*Something* happened last night."

Callee closed her eyes, embarrassed. It was a mistake. She was so tired, she had no impulse control, and images of Quint—naked, aroused, touching her, kissing her—scrolled across her closed lids, assailing, teasing, haunting. She shook her head, trying to eradicate the sizzling memories, but lost the battle.

Andrea caught her arm. "Come on. Put on your big-girl thong, girlfriend. Critiquing these pies is part of the process that will lead to finding a pastry chef and the only way you'll ever be free of that hunk in the other room. Besides, you know I can't judge a pie by its crust like you can."

"Only because I make such bad crust." Callee knew Andrea was right. Leaving without speaking to Quint would be childish. She had to face him. *Back on the horse that throws you.* Her knees trembled. She had listed her reasons for leaving Quint and her reasons for filing the divorce documents. According to Roxy that should have given her the armor she needed to resist his heady allure. Time to find out if that was true.

She followed Andrea to the kitchen, holding the journal, her lists of Quint's bad behavior within as though the hidden pages would shield her from temptation. Quint stood beside the Sub-Zero and greeted them with a big grin. "Afternoon, ladies."

His gaze flicked over his employee, but felt like a caress on Callee, like he was peeling her flannel shirt from her shoulders, lifting the t-shirt over her head, unhooking her bra, unzipping her jeans. She grappled to hold on to her composure.

She tore her gaze from his. It didn't help. So much for Roxy's theory. She blushed from head to toe, her heart racing. One look and she melted like chocolate to his sizzling heat.

She forced her mind and her attention to the three sample pies on the island. The bright overhead light glinted off the glossy filling that oozed thick and rich through the top crusts.

"How'd it go?" he asked, breaking the electric silence. "Did we find a pastry chef?"

Andrea waited a beat for Callee to respond, realized she wasn't going to, and said, "It was a mixed bag, McCoy. The mediocre, the overconfident, the no-show, and the runaway." She recounted the interviews, mentioned the applicants scheduled for morning, and expressed the possibility of more e-mail responses by tomorrow.

He rubbed his chin thoughtfully. "Hmm. It's not looking like we're going to have a chef by the pre-event."

Callee wondered if Andrea noticed he didn't seem to be as worried or stressed about that as he should. Didn't it occur to him that he would have to explain where the pies came from if he ended up making them? Once he did realize it, that sly smile on his seductive lips would vanish in a blink.

She wanted the smile gone now. Not later. "I have high hopes for one of our applicants. She's coming back tomorrow afternoon."

"Oh, yeah?" His smile didn't falter. It widened. "The runaway?"

A bubble of anger popped inside Callee. It had been a frustrating day, packed with dashed hopes and unfulfilled goals. She didn't want to lash out, but couldn't stop herself. "Would you rather bake all six pies for the pre-event yourself?"

"Quint make pies?" Andrea burst out laughing and couldn't seem to stop.

But Quint didn't laugh. He turned a satisfying shade of crimson. His eyes narrowed at Callee in a "you promised" look of disappointment. Callee didn't care. After thinking about it all day, she realized what had gone on after she'd made that promise negated the promise, in her book. Did she have to remind him that he'd promised not to touch her?

His mouth slipped into a tight line. He glanced at the wall clock, then at Andrea. "Can you stick around and help evaluate these pies? Or do you have to pick up the boys?"

Andrea seemed aware of the tension zinging between Callee and Quint, aware that damage might occur in the pie shop if she left them alone for long. "Yeah, er, give me a minute to phone the boys' sitter." Her look said: try not to kill each other while I'm out of the room. She ducked into the office to make the call.

The timbre of Quint's voice resonated off the cupboards, not loudly, but in a low vibration. "I remember when a promise was sacred to you, Callee."

Chapter Ten

$\sim$

"Where do you get off talking about promises? You said you wouldn't touch me or kiss me or..." Anger propelled her toward Quint, until she'd backed him into the counter. How many promises had he made and not kept? All of them cruel, thoughtless, and heartbreaking. Especially the biggest broken promise: *'Til death do us part.* "You said you'd handle the question-and-answer part of the interviews; instead you left it up to me, without any input from you. These people are your possible employees, not mine. You or your mother or her staff will have to work with them. I won't. I don't mind checking résumés and sitting in on the interviews, but that's it."

"Yeah, well, I didn't figure you'd be too thrilled to deal with me this morning after last night." His voice was throaty, his gaze smoldering.

Every sensation she'd felt the previous evening—the hot kisses, the thrill of touching his naked body, the fervent need—returned on a wave of desire. She swallowed hard. "Last night…that, that was a mistake."

"Are you sure, Callee? It didn't feel like a mistake." His mouth moved nearer to hers, his breath as feathery as his whisper. She stood there, too near him, yet unable to pull back. "It felt like the first time. Do you remember?"

Did she remember? She could never forget the explosion of irresistible eroticism ignited by their first kiss. She hadn't wanted a romance, or a marriage, or a man to fill her future. But those things found her. And it seemed like maybe she would end up with everything that had been denied her while growing up. Maybe she'd been blinded by love at first sight, or by his incredible sexiness, or her romantic longings.

But passion doesn't sustain romance if you aren't a priority in your man's life. Reality had cured her romantic notions. She said softly, "We aren't starting again, Quint. We're ending."

He leaned in and whispered in her ear. "You still want me."

Yes. No. No. No. She blamed last night's slip on her self-imposed celibacy. Her raging hormones. Her need for a man. But not any man. Just this man.

As if he read her thoughts, he said, "See? You can't even deny it, can you?"

His self-assurance stiffened her spine, roused what remained of her pride. "I can. I do. We are over. You wanted the divorce. Now that you've got it, you need to deal with it."

"How am I supposed to do that after last night?" He reached as if to stroke her face, and she made no attempt to back away, but when his touch came, it was not the loving caress she expected, but a gentle brushing at something on her cheek near the hairline.

His hand on her face felt so good and carried the scent that was all his, more savory than any cherry pie.

"Flour," he said, explaining what he'd brushed from her hairline.

Flour? Shit. She had bags under her eyes, the band on her ponytail was losing its grip, and she had flour on her face. Why would any man try to seduce her looking like this? And why were her hormones screaming for her to jump his bones? She needed to get a grip. She turned toward the Sub-Zero and pulled out a water bottle, thinking she should dump it on her head rather than drink it. "It's been a long day."

"It's not over yet, sweetheart."

She frowned at the endearment. "How's Molly?"

Hopefully thoughts of his mother would chill his jets. She reached to tighten the band holding the ponytail. It snapped. Her hair flopped to her shoulders. Great, just great. She shook it out, grappling with her composure...again. "Andrea says her surgery is scheduled?"

"It's the day after tomorrow." His damned grin was back. He was laughing at her dismay.

She stepped out of his reach, batting at his hand. "What time?"

"First thing in the morning." A wistful sigh escaped him. "I just came from the hospital. She looks about the same as she did when I visited her this morning."

Pain danced through his eyes, and despite herself, she ached with him.

"It's tough seeing her like that. She's so damned pale."

"I know." Callee nodded, hating the misery spreading

across his face. Her heart hitched, reawakening the urge to take him into her arms, only this time it would be to offer comfort. At least, she was pretty sure that was all she would offer. Oh, hell. Who was she kidding? Vulnerable, Quint was damn near impossible to resist. She'd rather deal with his cocky counterpart.

She put more distance between them. What was taking Andrea so long?

As if on cue, Andrea returned. "I can stay another hour, but that's it."

"Then let's get started." Quint moved to the island, suddenly all business.

Callee took a position between Quint and Andrea. She explained the colored toothpicks, passed around her notes on the applicants, and readied to take down the opinions about the pies. On a clean notebook page, she made two columns and wrote "Presentation" at the top of one, "Taste" above the other. She inserted the names of the bakers on the side, leaving enough room between each applicant's name for three comments.

The three pies were center stage on the island, every asset and flaw spotlighted in the incandescent glare. Quint rolled up the sleeves of his denim shirt as though he meant to dig into the task at hand. He said, "Before any taste test, we need to judge these pies on appearance. Pie number one. What do you think?"

"Seriously?" Andrea sounded like this was a complete waste of her time, since she had kids waiting on her and needed to go home. "Let's cut to the chase. None of these pies looks like one of Molly's pies. Not even close. I'd give them all a one out of ten for appearance."

"I agree." Callee stifled a yawn. "None compare with

Molly's, but number two isn't horrible. I'd give it a four."

"Is four good enough?" Andrea asked Quint. "Is that what you're aiming for?"

"No," Quint said. "I'd be happier with a seven or eight."

"There are none of those in this trio." Andrea hitched a hip against the island.

"Let's not get discouraged on the first day," Quint said. "I knew the odds of finding someone who makes pies up to Mama's standards on the first try was probably impossible. We'd have a better chance of hitting the Powerball."

Andrea pulled a tiny container of lip balm from her pocket and applied it with her pinkie. "We might need to settle for someone with lesser talent."

"I know I'm not going to be working here, but I need to weigh in on this," Callee said, sharing something she'd learned from Roxy. "Lesser talent is okay in an assistant. They can learn, grow, improve, and hone. They can be taught. But for the main pastry chef you have to shoot higher."

Quint swiped his hands down his jaw and over his mouth in frustration. "Okay, then let's consider this pie you'd give a four. The crust isn't beautiful, but it is flaky, and it looks as edible as most homemade pies across America. Which applicant baked it?"

Callee checked her notes. "BiBi Henderson. She is in her early twenties. Her father has something to do with the cooking industry. She was raised, she said, around chefs and bakers. I put eager beaver next to her name. I thought she might make a good assistant pastry chef."

"I don't know if she'd take that job if you offered it,"

Andrea said. "She seemed like she wanted to prove something to her father. She's after the main job."

"But she's not qualified for it based on the appearance of this crust," Quint said. "If, after we taste her pie, we still think it deserves a four, or higher, then make a note, and I'll call her in to discuss the assistant's job later. I want to hire the pastry chef first."

Or you could just be *the pastry chef,* Callee wanted to say.

Quint glanced at her, and his eyes narrowed into a glare. God, could he read her mind? Or was his conscience bothering him? "Okay, let's taste these pies, so Andrea can get home to her boys."

He dug through drawers and took out a pie server, a knife, and a tray. "You two go on into the café. I'd appreciate a cup of coffee if there is some."

"There is," Andrea said. "I made a fresh pot while Callee was with the last applicant."

"If you'll pour me a mug, I'll slice these pies and bring in samples. I want to mix up the numbers so you won't know whose pie you're judging. But I will. Since I didn't meet any of these applicants, but you have, you might be prejudiced against one or the other. This way, however, the taste test will be impartial."

It sounded reasonable, Callee thought, but to be honest, she was too wiped out to be sure. Maybe some sugar and caffeine would give her an energy boost. She told Andrea, "I could use a cup of coffee, too."

"Sure thing."

Callee gathered forks and napkins and took them to the café, sliding into the back booth. She made Andrea sit beside her. She needed a table between Quint and herself.

He entered the café hoisting a tray and set it in the center of the table. He took his mug from Andrea and settled into his side of the booth. Callee kept her gaze on the pies, wondering if she could still tell who had made which pie by looks alone. But she couldn't. Her mind was too much of a sieve after this crazy day.

On another clean page of her notebook, she wrote numbers next to the three colors and then left space again for each of their comments. Quint handed out the pie she'd marked number one.

They were silent as each of them took a bite.

"This crust isn't too bad." Quint shrugged. "Not Mama's crust, but it's...passable."

Andrea agreed. "Definitely a six for flakiness."

But then Callee realized what Quint had said. "Do you want passable?"

He shook his head "I know Mama wouldn't approve of passable. This is a possible for the assistant chef, but that's all."

BiBi Henderson's pie, Callee guessed.

They moved on to pie number two. Quint took a bite and spat it out immediately, looking accusatorily at Callee. "Who made this dough?"

She knew without tasting, but had to ask, "Is the dough tough?"

"As a calloused heel."

"Francis Bronkowski," Andrea said. "The woman has the right credentials—if this was a cupcake shop."

Quint dipped his fork into the filling and tasted. He made a face. "The filling doesn't even taste like Mama's. Didn't they all have the same measurements for the ingredients?"

"They did," Callee assured him.

"Then how could she have screwed this up?"

"I saw her add extra lemon juice. I think she *preferred* less sweet cherries."

Andrea spit the bite of Francis's pie into her napkin and laughed at Callee's inside joke, a joke they explained to Quint.

Callee's notes made it clear. "Things are not looking good, guys."

"One more to go." Quint handed each of them a sampling of pie number three.

As the light caught the sugary top crust, Callee stayed her fork. The others dug in, but she puzzled over the appearance of this crust. The rich golden color was nothing like the three pies she'd assessed in the kitchen. What the hell? She poked the crust with her fork. It flaked apart like layers of baklava. Her mouth watered. She stole a suspicious glance at Quint.

Head down, he kept eating.

She stared at him as she raised her fork and slipped a bite of pie into her mouth. The buttery crust melted on her tongue, the sweet sugary cherries adding to the delight. Dear God, this pie was absolutely delectable...and the filling...oh, my, it tasted exactly like what she'd made last night for Quint. "Is this—"

"Delicious or what?" He glanced up sharply, cutting her off.

"If I didn't know better, I'd think this was one of Molly's pies." Andrea beamed.

"Quint," Callee said, "whose pie is this...?"

Quint stiffened. Satisfaction arrowed through Callee. She knew it. He made this pie—with her help—and it was every bit as good as one of Molly's. She wanted to tell him that. Tell him to embrace this natural talent he had inherited. Contrary to what he thought, or what all of his redneck buddies thought, she found men who could bake about the sexiest thing ever. But unless he confessed this hidden talent to Andrea, she, in good conscience, could not.

"Whoever baked this is our new pastry chef!" Andrea whooped.

"Whoa." He seemed not to have expected this reaction. How shortsighted of him, Callee thought, figuring he deserved to talk his way out of it. Didn't he realize the pie was too good not to elicit excitement? He looked dismayed, scrambling for an answer Andrea might believe. "I'm sorry. I played a bit of a trick on you. This is a pie I brought from Mama's house. She made it the day before her heart attack. I thought we should have a comparison to Mama's before making a decision on any of these others."

One of Molly's pies? *Liar!* Though she wanted to, Callee decided not to call him out on it, if Andrea didn't. But why had he really included his pie with these others? Her stomach clutched. Of course. He wanted her to know that he had come back and finished baking this pie last night. Her gaze fell on the crust, on the uniquely crimped edge. It looked kind of like…Her eyes widened as an image of the floured chopstick returned. *Well, I'll be damned.* This man had more talents than she ever knew or suspected. How had they never taken time to discover this sort of thing about each other?

And why did he need to brag to her about it, even in this sneaky manner? Such a boy thing to do. Wanting to show his accomplishments, large or small, off to the woman in his life. *Hon, come look at how well I washed and polished the car. Hon, come look at how good the yard I mowed looks.* Like a kid: *Mommy, Mommy, look, no hands.*

Did men ever outgrow that show-off impulse? Probably not. She found it equal parts annoying and engaging. But she was no longer the woman in his life. In twenty days, their divorce would be final. A divorce he'd wanted. He'd hurt her, sent her away, and he had no business trying to impress her. Especially after what went down between them last night.

She met his gaze, trying to silently convey that he should not be feeling so very smug. If he still hadn't hired a pastry chef by tomorrow, he would have six pies to bake all by himself. She wouldn't play assistant again. Not after last night. She'd agreed to help him find a pastry chef, not play patty cake with him.

"What about the third pie?" Andrea asked. "We owe it to the applicant to at least taste it, don't we?"

"It was so-so. Crust was too thick." Quint finished the last bite of his wonderful pie. "I tossed it out."

Callee poked her fork into the slice of pie that she and Quint had made and ate another bite, enjoying the thick, gooey sweetness. As she swallowed, a thought struck her. This filling was not runny. The realization sent her reeling back against the booth, and an odd sensation welled up from deep inside her, something that made her feel so good she smiled. Oh my God, she could actually make pie filling. She almost said it out loud, catching herself just in time.

"Well, tomorrow's another day. And a new group of

applicants." Andrea sounded weary and dispirited despite Quint's earlier pep talk about not setting their expectations too high. She got up and began putting the plates and mugs onto the tray. "Not that I want to stress anyone out, but what if we can't find anyone who measures up to Molly's pie-baking skills? Big Sky Pie will go under before it's opened."

"Let's not worry about that until we do tomorrow's interviews." Quint swiped his mouth with his napkin, then tossed it onto the tray. "Maybe one of them will be the one. We need to keep a positive vibe going."

Callee wanted to tell Andrea not to worry. If all else failed, she "knew someone" who could bake pies as good as his mama's. Maybe better. But since Quint was probably going to be up all night making pies, she figured that was enough punishment for one day. She didn't know, though, how he thought he'd get away with pretending he found the pies at his mother's.

He said, "Callee, may I have your notes and the résumés? I want to put them into a file. I'll wait a few days more, until new applicants trickle down or fall off completely, before notifying anyone."

"Sure. I'll put a star on the potential applicant for the assistant job." Callee pulled the folded résumés from a pocket in her journal, added the star to BiBi Henderson's résumé, and gave them to him. As she readied to leave, she said, "Oh, Quint, since there are more applicants coming in the morning, you might want to cube some butter and stick it in the freezer."

Andrea glanced at Quint, and Callee watched his neck grow red as he glared at her. She smiled her sweetest smile. "Good night."

As she went out the door, she heard Andrea ask, "Why would she expect you to cube butter?"

"It's payback for bailing on the interviews today," Quint said. "Callee used to tease me about my lack of kitchen skills when we were first married. But how hard can cubing butter be? Just cut the sticks into chunks, right?"

"How should I know?" Andrea laughed and took another sip of coffee. "I'm not a cook. Or a pastry chef. How did the two of us end up running a pie shop, McCoy? Maybe you should call Callee back in here and ask her how to cube butter."

"Naw." He shoved his long legs out and crossed his feet at the ankles. "If I don't do it right, she can fix it tomorrow."

Andrea got up from the booth, went to the coffee machines, and unplugged them. "I'll clean them in the morning and have the coffee made by the time you show up for the first interview."

He nodded, listening with half his mind. The other half was on Callee. "Lovette, tell me something, would you?"

"Depends on what it is."

He shoved his hand through his hair. "How do I win back the woman I love?"

"Oh, no." The question seemed to startle Andrea. "Are you serious?"

"Absolutely. I really screwed up. I don't want the divorce, and I don't know if I deserve to have Callee forgive me. I'm not even sure she can."

Andrea shook her head. "Much as I'd cheer your reunion, if you *both* want that, I'm not getting in the middle of it. She's my friend, you're my boss and my friend, and I am not choosing sides. Uh-uh. Don't ask me to."

He heaved his shoulders, dejection falling on him like a weight he couldn't shake. "You better get going. Your hour is gone."

Andrea hurried to the office for her coat and purse and returned a minute later holding Callee's handbag. "I don't know why she didn't come back for this. Her hotel key is probably inside." She gave it to Quint with an encouraging smile. "You might want to take it to her."

Chapter Eleven

〜

Callee languished in a bubble bath, letting the sweet scent of peaches and cream invade her pores and her senses. She closed her eyes, drifted off, and dreamed of making love with Quint in their master bathroom. She awoke, touching herself, lingering sexual sensations flowing through her veins. As her eyes eased open in that first stirring of awareness, she swore she saw him there, through the steamy mist. She started up in the tub, water sloshing and splashing over the edge and onto the tile floor. But it wasn't Quint, just her own reflection in the fogged mirror.

She toweled off, dried her hair, and put on fresh makeup. She was starving. Tonight, she would treat herself to pepperoni pizza with olives and peppers and onions and extra cheese. Or maybe Chicken Parmesan. Anything Italian. Her mouth watered with anticipation. After she ate, she would visit Molly. But she could do none of that without her handbag. Her credit card, cash, and her driver's license were all in her wallet.

She was halfway across the mall parking lot when she realized she'd left her handbag at the pie shop. No way was she going back for it. The front desk clerk recognized her and issued her a second room key. Once she was in her room, she'd called Andrea. The call went to voice mail. She left a message and begged her to take the bag with her. Said she'd swing by for it on her way to dinner. She was pleased to see she had a message on the hotel phone, more so when she found it was from Andrea. But the message displeased her. "Sorry, I was running late. Quint is bringing your purse to you. He'll be by within the hour. Maybe sooner. See you tomorrow."

Quint? Callee hung up and glanced around the room, realizing she had forgotten to put the chain on the door. He could have let himself in with her room card. Had he? Was that why the vision she thought she saw in the mirror as she was waking up had seemed so real?

She checked everywhere in the room. No purse. She called the front desk, thinking he might have left her purse with the bell clerk. He hadn't. But she discovered he was in his room. The desk clerk gave her the room number, and she realized he was actually just down the hall from her. She took one last look at herself in the mirror. What stared back at her was a definite improvement on the earlier version of herself. Fresh jeans, her red Dingos, and a matching sweater that picked up the auburn tones in her chestnut hair.

She grabbed a favorite denim jacket with rhinestones decorating the lapels and back. She strode down the hallway, confident in her look, and found Quint's room. Her pulse had decided to run a race with every step she'd made toward this door. Now her heart seemed to have climbed into her throat. So much for confidence. She knocked. No answer. Maybe she should have called first. She knocked again. A little louder. Maybe he'd left without the front desk knowing about it. She lifted her hand to knock again, and the door swung inward.

Quint stood there naked except for a towel around his taut waist. Her gaze went to his chest, to the swirls of ebony hair between his pecs, to the trail of fuzz that ran down to his six-pack flat belly. She caught herself and raised her eyes to his face. His hair was damp, and he smelled of his favorite aftershave and soap, and just looking at him roused memories of sex in a steamy bathroom.

Callee struggled to find her tongue, which seemed to be fantasizing on its own about tasting him—here, there, and everywhere. "Uh, Andrea said you were bringing my purse to my room?"

"Come on in."

"No, that's okay. I'll wait out here."

"Suit yourself."

He shut the door and left her standing there. Hopefully while he put on pants. And a shirt. After five minutes, she pounded on the door with her fist. "Quint. Come on."

He opened the door again. Still wearing the towel... and nothing else.

She shoved past him and into the room. "Where is my purse, and why didn't you bring it to my room?"

"I did." He said, his voice gravelly and mind-bendingly sexy. "You didn't answer the door."

She hadn't heard anyone knock. Of course, she had been soaking in a bubble bath. Sleeping in it, actually. She stared at his body again.

He grinned that wide, disarming McCoy grin. His gaze

slid over her, igniting tiny fires everywhere inside her. Why did he have to look so great in anything, dressed, undressed? Damn him.

He asked, "How'd you get in the room without your key?"

She'd gotten another key from the front desk, of course, but since that was such an obvious thing to do, she ignored the question. "Why didn't you leave the purse in my room, since the key was in it?"

He lifted an eyebrow, realizing what she meant. "You mean let myself in... ?"

"Did you?"

"Did you want me to?"

That was no answer. Had she imagined him there? Or had he been there? She blinked, remembering where her hands were when she'd awakened. She blushed, cursing her desire for this man she didn't want to need, but ached for.

Quint took a step toward her. "For the record, I don't enter ladies' hotel rooms uninvited."

His smoldering gaze said he'd once had no trouble getting those kinds of invitations. Lots of them. She swallowed back unwanted images. The way he looked in that towel... "My handbag?"

He pointed, and the towel dipped dangerously low, revealing a dark, dense hairline. Her gaze went there and not to where he pointed. "It's on the bed."

It? She glanced at the bed, realized he meant her purse, and blushed. She scooted over and grabbed the bag by the handle, then faced him again.

"I didn't look inside, in case you're wondering," he said.

"I—I wasn't wondering," Callee lied. Not that she had anything in her bag that she'd mind him seeing. Her journal was safe in her room.

"Out of curiosity, do you have a radio or something in there?"

"No, why?"

"I swear I heard singing that sounded like Carrie Underwood." Quint pulled clothes from a drawer and then placed clean jeans and boxers on the bed, boxers she'd bought him for Valentine's Day last year. Navy blue with tiny red hearts.

"That's my ringtone." Callee sank to the bed and found her phone, but didn't even glance at the screen. Her gaze was glued on those boxers, her mind awash with the memory of stripping them from him, on what had ensued after. Delicious tingles raced through her. A glimpse in the dresser mirror showed her nipples stood proud against the soft plush of her sweater.

Quint noticed, and the blue of his eyes darkened. Beneath the towel, she saw the signs of arousal.

Dear God, she was sitting on his bed, all but inviting him to drop that towel and join her.

"I have to go." She shot to her feet, her phone gripped in one hand and the handle of her purse in the other. He strode to the open closet, standing between Callee and the exit. As she neared, he pointed to three of his shirts. "Which one? The white? The blue? Or the striped?"

"Hot date?" Callee asked, wondering why he would ask her what shirt to wear. He'd never done so while they were married. A stall tactic, she decided, when he only grinned at her question. She shook her head. "No?

Well, I do have one . . . a hot date, that is, so if you'll excuse me . . ."

It wasn't a lie. She had a date with some spicy Italian
food. She started past him.

"Callee," he said so softly that it stopped her in her
tracks. His eyes were twin blue flames, as mesmerizing as
fire on ice. If she weren't careful, she could burn up just
looking at him, especially given his current attire.

"What?" she managed, her voice raspy.

"Thank you."

She frowned, clear thought clouded by the charged fog
of energy between them. "For what?"

He dipped his head toward her, a lock of hair falling
across his forehead, his breath minty, his aftershave
heady. "You know . . . everything."

Did "everything" include how she'd left him in the pie
shop the night before? Probably not. "Okay, sure."

"Handling the applicant interviews today allowed me
to see the cardiologist about Mama's surgery, get some
realty business done, and check on Mama a couple of
times. I appreciate it. I'll be there tomorrow to do the
question-and-answer part of the interviews," he said.
"And to observe the pie making."

"Good." She moved to the door, then turned back and
said, "The striped."

"Yeah, that's what I was thinking, too." He reached for
the hanger, and the towel hit the floor.

* * *

Molly looked marginally better than the last time Callee
visited, but the machines still beeped and IV tubes still

snaked from her arms. She still lacked sparkle. It was as if all her color had washed away with her health, leaving her complexion the color of paste and dark circles under her blue eyes. Her usually spiky red hairdo resembled matted monkey fur. Callee wept inwardly, but forced a big, bright smile.

Surgery was less than forty-eight hours away, Callee reminded herself, and as scary as the operation was, it was also welcome. Callee kissed Molly's cheek, held her hand, and asked if she needed anything. "A book or magazine?"

"No. Too sleepy to read." Molly raised her bed to a semi-sitting position, an eager expression in her eyes. "What I want to know is are you ready for the pre-event?"

"Almost." *As ready as we can be without a pastry chef.*

"See, I knew you could do it."

A lot of responses to this occurred to Callee, but none of them were good for Molly's health, so Callee adopted a soft expression and a teasing attitude. "You know darn well that I am not making pies."

Molly looked contrite. "I'm sorry for any and all emotional hardships this favor may be putting on you, Callee, but you were the only one of the bunch with restaurant experience."

"Don't you worry about me. I'm doing just fine." Callee squeezed her hand. "Besides, I didn't have anything better to do. It's not like I would have left for Seattle anyway knowing you were here."

Molly gave her an "I love you too" grin, then said, "Well, if any good has come out of this crisis of mine, it's that Quint finally 'fessed up about inheriting my pie-baking skills." Something flashed across her face, a hint of her old sparkle, but it was gone as quickly as it had come. Molly sighed and laid her head back on the pillow. "Did he tell you that he brought the pie you made together to show me this morning?"

"No, he didn't." Callee shook her head. "Your son is full of surprises."

Molly ignored that and said, "Callee, am I imagining it, or does he seem to be getting some of his emotional footing back?"

Callee considered that, deciding she couldn't be sure, but for his mother's sake, she hoped it was true. "Maybe so."

That seemed to please Molly. She asked for a sip from her water cup. Callee obliged. Molly thanked her and lay back on the pillow. "Tell me about the pre-event. What pies is he baking for it?"

Callee said, "I'm not sure he's decided yet. The cherry pie, for sure, though."

"Of course. He gave me a tiny taste of his pie, and I must say it was every bit as good as mine."

Callee concurred. The apple didn't fall far from the tree. "We couldn't go wrong with your recipe."

"That's true." She chuckled. "What other pies?"

Callee scrambled to think of pies that would be appropriate for this time of year or that Molly had the ingredients for in the freezer. Her mind went blank. She couldn't come up with one label she'd seen on frozen packages. And then it struck her that maybe Molly could participate in the pre-event even from this hospital bed. "What would you suggest?"

"Blackberry," Molly answered immediately. "And strawberry rhubarb."

"Wait," Callee said, pulling an envelope and a pen from her purse. "Let me write these down. What about the pies you had us taste test the other day? The Daiquiri, the Tar Heel, and the Key Lime?"

Molly nodded, pleased. "Good choices. Oh, it's going to be a great event. I hate not attending, but I know you and Quint will do Big Sky Pie proud. I was so looking forward to the mayor's dinner and the food the others will be bringing. Sharla has lined up Kalispell's best restaurateurs to participate. Dear me, I'm making myself hungry just thinking about it. Probably because that doctor of mine has me on a cardboard and mush diet. I swear he's set on ruining my taste buds."

Callee assured her that was not likely to happen and that she would be able to have real food again soon. "I need to go. They don't like me to stay too long."

"I'm very proud of you, Callee."

Callee didn't know why Molly should be proud of her. She hadn't done anything to deserve it. Nothing Molly wouldn't have done for her, if she were the one in this hospital bed.

"Oh look," Molly said. "Here's Quint. Oh my, isn't he handsome in that striped shirt?"

Callee spun, her eyes filling with the tall, strong man in the doorway. He grinned the same grin he'd worn when the towel dropped to the floor. And now, that was all she could see. His gorgeous, naked body. She wanted to rub her eyes to eradicate the image.

Concentrate on how he looks now. Fully clothed. But one glimpse at those blue jeans drew a picture of the navy boxers beneath, and that brought the earlier memory.

She hastily kissed Molly's cheek and said good night

to them both. As she passed Quint, he said, "See you in the morning," then mouthed, "if not later tonight."

She whispered, "Only in your dreams."

* * *

But it was Callee arriving at the pie shop exhausted, yet again, from tossing and turning during a night of dreaming about Quint. Her sexy dreams convinced her that this insane reaction to him meant she had a case of the "go backs." A really bad case.

Andrea and Quint were seated at one of the round tables with coffee cups at hand and résumés for the upcoming interviews between them. Callee greeted them, went straight to the coffee machine, and then joined their conversation. Andrea was going to be in and out of the office, catching up on paperwork. Callee would sit in on the question-and-answer part of the interviews and take notes for Quint. And all three would discuss each applicant after they left.

The two morning applicants showed promise in the first part of the interviews, but were less impressive making pies. Quint pulled the second pie from the oven and set it on a rack to cool. "This is pathetic."

"Even I could make a pie that looked that bad," Callee said.

Andrea just *tsk*ed. "I had high hopes for this one. Some people sure can talk a good game, but don't look so discouraged, you two. There might be another applicant. I'm waiting to hear back from him so I can set up an appointment."

"Great," Quint said. "Where's the résumé?"

Andrea had it ready. "Right here. As you can see, he worked at a bakery in Billings." Quint walked away reading the résumé.

"Have you heard anything from Jane Wilson?" Callee asked Andrea.

"Nothing." Andrea pushed her hair behind one ear. "I think we can forget about that one."

Maybe Andrea was right about Jane, Callee thought, taking her phone and journal outside into the back parking lot to stretch her legs. Sunshine spilled over her, warm and welcome, and the air smelled sweet with the promise of summer. Callee would miss not being in Montana for summer. The Seattle waterfront smelled of brine and creosote and fish. Quint would probably love it.

As she walked, her mind kept returning to thoughts of Jane. She couldn't shake the sense that there was something special about that young woman, but if Jane wanted the job as much as she'd said she did, wouldn't she have phoned by now?

I would have.

Callee debated calling Jane. Finally she decided she owed it to Molly to go the extra mile, if that's what it took. She found Jane's number and phoned. Don't seem too eager, she cautioned herself. The phone rang and rang again. Jane didn't answer. Callee didn't leave a voice message.

But she wasn't ruling out calling later if Jane didn't call first.

She went back into the pie shop café and saw a car pulling in. Maybe it was Jane. She hurried to the front door, renewed hope tripping through her. It fled the second she saw who it was.

A twenty-something guy with dirty blond hair, baggy

cammo pants, a grimy muscle tee, and flip-flops. She tried not to look at his filthy feet. The stench of deep-fried fish came at her, pitching her mentally back to another place and time, another life. To her years working in Twangy's Bar and Grill.

"Calleeee," Milo Keech, her former coworker, gushed through a flash of yellowed teeth.

Callee didn't share Milo's enthusiasm for this reunion. "What are you doing here?"

"Ain't you gonna invite me in?"

"Are you here about the job?"

He shrugged. "Yeah, maybe."

Callee's bullshit meter pinged off the charts. She would stake every item in the U-Haul truck that Milo was lying. If he was a pastry chef, she was the first lady.

"I didn't have no clue this was your pie shop," he said, shoving past her and into the shop.

Milo nodded to Quint as he looked around the café. "You come up in the world, girl. Owning your own place, and ain't it shiny new?"

"It's my mother-in-law's pie shop."

He went quiet, and then said, "I heard a rumor she died."

"Where'd you hear that?" Callee asked.

"Ain't it so?"

"No," Quint said, his arms folded across his chest. He eyed Milo with curiosity. "She had a heart attack. She's having surgery tomorrow."

Milo sighed loudly. "Ah, that's great, man."

Suspicion darted through Callee. Why was he so relieved that Molly hadn't died? She asked again, "Why are you here, Milo? The truth this time."

He gave a shake of his long hair, sending the fried-fish odor at her. "I come "'cause a guy I know, he thinks maybe he killed your mama-in-law."

"What?" Quint said so loudly everyone jumped. "What the hell are you talking about?"

Milo shied away from Quint, but Callee stepped into his personal space. "Who is this guy you know? What's his name?"

Milo shrugged, like he didn't want to say. Callee pressed the point. Milo raised his hands in a "giving it up" gesture. "Okay, okay. Name's Sanchez. Rafael."

Quint's brows lifted. "Rafe? Our Rafe?"

Callee couldn't get past the fact that Rafe thought he'd killed Molly. "Is the Rafe you're talking about tall and extremely handsome?"

"I ain't into guys." Milo made a face. "But, yeah, I guess he's okay looking."

"Does he have a tiny scar beside one corner of his mouth?" Andrea asked.

"Yeah. That's him." Milo nodded, pointing at Andrea. "Man, he's gonna be a happy dude."

"Where can we find him?" Quint seemed ready to shake the information out of Milo.

"Why did he think he killed Molly?" Andrea and Callee asked in unison.

Milo laughed. "It's kinda funny. He says they was working on which pies should go on the menu. He told her 'bout a old family recipe he has for some kinda meat pie. He says it's mucho spicy. He made one, and she took a bite just before she died."

"She's not dead," Quint reminded Milo.

"I'm just sayin' what he says. He thinks his pie killed her."

"Well, it didn't, and we need to let Rafael know that he still has his job. With my mama having surgery, we want him to come back here and start working again. Right away."

Milo smiled. "Ah, that's nice."

"Where can we reach him?" Quint's impatience showed in the tense set of his brows.

"Do you have a working phone number for him?" Callee asked, trying to defuse the tension.

"Naw, but this here's his sister's address over on Railroad." He handed Quint a slip of grimy paper.

As soon as Milo was gone, Andrea said, "I live near Railroad. Let me see that address."

Quint handed her the paper. "Wow. This is very near my apartment. Want me to run over and see if I can talk to Rafe on my way home?"

"I'll drive you now," Quint said, digging his keys from his pocket.

"Oh, that's not a good idea." Andrea stopped him with a raised hand. "As jumpy as he must be, thinking he's about to be arrested for killing your mother, he might assume you're there to haul him to the police. Or seek vengeance. He could run at the sight of you—before you can tell him otherwise."

Quint didn't like it, but he nodded. "Okay. You're probably right. Go. Find him. Convince him to come back to work."

"I'll do my best."

As Andrea drove off, Quint turned to Callee. "I don't know about you, but I could use some lunch."

Men and their stomachs. "Aren't you the least bit worried about the pies for the event tonight?"

He shrugged. "Not yet. It's only noon. I'm getting something to eat." He indicated he was heading to the mall. "Want to come with?"

"No, maybe Jane Wilson will show up. Someone should be here just in case."

"I think that's a lost cause," he said. "I'll bring you back something."

Callee paced through the kitchen and the café, willing Jane Wilson to call, periodically checking the wall clock, her nerves winding tighter with every cycle of the rooms. As the time neared one, she started to believe Quint was right; Jane was not coming. But damn it all, call it woman's intuition or a gut instinct, something told her that Jane might be their only real candidate for the pastry chef job.

One o'clock. No Jane. No new applicant e-mails. No response yet from the guy from Billings. Quint hadn't returned either. And Andrea hadn't phoned or come back. Callee decided to bite the bullet and call Jane again. Nothing to lose if she said no. But what if she just needed some encouragement?

The call didn't go straight to voice mail this time. "Hello?"

"Jane Wilson?"

"Who is this?"

"Callee McCoy, from Big Sky Pie." She waited for Jane to respond, but when she said nothing, Callee continued, "You said you'd be back this afternoon to finish your interview. Are you still planning to do that?"

Jane said nothing. Callee's heart dipped to her stomach. "Jane? Are you still there?"

"Yes. I—I'm so embarrassed about yesterday. It's not

the impression I planned on making. My nerves just got the better of me. I don't usually get sick like that. And anyway, well, I figured you wouldn't want me to come back."

"But I do." Callee breathed easier. Jane still wanted the job, but she seemed to have weighed good manners against the chance of a lifetime, and wrongly come in on the side of manners. She needed a reality check. "Jane, opportunities like this aren't going to drop into your lap very often. If you want all that you told me about yesterday, then you need to get down here and fight for this job."

Callee saw no reason to reveal how weak her competition was. Or that if she could bake a decent pie, the job was hers hands down.

Jane was silent another long minute. Callee wanted to reach through the line and shake her. Had no one ever explained the concept of golden opportunity to this woman? "What do you say, Jane? Are you coming?"

"Oh, yes, I'm sorry, I was hunting for my car keys. Oh, and I have to take a couple of pies out of the oven. I bake when I'm anxious. I'll be there in fifteen minutes."

Ten minutes later, a minivan pulled into one of the parking spaces out front. Behind the wheel was a strawberry blonde. Relief and anticipation collided inside Callee.

Quint was just crossing the street. He arrived before Jane got out of her vehicle. Callee grinned at him. "Oh, Quint, this is the woman I told you about who I think might be the answer to our prayers."

"I brought you a chicken wrap. Why don't you eat while I talk to her?" He welcomed Jane into the shop, introduced himself, and directed her to one of the round tables. Callee sat nearby, eating and observing.

Jane looked even more ready to cook today than she had yesterday. Perhaps because she had been baking. French braid tight, cheeks peachy pink, chef pants, t-shirt. She took off her jacket and underneath she wore an apron that read: FEELING CRUSTY? BAKE A PIE.

Quint smiled when he saw that, but Callee could tell he was thinking Jane looked too young to be all Callee claimed. Perhaps he'd forgotten that he'd started young, too. He went over her résumé again, asked a couple of other questions, then said, "Let's see what you can do, then."

Jane's first sight of the kitchen produced a small gasp, the sound resonating through the room like a hum of joy. Her gaze moved from one corner to the other, and a smile of awe started and spread across her face. She actually stroked the marble countertop with a reverence that suggested it was chinchilla. The top-of-the-line appliances widened her big, blue eyes. She glanced at Callee, then Quint. She asked, "You're going to let me bake a pie in this kitchen?" When clearly her expression shouted, *Are you telling me if I pass this test, you'll actually pay me to work here?* When even more clearly she'd likely do it for free.

Callee had placed the ingredients on the counter, already measured for her, along with the large bowl. Now she stepped back to let Jane show them what she could do.

Quint watched from the doorway like someone monitoring a college class, his expression leery, but curious. Callee crossed her fingers behind her back. Jane began to talk, telling them what she was doing and why. She gave the same spiel Quint had given Callee when he'd been making dough, and as he watched and listened, Quint lost his scowl. He was coming around.

Jane mixed the thawed Bing cherries as Callee had done the other night, tasting the finished mixture to be certain it was what she expected. She smiled. "Oh, yes, this is delicious. I never thought about freezing the cherries. But it works. Is this your mother's recipe, Mr. McCoy?"

"Quint," he said, beaming. "Yes, it's been handed down for three generations."

Four generations, Callee thought.

Jane smiled. "I have a couple of recipes like that, too. Our family favorite is Cottage Cheese Pie. It tastes like custard pie, but we like it even more."

Jane rolled the dough with an expert's touch. She placed the bottom crust into the pan, poured in the filling, and added bits of butter on top. Then she quickly sliced the top crust into long strips, crisscrossing the strips over the filling to form a decorative lattice crust. She crimped the edges, her little hands as creative with the dough as a sculptor's with clay. A sugary glaze finished her handiwork. None of the other applicants had done anything like this.

"Wow," Quint mouthed to Callee. She nodded and felt something warm and pleasant settle into her. Satisfaction, maybe. They had found their pastry chef. Jane was efficient, fast, and the resulting pie looked scrumptious. She placed the pie in one of the wall ovens and set the timer on the stove as though she'd been working in this kitchen for years.

The confidence Jane exuded creating the pie seemed to

float off on a wave of new anxiety. "When is the shop going to open?"

Quint told her, which led him to mention the pre-event at the mayor's ranch that evening.

"Oh, I've heard about that." Jane began cleaning up the mess on the island. "Sharla Tucker goes to our church. According to her, it's supposed to be something pretty special."

Callee could see Quint was charmed, by Jane and by the appearance of her pie. He seemed about to ask if she wanted to participate in the pre-event as the new pastry chef for Big Sky Pie—if she agreed to the salary and hours. But before he could say anything, the sound of a phone ringing in the café caught his attention.

He went to answer his cell. Callee chatted with Jane, small talk, garnering more information about her family and background. Quint walked back into the kitchen, pale and obviously shaken. Callee's heart began to thud. "What is it?"

"Mama's surgery. We need to get to the hospital now." He hurried to the office, moving like a man in a panic, speaking as he went, "There was a cancellation about an hour ago, and they've prepped her and are taking her in in a few minutes."

Quint grabbed his keys, telling Callee to hurry. He seemed oblivious of Jane and the baking pie.

"I need to get my handbag," Callee said. "I'll meet you at the SUV."

He hurried out, and as she struggled into her coat, she explained the situation to Jane and begged a huge favor. "I hate to ask you this, but can you stay until your pie is done baking, then lock up the shop for the night?"

"Of course. Don't worry."

Callee handed Jane her key. "Put it in the decorative mailbox out front when you leave."

A horn honked from outside.

"Go," Jane said. "I'll close the blinds and turn off the lights and make sure everything is shut down."

"Thank you." Callee started toward the café, then stopped. "Oh, and Jane, I'd say this job is yours. Quint will need to confirm it, of course, but he can't think about anything but his mother right now."

"Oh, wow. Thank you." Jane looked over the moon.

Callee hurried out to Quint, terrified. Thoughts of Jane, the pies for the pre-event, and the pie shop faded as soon as she buckled her seat belt and they pulled out of the parking lot, headed for the hospital.

Chapter Twelve

～⌒～

Quint felt cold one minute, hot the next. Everything the doctor told him that could or might go wrong during his mama's surgery sailed through his mind like signs on a road trip. "Bad reaction to anesthesia, heart attack or stroke during or after the procedure, postoperative infection. Even weeks after the surgery something could go wrong."

Callee stomped her foot. The heel of her boot hitting the flooring felt like a cymbal to his ears. He looked up into her green eyes and felt his breath catch.

She said, "Stop being such a gloomy Gus and quit dwelling on everything that can go wrong. It won't do Mama any good if you get sick from worrying."

True, but he couldn't seem to help it. Until his dad died, he'd never even thought about mortality. Now every time he turned around, it seemed about to tackle him. He wanted to shout: "I got it. Nobody lives forever!" But damn, he still found himself dialing his dad's number, before hurt and loss brought back the realization that Jimmy McCoy was no longer reachable by phone.

He glanced at Callee, wondering how she had coped with losing her mother as a kid. How did a child figure out that her mommy wasn't ever coming back? How did she learn to even trust loving someone again? Hell, how had losing his dad led to losing Callee? He'd gone into their marriage planning on them growing old together, still as in love as Mama and Dad were. *Until death do we part.*

It occurred to him now that all of life's important relationships were based on that phrase. You had friends until death do we part. Pets. Parents. Mortality was everywhere. He couldn't outrun it or out-fish it. Or curse it away. He could only face it head-on and deal with whatever hand it dealt him.

Was he man enough?

He glanced at the clock. He didn't expect the surgeon for another hour or two. Any sooner meant bad news. Callee shook her head, sending the scent of peaches through the air, and her words came back to him. *Stop dwelling on everything that can go wrong.* He ached to reach for her. To hold her hand. To hold her. He closed his eyes, leaned his head back, and wracked his brain to recall what the doctor told him would occur after surgery. Nothing came to mind. "I can't remember what else Dr. Flynn said."

"Good thing I'm here then." Callee smiled. He could see the worry lurking deep in her eyes, knew she feared something would go wrong as much as he did, but she refused to go there. Here and now they were in the hope zone. He needed to get on board with her or she'd kick his ass.

She gestured as she spoke, her voice low, he assumed, out of respect for the other families in the waiting area.

"Dr Flynn said if everything goes as it should, and we need to keep thinking it will, Molly will spend two or so days in the ICU, then be moved to another wing in the hospital for three to five more days before recovering enough to go home. And in twelve weeks, she will be fully recovered. Imagine. When she was our age, this kind of life-saving surgery would have only been possible with the use of things like pig valves."

"Are they still using pig valves?"

She shrugged. "I'm not sure. I haven't researched it. You could probably search the Web for the answer."

"They're using Mama's own veins."

"I know." Callee nodded, then a teasing grin lifted the corners of her kissable lips. "Do you think she'd rather have pig valves?"

That coaxed a smile out him. "Knowing Mama, she'd rather have pie-dough valves."

They shared a quiet chuckle, and as the tension eased throughout him, he remembered Jane Wilson. "Holy shit, we left Jane alone at the pie shop."

Callee sighed. "We did. But don't worry; she said she'd stay until her pie finished baking and then lock up. I gave her my key. She'll leave it where I can find it."

He didn't seem to think that was a great idea. "You sure she's trustworthy?"

"I am."

"She's definitely a surprise. I liked how she came in prepared to bake pies, apron and all."

"Plus she's fast, and when orders start coming in, that will be an important asset for your pastry chef to have," Callee said. "She started baking pies younger than you did. It's what she wants to do the rest of her life."

"I can't fault her enthusiasm, instinct, or skill. My only reservation about her is her age and management experience. The main pastry chef will have a lot of responsibility on his or her shoulders. The job is more than baking pies. It's running that kitchen and the kitchen staff."

"I think she deserves a shot."

"I'm not saying no to her." Yet. So why did Callee look as though she might punch him if he didn't hire Jane? Was she thinking of her own desire to get to Seattle? Probably, since Mama's surgery and finding a pastry chef for the pie shop were the only two reasons she was still in Kalispell.

"Speaking of pastry chefs, did Andrea ever get back to you about Rafe?" Callee asked.

"I talked to her last night. Rafe took one look at her and tore out of there. I'm guessing Milo hadn't spoken to him yet. So she explained to his sister what was going on."

"I'm surprised she's not here. Did you tell her about the surgery?"

"I didn't think to let anyone know but you."

Callee said, "I'll step out and phone her. I don't want to tell her this in a text." When she came back, she sank onto the seat beside him.

He asked, "Is Andrea coming?"

"No. Now both her boys are sick, and she's feeling like she's coming down with their bug. She doesn't want to give it to us."

"If she hasn't already." He couldn't afford to catch a cold or flu bug. Not right now.

As he thought this, Dr. Flynn appeared. A moment later, Callee was in Quint's arms, sobbing.

Chapter Thirteen

$\sim$

An occasion like this called for only one thing, Callee thought, and apparently Quint agreed.

"I want some of Mama's sweet cherry pie," Quint roared. "To go along with this champagne."

"And I know where we can get some." Callee laughed as tears of joy filled her eyes again. She thought her tears were spent, but the relief and delight felt boundless.

The moment Dr. Flynn had said Molly's surgery was textbook, that he was cautiously optimistic of a full recovery, Callee had collapsed against Quint, unable to stop her tears.

Quint didn't cry. He laughed and laughed, and hugging her, spun her around in celebration...until the waterworks subsided. This had gone on for less than a minute, yet it felt as though they'd clung to each other for an eon. Even afterward, as the doctor cautioned that the next couple of days were critical, Callee had stayed spinning on an emotional cloud.

She said, "The pie I have in mind wasn't made by your mother, but Jane's pie looked like it could be of the same caliber."

"Big Sky Pie, it is," Quint said, steering the SUV toward Center Street.

It had been hours since they'd grabbed something to eat in the hospital cafeteria, hours more until they could see Molly, hours spent in the waiting area quietly leaning on each other, words unnecessary in their bubble of gratitude and hope. Finally Molly arrived back in the ICU. Tubes and wires and IVs had been reattached by the time they were allowed to peek in on her. She slept, unaware of their visit, but Callee noted her coloring was already better.

It was after eleven p.m. when they left the hospital, both too wired to call it a night. They'd secured a bottle of Cold Duck, not exactly expensive bubbly—more like the dregs—but the one sparkling wine Quint actually liked.

When he pulled the SUV into the parking space, Callee saw the pie shop had the proper night lights on inside, as well as the outside lights. If this was any indication, Jane had not only locked up, she'd done a stellar job of it. She found her key in the mailbox. Her faith in the woman boosted her already high spirits. She was certain that when Quint tasted Jane's pie, the job would be a lock for Ms. Wilson.

They went inside, switched on lights, and locked the door behind them. The scent of sweet cherry pie hung in the air, making her mouth water in anticipation.

Quint surveyed the café. "Looks just as we left it."

The kitchen, however, was not as they'd left it. "Wow," Callee said, impressed. "Jane not only stayed until her pie was done baking, she put the supplies away, did the dishes, and cleaned off the counters. Pretty responsible for someone without a lot of experience under her chef cap."

But Quint was frowning as he dug through cupboards, then looked into ovens and the Sub-Zero. "Only one thing wrong."

"Oh?" Callee removed her jacket, trying to figure out what he referred to, but not finding anything amiss. She couldn't have done a better job herself of cleaning up.

Quint placed two clean coffee cups on the island beside the wine. "What did she do with her pie?"

Callee's eyebrows lifted. "It isn't here?"

"Nope." He levered the plastic cork from the Cold Duck bottle with both thumbs. The ensuing "pop" underscored his words. "Not on the counter or in the refrigerator. And not in any of the ovens."

"Hmm." Reasons why the pie wouldn't be there raced through Callee's mind. Maybe it hadn't turned out as well as it looked like it was going to. Maybe Jane dropped it when removing it from the oven. Maybe she tossed it out. Callee did a quick check of the garbage and the disposal for signs of the pie. Nothing. She shrugged, perplexed. "I guess she took it with her."

"Why would she do that, knowing the pie was the final test as to whether or not she gets the job?"

Callee had no answer. "I can't explain it. It's not like she doesn't know how to bake a pie. We both watched her. She did everything you did with the crust, and everything I did with the filling. That pie was perfection before it was baked."

Quint poured wine into the mugs and handed one to

Callee. "Maybe she was so busy cleaning up, she forgot to take it out in time, and it burned."

"I saw her set the timer." Callee shook her head. "Besides, do you smell burned pie in here? No. Just delicious pie."

"Well, it's irresponsible of her and just exactly what I worried about given her lack of work experience. But given my good mood, I'm willing to hear her explanation before I make a final decision. She is, so far, the best applicant we've interviewed."

"Yes, but now we have no celebration pie."

"Wipe that let-down look off your face, Callee." He pulled a pie box from the refrigerator and produced half a sweet cherry pie. Their pie. Quint heated the pie in the microwave just long enough to make the filling warm and gooey, then carried it to the island. Callee laughed as he lifted his mug to hers. "To Mama's full recovery."

They clinked and drank.

"To Big Sky Pie," Callee said.

They clinked and drank, and offered up a few more toasts, the bubbly wine easing away the stresses of this long day. Quint turned on the CD player, and the soft sounds of Latin music floated through the room, a delicious accompaniment to her celebratory spirit, seductive even. They stood side by side at the island, digging in to the pie straight from the dish. He cut into the pie with his fork, fed a bite-sized piece to Callee, and wiped sweet sticky filling from the edge of her mouth with his thumb. The intimate contact sent delicious slivers of desire to her toes.

The reaction jarred her as she realized she and Quint were back at the scene of the crime, letting their guards down, and enjoying time together in the kitchen, something she'd found sexy as hell the other night. But the chain reaction that followed had ended badly. She warned herself not to let things escalate again. *Just store this moment in your memory banks.* It was likely to be the last sweet one she would have with Quint.

Her new future loomed large now that Molly was on the road to recovery, and the pie shop had likely found a pastry chef. In the next day or so, she could head to Seattle and never look back. A week ago, this would have been so easy for her. But now…like in the song, "Regrets, she had a few," but in her case, not too few to mention.

Even the sugary heaven attacking her taste buds couldn't erase the bitter taste of her regrets, but before she could voice even one, Quint asked, "Do you like to fish?"

"What?" The question seemed to come out of nowhere. Was he thinking of going fishing again? Right now, maybe? She continued to frown at him.

"Do you like to fish?" he asked, waiting for her answer as though it were of monumental importance, and she realized that he was being serious.

"I don't know." She shrugged. "I've never been fishing."

"I should have taken you." A look of pure regret crossed his face. "Or, at least, asked if you wanted to go. I should have taught you how to fish."

The remorse in his words touched a chord inside Callee, surprising her. "I'm not sure I'd like putting a worm on a hook…"

He grinned, his voice low and husky. "I'd do that for you."

"You would?"

He nodded, reaching as if to touch her hair, but not touching it. "I'm so sorry, Callee. For everything I didn't do and for everything I put you through."

She hadn't expected this admission, and it stole her breath and made her nerves twitch. Things were getting a little too serious. Entirely too serious. She gulped some wine.

"Losing Dad..." Quint choked, looking as though the impact of all that had happened that afternoon had finally caught up to him. He seemed unable to swallow, his eyes gleaming wet, his expression one of unbearable pain.

Callee felt her own throat constricting as tears sprang to her eyes and began rolling down her cheeks. She cupped his cheek in her hand and sputtered, "I—I lost him, too."

Misery and grief welled up from deep inside, releasing the anger and sorrow and fear she'd held at bay. Words began to tumble out. "Jimmy treated me like his natural-born daughter almost from the first day we met. Did you know he used to phone me every few days to ask how I was doing, to see if there was anything he could do for me? Or that he sent me a bouquet of flowers every now and again? Just because. Or that on my days off, he would often call and ask me to lunch or to take a walk so we could catch up?"

Quint shook his head in wonder, his eyes awash with regret and guilt. "He was such a great guy."

"He was the sweetest, most thoughtful man I've ever known." She choked, the tears falling faster now.

"He was," Quint said, his voice gravelly.

Callee gazed up at him through scalding tears. "He wasn't just your dad, Quint; he was my dad, too, the only one I ever knew."

"I know…"

"We—" Callee said, her voice breaking as badly as her heart was at the memories that assailed her, at the loss of Jimmy McCoy, but she couldn't stop the flow of words. "We shared a special bond that I can only assume is what little girls are born having with their fathers." She'd relied on that fatherly affection, even taken it for granted, but it had been snatched from her way too soon, reminding her that nothing and no one stays for long. "Losing Jimmy was like losing my mother all over again."

Her knees wobbled as she began sobbing.

"Oh, God, Callee." Quint pulled her into his arms, holding onto her as she'd wanted him to do when Jimmy died, and she clung to him as he muttered, "I should have realized. I should have…I'm so sorry…"

Callee wept uncontrollably, her face buried against Quint's chest, her tears wetting his shirt. As her tears began to subside, she realized that he was trembling, too. She felt his heart thudding beneath her cheek, heard his tender words of commiseration, and her sense of loneliness decreased. When she lifted her head and gazed at Quint through wet lashes, she saw a watery sheen in his eyes. Her heart ached for him, for both of them, and for Jimmy McCoy.

"I'm so sorry," Quint repeated, the sincerity in his voice setting off a primal urge in Callee. She reached her hand to his face, then slid her fingers into his hair, and pulled him to her, wanting to curl inside him, wanting him inside of her, wanting to feel alive.

Needing it so much she thought she'd die if it didn't happen.

She lifted her mouth to meet his kiss. At his hesitation, she whispered, "Please."

"Are you sure?"

She nodded, and although his lips met hers, he still held back, his kiss as soft as a butterfly wing, a wispy breeze. She started touching him and with a groan, Quint claimed her mouth and deepened the kiss, bringing his arms around her possessively, imbuing her senses with the rich scent that belonged to him alone.

"Oh, Callee…" He caressed her back, her waist, her bottom, pulling her impossibly closer, his erection solid against her thigh, their tongues twining in a joyous dance that tasted of Cold Duck and cherries and desire.

And then his hands were under her sweater, grazing her belly, singeing her naked flesh everywhere he touched, until he stroked her sensitive, budded nipples and she gasped, her pulse exploding as though shocked with a live wire.

With her breath coming in short, sweet gasps, she tore at his shirt and helped him remove her top. Clothes hit the floor, his shirt, her sweater, his jeans, her bra, and soon Quint was nibbling a sensuous trail from her earlobe down the most sensitive areas of her neck, finding her eager breasts, and sucking. Erotic tingles surged through her body, trying her patience to its limits.

Quint unzipped her jeans and shoved her panties to the floor, his eyes heating from warm to smoldering blue flames at the sight of her totally undressed. He said in a low, husky voice, "Damn, woman, you're the most beautiful thing on this earth."

Callee savored the bliss sweeping through her as he pulled her into another kiss, caressing, stroking, his finger slipping between her thighs to fondle her most sensitive spot until he elicited a jarring climax. She cried his name, and he moaned loudly as if her pleasure were also his pleasure.

The need to feel him inside of her grew more urgent with every passing second, and she tugged at his boxers, taking his arousal into her hand, and then into her mouth. He moaned her name, conveying to her in the language of lovers that his control was slipping dangerously, quickly. She met his kiss as he scooped her up in both hands, lifting her to wrap her legs around his hips, and then finally, he entered her, the joining a shock of joyous rapture, too long denied.

Electric impulses zigzagged through her senses, her body seeming to be liquid and fire and music. Need spiraled tighter and deeper and then began lifting up and up and up with each thrust until it exploded into starbursts of pleasure. Until she screamed his name, and he screamed hers.

She collapsed against him, spent, yet not done, fulfilled for the moment only, breathless, panting, her head on his shoulder, their bodies still joined. She didn't care that they were divorcing or that she might later regret this; all that mattered was this moment and how healing it felt.

Her gaze fell to the dregs of Cold Duck and the abandoned pie, and an awful thought struck Callee. "Oh my God, Quint, we missed the pre-event."

He leaned back and looked at her, a lazy smile on his sexy mouth. "Seriously? That's where your mind went after our lovemaking? I must be slipping."

She laughed and kissed him again. "As if you need to worry about that."

"Good to know." He grinned wider. "I suppose I'll need to call the mayor and Sharla tomorrow and explain. Nothing we could've done about it, and frankly, right now, this is all I care about."

He began nibbling her neck, and Callee sighed with desire, but pushed him away. "Not here."

Catching her meaning, he released her. Without even speaking, they dressed, locked the pie shop, and within minutes were naked again in her hotel room shower. She spread peach-scented bath gel through the black hair on his chest, over his strong shoulders, down his muscled arms, his solid back, over his tight butt, and his erect penis. She savored every stroke, sighing as he returned the favor, her body coming alive beneath his hands.

She couldn't get enough of him. She went down on her knees, warm water raining over her, as she took him into her mouth again and again until he groaned in ecstasy, lifting her off her knees and spinning her around to face the shower wall. He entered her, his arm around her waist, his hands on her breasts. She met his thrusts with equal passion and felt the world giving way. They seemed to climax together, their cries of euphoria a melodious duet.

They finished showering, toweled each other dry, and once again, desire overtook them. Afterward, she snuggled with him in her bed, dreamy, dreaming, lost in an afterglow of pure satisfaction. As though the past months hadn't happened, they curled together and slept the night through, wrapped in each other's arms.

In the morning, they made love again.

Afterward, Quint caught a strand of her hair between his fingers, sniffed it, and smiled. "God, woman, I missed you."

"I've missed you, too," she whispered. "If this is the 'go-backs,' no wonder couples do it."

"What are you talking about?" Quint propped himself on one elbow and stared into her eyes, wearing nothing but a sated smile.

Callee reached up to brush aside a lock of his ebony hair, then traced her fingertip down the side of his face. "It's something Roxy told me about." She explained it to him.

Quint listened, his expression disconcerted. "You think this is the 'go-backs'?"

She'd been too busy enjoying the ride to consider where things went from here. "I don't know. Can we go back? Do you want to go back?"

"No. I want to go forward. From here."

"And just pretend the past months didn't happen?"

"No. That would be a mistake. But what's not a mistake is us." His expression grew pensive. "I know now that I let my grief isolate me, that I shut you out when what we both needed was to deal with Dad's loss together. If I could go back and change that, I would, but I can't. All I can do is beg your forgiveness and promise that I will never again turn away when you need me. I love you, Callee, with all my heart and soul. I want to spend the rest of my life making up for these past months, if you can forgive me, and if it's what you want, too."

She hadn't thought she could be any happier than she was when she woke up wrapped in Quint's arms, but his words filled her with such gladness. "I love you so much, Quint."

Quint let out a cowboy whoop and kissed her again,

then pulled back, grinning, already breathing faster. "Whoa, I think we better save that for later. I have business decisions and phone calls to make about the pie shop."

"Then get dressed and go." Callee snuggled into the sheet. She needed to shower and dress, too, but for a while longer, she wanted to nestle beneath the covers, still warm from his body heat.

"Meet me at the pie shop in a little while, okay? And then we'll go visit Mama." Quint pulled on his shirt and jeans and began stuffing his feet into his boots. "She's going to be thrilled that we're calling off the divorce. Oh, call your lawyer and do that, okay?"

"Okay." Callee laughed, shooing him toward the door. "And make sure you phone Sharla Tucker about the pre-event."

"Will do." He kissed her once more, a sweet kiss on the lips, and left.

Callee hugged herself, savoring the warm wonder of the past forty-eight hours and all the sweet possibilities that loomed on her horizon. Life was a constant surprise. She reached for her phone to call her lawyer, but before she could find his number in contacts, a call came in. "Roxy, I'm so glad you called."

Callee brought Roxy up to date on her relationship with Quint. The announcement was met with silence. A shiver went through Callee, something her grandmother would have called a shadow passing over her grave. "What's the matter, Roxy?"

"Oh my God, you do have the go-backs."

"No, it's not that." Callee felt defensive, grabbing at everything she could to make her best friend understand how much she and Quint had worked out, the promises he'd made, their grieving over Jimmy. "We made love all night long and again this morning. I'm deliriously happy."

Silence again.

Callee was getting annoyed. "Roxy, whatever you have to say, just say it, okay?"

"You're in the honeymoon phase of the go-backs. Remember when Ty and I reconciled? He made all those promises? I think he even meant to keep them, and I admit, it was pure bliss for about two weeks. But the man is who he is... and I am who I am. Can't fix what's broken. I'm sure Quint means all those promises he's made you, too, but give him a few days and he'll revert to his old workaholic self. You can't change the stripes on a tiger, girlfriend."

As she showered, Callee thought long and hard about her best friend's warning. She knew Roxy might be right, but that wasn't really what kept gnawing at Callee. She'd told Quint that losing his father was like losing her mother. And it was. But if she loved Quint like she thought she did, shouldn't losing him have been the most devastating loss of all?

Chapter Fourteen

Quint went back to his hotel room. He showered, shaved, and dressed, feeling like a man finally touching down to earth after a long, free skyfall. He stared at the man in the mirror. Had he gone insane after his dad died? All signs pointed to it. But today was a new day, a new start. He'd begun to reclaim his life. Only this time, he wasn't going to take it for granted. Not ever again.

He phoned the hospital. Mama had had a good night and was sleeping. Quint said a silent prayer of thanks, then asked the nurse to let his mother know that he'd be by later. As he passed Callee's room, a Rascal Flatts love song popped into his head. He rode the elevator humming the upbeat tune, ignoring the odd looks from his fellow passengers. Nothing was going to bring him down today. Nothing.

He grabbed a copy of the local newspaper in the lobby, stopped in the breakfast area for some scrambled eggs and toast, and caught up on his hometown sports. Afterward, he hurried to the pie shop. The morning was getting away from him, and he had decisions to make, applicants to phone. Big Sky Pie would open its doors in a few short days; staff had to be in place as well as baked goods ready to sell.

He let himself in, switched on the lights, raised the blinds, and turned up the heat. He started the coffeemaker and went into the kitchen. The pie plate, empty bottle of Cold Duck, and their mugs still littered the island. Everything was as they'd left it last night before going to the hotel. Lusty images filled his mind, every excruciatingly wonderful second of their lovemaking recalled with pleasure. He didn't try to banish the memories or the accompanying hard-on.

This kitchen had offered him some horrible moments, and some he would always treasure. Especially making a pie with Callee...and making love with her after eating that pie. A feeling as good as hot cherry pie went through him. He started whistling the Rascal Flatts song again as he gathered the empty bottle and pie box and tossed them into the garbage, and put the pie plate, silverware, and cups into the dishwasher.

He was drying his hands when Andrea phoned. She sounded like someone had scraped her throat with sandpaper. "Stay in bed and get well, Lovette. Mama had a good night. I'm feeling hopeful. I'll text you an update later today."

He disconnected and went into the office. The first thing he did was check for new responses to the ads, but there were none. No e-mail from the Billings applicant either. He collected the résumés, read through Callee's notes on the applicants, and began his calls. Although he tried being tactful, Francis Bronkowski was livid. She said he'd never find anyone more qualified for the job. Quint reined in the urge to tell the woman her pie dough could pass for shoe leather. He moved on to the others and thanked them for coming in, letting them down as easy as he could.

He left a voice mail for BiBi Henderson to call if she was interested in an assistant pastry chef position. Then he left another voice mail for Sharla Tucker apologizing for not making it to the pre-event and asking her to phone, at her convenience, to discuss the main event.

By the time Callee let herself in the front door, he still hadn't decided what to do about Jane, and one look at Callee sent everything else out of his head. She wore a summery dress with a denim jacket and red Dingo boots. Her hair was down, shiny and wavy, to her shoulders. His heart did a handspring. "Hey, pretty lady."

She stayed in the office doorway, tilting her head to one side. "What are you doing?"

He caught Callee up on the calls he'd made, doing his best to concentrate on that and not give in to the desire coursing through his veins. But damn it, she could distract a stampede of wild horses.

"I've phoned everyone but Jane Wilson. Still trying to decide if I can trust the running of the kitchen to her."

"Then I'd say you have only one other choice. Take the job yourself."

"I don't want to be a pastry chef. I'd rather keep that as one of my hobbies. Something we could do together whenever the mood strikes us."

"I'd like that," she said, then frowned. "As long as

you've got time. I mean, once this shop is open and you add in getting the realty office restarted..."

He could see the worry and realized she knew that, if he meant to get his business up and running, it would mean more hours spent apart, the same old, same old. He didn't want that either. "I haven't had time to talk to you about this yet, but I'm considering switching up my realty business, getting into remodeling and selling some of the old buildings Mama owns around town instead. It would be something where I could control the hours."

"Ooh, more of a nine-to-five job with evenings and weekends off...I could get used to that."

He smiled, but before he could continue this conversation, he heard a car pull into the back parking lot. Callee glanced toward the windows. "Uh-oh, Sharla Tucker is here."

Sharla's brown hair looked even bigger than usual as she swept inside, her gigantic handbag in tow. Her black dress seemed appropriate for a funeral. Hopefully not Big Sky Pie's funeral, Quint thought. "Come on in, Sharla. How are you today?"

"Well, goodness, I'm just wonderful," she said, sweeping inside and plunking her bag onto the island. "But the better question is, how's your mother? I pray the surgery went well."

How had she heard about the surgery already? Quint frowned, but decided to roll with it. "The doctor said it was textbook. He expects a full recovery."

"Oh, that's such great news. Molly is in my prayers."

"Thank you. I appreciate that," he said. She must be here for an apology, Quint decided. He needed to mend

fences in this town. Might as well start here and now.
"Look, about the pre-event—"

"Oh, it was excellent. I'm sorry you two had to miss it,
but, of course, everyone understood."

Everyone? All the folks at the pre-event? Quint
couldn't believe how fast gossip spread in this town.

"Could I get you a cup of coffee, Sharla?" Callee said.

"Oh, no, no, I can't stay." She glanced from Callee to
Quint. "I don't suppose you've heard yet?"

"Heard . . . ?" Quint said.

"Your pies, of course."

She meant their pies were banned from the big event.
He got it. He started on his apology again. "Yeah, about
that—"

"Well, goodness, let me tell you both, they were the hit
of the night," Sharla gushed. "Everyone raved about the
variety you provided, so tasty, especially the sweet cherry
pie. I think the mayor ate three slices himself of that one."

"Pies?" Quint glanced at Callee in confusion. She
shook her head slightly and shrugged, looking as clueless
as he felt. What the hell was Sharla talking about?

Sharla said, "Given all that you're juggling right at this
moment, well, I don't know how you managed, but I'm
impressed. Everyone is impressed. Big Sky Pie is the talk
of the town this morning. Stan Byers from the *Gazette*
will be calling for an interview. You've got a success on
your hands, Mr. McCoy."

"Um, how, who, how did the pies get to the event?"
Callee asked, obviously as much at a loss to explain this
apparent miracle as Quint was.

Sharla paused, then smiled. "Why, your pastry chef
delivered them to the mayor's ranch late yesterday af-

ternoon. I didn't see her, but he said she's a pretty little thing. Reminded him of a Kewpie doll. Strawberry blond, big blue eyes."

"Jane Wilson," Quint said, sounding like he'd known the whole time who and what she was talking about. Callee, he realized, was giving him a huge "I told you so" grin.

He met that grin with an "I'll be damned" one.

"Well, goodness, I know Jane Wilson. Her family attends my church. She's been baking pies almost since she was a baby." Sharla gathered her purse. "Aren't you the sly ones snatching her up for this shop? She's a gem. I am really looking forward to the big event, and thanks to your pies, so is everyone else who was at the mayor's dinner."

Quint didn't think his day could get much better. Everything was going his way. Damn. He was glad to be alive. "Thank you, Sharla, for stopping by."

"Of course. Oh dear, look how late it's getting. I won't bother you any longer. I know you've got a full plate at the moment, as do I."

With that, she blew out as fast as she'd blown in.

Quint grabbed Callee and spun her in happy circles, their laughter ringing off the cabinets. "Wait'll Mama hears. She'll explode with all our good news."

Callee shoved out of his arms. "Quint, I need to talk to you about that."

"About Mama or the good news?"

"About telling everyone about us." She was biting her bottom lip, a sign she wasn't sure how to say what she wanted to tell him. Quint felt unease slip through his belly. She said, "I'm not sure Molly is well enough for an overload of good news yet."

"You don't want to tell Mama that we're back together? Why not?"

"I, er, I want to keep it between us for now."

Quint frowned so hard it hurt his head. "What? Why? I want to shout it to the world."

Callee hesitated, licked her lips, then said, "We jumped into our relationship too quickly the first time around. I don't want this time to end up like last time. I don't want us to be a 'go-backs' statistic."

Quint laughed, hugging her again. "I swear I won't let that happen, sweetheart."

She didn't seem reassured. "Please, Quint, I don't want our big news getting lost in the launch of the pie shop."

He hadn't thought about that, but now realized she had a point. He didn't want to share their reunion with the opening of Big Sky Pie either. Hell, what difference would a few more days make? He tilted her chin and grinned down at her. "I kind of like the idea of us sharing a sexy secret, but once this pie shop opens, we're gonna celebrate like New Year's Eve and Christmas all rolled into one."

"It's a deal." Callee smiled and kissed him, acting as though a weight had lifted from her. "Meanwhile, shouldn't you be calling Jane Wilson before someone else hires her?"

"Hell yes," he said, starting for the office. "I should have trusted your instincts. You were right about Jane from the get-go."

Callee beamed at the praise. "I'd say she's proven she can more than handle this kitchen."

"Agreed. And it explains what she did with the cherry pie she baked. But where do you suppose she got the other pies?"

"I wonder," Callee said. "When I phoned her yesterday, she said she was baking pies. She said she bakes when she's anxious. And she'd been afraid she'd made a bad impression at her first interview and was debating whether or not to try again."

"I'm grateful you talked her into it."

"I'll bet she took the pies she made at home to the mayor's ranch and presented them as our pies."

"And I have her reward." Quint smiled. "Would you like to be the one to tell her?"

Callee shook her head. "Nope. I think she deserves to get the job offer from you."

"Okay, but let's put this on speaker phone, and we can both talk to her." He dialed the number. Jane answered. He identified himself, and after answering her inquiries about his mother, he told Jane that she'd nailed the interview with her ingenuity and her skills. And that by going the extra mile for the pie shop, she'd made Big Sky Pie the hit of the pre-event and the talk of the town. The pastry chef job was hers—with one proviso. She would need to make her recipes part of the menu.

Jane laughed, screamed, apologized, and then screamed again. He set up an appointment to meet with her later that day to discuss salary and hours and do the paperwork to make the job official.

"Do you think her neighbors will call the cops thinking she's being murdered?" Quint said, disconnecting.

"Probably." Callee laughed.

"Let's head to the hospital. I can't wait to tell Mama all this good news."

"Sure. I'll get my purse. It's in the café." Callee left the office.

Quint's cell phone buzzed. He checked the screen. He'd missed a call and had a new voice message. The call was from Dave the Realtor. He listened to the voice mail, then tried calling Dave back as he strode toward the café. The call went to Dave's voice mail. Quint said, "Tag. You're it."

As he drove the ten minutes to the hospital, Callee filled the miles with talk about Jane and the pie shop's promising future.

His mind was on Dave's voice message.

Chapter Fifteen

⁓

In just three days, Big Sky Pie had transformed from an almost-open business into a viable entity with a steady stream of customers. Sweet aromas teased the air as Jane worked her magic in the kitchen and Andrea handled sales at the counter.

The official grand opening was delayed until Molly could attend, the tentative date coinciding with the twelve-week recovery estimate given for triple bypass patients. Her doctor continued to rave about her progress and said he would release her from the hospital in another day or two.

Callee and Quint spent their days working together, yet apart, exchanging the occasional secret glance or smile. He'd dealt with getting the pie shop staff hired, figuring out the volume of pies that would be needed on a weekly basis and pricing the pies, cobblers, and tarts. He also saw to the installation of an à la mode dispensary behind the café counter with a choice of either vanilla or cinnamon ice cream.

Andrea jumped between the front counter, the café, and the office, selling pies and juggling accounts payable, and holding everything together as assistant manager whenever Quint couldn't be there.

Jane ran the kitchen like a pro with her new assistant pastry chef BiBi, producing samples, refining recipes, selecting the variety of pies, and deciding to do a feature pie each month. This month's pie was Frozen Sweet Bing Cherry Pie.

Callee designed brochures and albums for parties, weddings, and other special occasions and events, and she created the café menus. The work, while exhausting, gave Callee much satisfaction. She dropped into bed each night worn out, yet loving the sense of seeing her ideas come to fruition.

Quint, on the other hand, seemed so immersed in operating the pie shop that he had little time for her, and he hadn't even started doing anything about his realty business—except to have his huge billboard on the way into town transformed into one for Molly McCoy's Big Sky Pie.

Every night that he arrived late to their bed, Callee's sense of déjà vu grew. Like tonight. She checked the bedside clock. After ten. She'd hardly exchanged two words with him all day, and she was starting to worry that they were falling back into the old, dreaded routine. It didn't help that Roxy's words of warning kept spinning through her mind. *I'm sure Quint means all those promises he's made you, but give him a few days and he'll revert to his old workaholic self. You can't change the stripes on a tiger, girlfriend.*

Callee nibbled her fingernail. If he was too busy for her now, it would only get worse when he began splitting his time between the realty office and the pie shop, and when that happened, they would once again be sharing a bed, but nothing else. She couldn't go back to that loneliness. She needed something more from this life.

* * *

Cell phone to his ear, Quint pulled the pie he'd just baked from the oven with his free hand. He'd planned to take it to Callee tonight as a surprise. But she was the one with the surprise for him.

"Are you sure?" Quint said into the phone, feeling as if he'd touched a live wire.

"Positive," his lawyer said. "Got it directly from her attorney."

"Shit." Quint couldn't wrap his head around this news. "What do you want me to do?"

"I'll let you know." Quint disconnected, fear lodging in his chest, the world falling away from him all over again. He'd been so certain that Callee had forgiven him. That she wanted to go forward with their marriage. *Except she didn't want you to tell anyone you were back together. Let's keep it a secret, she'd said, between the two of us.*

His legs seemed rubbery. He needed to sit down and think about this, not lose his temper, not go off half-cocked. He pulled a beer from the fridge, downed a swig, and sank onto a stool. Another swallow did nothing to ease his distress. "What the hell?"

Why would she take him back into her bed, but not into her heart? Was this his punishment for what he'd put her through? Or was this that bitch Fate teasing him with how wonderful his life could be, then kicking him in the balls and ripping it all away just as he was starting to regain his self-respect? He chugged a second beer and reached for a third, trying to drown the monster clawing its way through his heart.

* * *

Callee let herself into the pie shop. The café was dark, the blinds closed against the night, the staff gone home hours earlier. They would return and begin baking pies while most of Kalispell slept. Big Sky Pie opened daily at eight a.m. with a fresh stock of pies ready for sale and consumption.

She found Quint in the kitchen, sitting at the island, near the Sub-Zero, several beer bottles at hand, a couple of them on their sides. What was this? A private beer party? Why? "Quint, what are you doing?"

"Hi." He glanced up. His mussed ebony hair still needed cutting, but he looked more delicious than any dessert offered at the pie shop, and she fought the urge to go to him. A piece of Sweet Bing Cherry Pie sat on the counter in front of him. Two forks nearby. He lifted a fork toward her. "Join me?"

"Did you bake that?"

"Maybe..."

Callee cocked her head. "Don't tell me you're starting to embrace your legacy?"

"Maybe," he said around a bite.

"Next thing I know, you'll be announcing it at the Center Mall during the big event."

"I might. It would be worth it to see the look of surprise on Lovette's face." He gestured toward the second piece of pie.

She stayed where she was, reading his mood. His smoky blue eyes said something was wrong. Very wrong. He set the fork down and cleared his throat. "My lawyer phoned a while ago. He'd spoken with your lawyer earlier and found out that you haven't called off the divorce."

Callee's breath caught in her throat. "I—I—"

"Still want the divorce?" He planted his palms on the marble countertop. "I thought we...you...loved me..."

She felt something hard crack apart inside her. Tears blurred her vision. "I do love you, Quint, I probably always will, but I...don't love you as much as you deserve to be loved."

"What the hell does that mean?"

She set her purse on the island and met his gaze, praying for understanding. "Remember when I told you that losing Jimmy was like losing my mother all over again?"

He nodded, but seemed to be struggling to keep a rein on his temper. "I remember every second of that night."

So did she, which made what she had to tell him so much more difficult. "I realized the next morning, after you left for the pie shop, that losing you should have been even worse, but it wasn't. And when I realized that, I began asking myself, Why not? Why didn't I fight for our marriage? Why didn't I call you on your bullshit?"

He took a swallow of beer and set the bottle down with a clink. "And did you figure it out?"

"Yes." She took a bracing breath, caught the heady mix of scents—beer and cherry pie tangled with Quint's aftershave—and her nerve threatened to desert her, but she had to explain, had to make him understand it wasn't him, but her. "I was only seven when Mommy died, but old enough to discern nothing good lasts for long, that death is inevitable, whether it's the loss of life or the loss of a relationship. As long as I don't invest my whole heart, I can't be devastated when the end predictably comes."

He looked baffled. "Let's see if I have that. You gave my dad your whole heart, but not me?"

Callee wanted to cry for hurting Quint like this, but it was true. She'd longed for a father her whole life, never guarding her heart against the possibility, but she should have. Otherwise losing Jimmy wouldn't have been so damned tough. Romantic love, however, was another matter. "When we met, Quint, I felt such a connection with you that I was on high alert. If I had given you my whole heart, then your leaving would probably have killed me."

He took another long pull on his beer. "So then, you don't love me?"

She did love him, so much so she couldn't bear seeing him so distraught. "I can't risk loving you the way you want me to without a guarantee that you aren't ever going to leave me again." She raised her hands to ward off his protest. "I know, I know. That's totally unreasonable, but that's how I feel."

He looked gut-shot and angry. "So you're going through with the divorce and what? Moving to Seattle?"

She hadn't thought things through that far, but pushed for an answer, she said, "Yes. I'm leaving in the morning."

He didn't say anything, just nodded as though it were

inevitable. He yanked a slip of paper from his pocket and held it up. "This is yours."

It looked like a check.

Quint rose, cut the difference between them in three strides, and dropped the check on the counter. "It's your settlement in the divorce. We sold our house. All-cash deal. Dave brought the check by tonight."

He grabbed her, kissed her with such passion her toes curled, and then released her just as quickly and headed out the back door. "I hope you find what you're looking for in Seattle, Callee."

* * *

Quint woke with a brick on his heart, his head pounding. After kissing Callee good-bye, he'd gone to Moose's Tavern and gotten falling-down drunk. He might do the same tonight. The U-Haul was gone when he walked to the pie shop. He checked on his employees and then went to see his mother. Molly was propped up in bed, watching a reality TV show about a cupcake shop. She was still weak, but a natural pink hue colored her cheeks, and some of her spunk was back. It warmed his heart. He took her hand and planted a kiss on her forehead.

She studied him, concern pulling her brows low. "You look like hell."

"Callee's gone, Mama," Quint said, his voice cracking. "Left for Seattle this morning."

His mother squeezed his hand. "I know. She came to see me before heading out. I love her, too, Quint. I tried to get her to stay, but…"

"Not me, Mama. I didn't even try. Maybe I should

have, but I'd already done too much to her. I have to let her figure it out for herself." His only consolation was that he'd done the right thing by the woman he loved. Let her go. "So why does it hurt like hell, yet also feel right?"

"You redeemed yourself. That's why." His mother smiled and patted his hand.

He nodded, glad she thought so highly of his efforts. He wouldn't say he'd redeemed himself exactly. He'd made some amends. But he had more to make. Still, he felt better about himself than he had in a long, long time. He could even look himself in the mirror without cringing. Positive steps.

"If she never comes back to me, Mama, how do I get over Callee?" A tear slipped down his face.

His mother sighed. "Well, your daddy always claimed fishing and pie could heal all things. We could sure tell him otherwise, couldn't we?"

Quint grinned wryly, but said nothing.

"When I lost Jimmy, everyone kept telling me time would heal my broken heart," Molly said. "But if you ask me, that's a crock. Time just puts distance between you and the rawness of the pain. It doesn't stop you missing someone. Keeping busy is what helps fill the loneliness."

He ran his hand through his hair and grinned. "Well, damn, Mama. That's not much help."

"Sure it is. You've got two businesses and your mama to take care of right now, Quint. I'd say that's enough to keep your mind occupied for the near future. You should drop into bed too exhausted each night to think about anything else. At least, it's worth a try."

* * *

Quint had been trying Mama's advice for ten days now, but as the divorce loomed closer, he hadn't dropped into bed once without thinking about Callee. Or without dreaming about her. During the day, he could keep his mind occupied enough, but in bed, in the hotel room bed he'd shared with her, there was no way to banish the sexy images and memories that assailed him. Nothing to ease his heartache. Or his longing for her.

He needed to be somewhere that didn't remind him of Callee everywhere he turned. He'd moved out of the hotel room the second night, right after discovering one of the properties he wanted to remodel in town had a twenty-three-hundred-square-foot, three-bedroom apartment on the top level that was in pretty decent shape. He'd hired a crew to give it a thorough cleaning, retrieved his belongs from storage, and moved in. It had the look and feel of a dorm at the moment, and it needed a renovation, but he'd get around to that later.

His mother was at home, her recovery on track, and live-in nurses tended to her needs, allowing Quint to take care of the pie shop without worrying about her every minute of the day and night. He walked to Big Sky Pie, the sun warm on his shoulders, but not warm enough to thaw the constant chill of missing Callee. In six days, the divorce would be final. He'd hoped to hear from her, but she hadn't even sent a text.

Ahead of him, he caught sight of a chestnut-haired woman, and for a moment he thought it was Callee, but as he neared the woman turned and his hope dissolved into disappointment. *Get your mind on business*, he told himself, glad to see the pie shop parking lot was full. Inside the café, tables and booths held customers, a queue led to the sales counter, and mouthwatering aromas tempted the hungry.

He greeted friends, neighbors, and strangers with handshakes, nods, and smiles. He filled a mug with fresh coffee then settled into his reserved booth. He and Callee had done a great job getting this shop up and running.

Callee. His heart squeezed. *Get your mind on something else, McCoy.* He pulled out his pen and started on his to-do list. First up: call Nick Taziano at Adz R Taz and discuss expanding the advertising for the pie shop with some online presence. Second: hire a waitperson for the café. He was pretty sure he had the employment agency's number in his contact list.

As he began searching for it, the bell over the café door announced another customer. He glanced up. A gorgeous woman with chestnut curls was just coming inside. His heart stalled, then jerk-started and began to race. Callee? Or just another woman who might be Callee? He was afraid to move. Or blink, for fear she was only a vision. That she'd disappear. But she was wearing those red Dingos, and they were tap-tapping across the wood floor straight to his booth.

Don't get your hopes up, Quint old boy. He asked in a husky voice, "Seattle too rainy for you?"

"Nope." She scooted into the booth beside him.

Then what? "I thought you were starting college this week."

"I was going to go to cooking school, but, well, after working here and in the kitchen of Roxy's bistro, I realized I don't have the passion I should for a career as a chef. I'd rather pursue my love of decorating."

"Really? I didn't know you wanted to be a decorator. Why didn't you ever tell me?"

"I'm telling you now."

"As it happens, I'm in the market for a decorator."

"Small world." She pressed herself against him, her lips brushing his. She whispered, "I called my attorney and canceled the divorce."

Quint sucked in a breath. He was terrified he'd heard wrong. "You did?"

"Yep." She sighed. "Turns out Seattle doesn't have what I'm looking for, after all."

"What's that?"

"A man who does things with pie dough that make my toes curl." She leaned back, just enough to look at him, her green eyes warm and inviting. "You know anyone like that?"

His pulse roared in his ears. "I might, but he's kind of particular about the woman he wants in his life. She has to love him with all of her heart. You know anyone like that?"

"Turns out I do. She didn't know it, however, until she left him and couldn't stop crying for days on end. Seems as though something happened in this pie shop that opened her heart to this man, and he filled every last corner of it with his love, claiming her as no other ever has."

It took everything in him not to grab her then. He was too distrustful that this answer to his prayers wasn't another trick of Fate. "What could cause such a change?"

"He opened his heart to her. He showed her his vulnerabilities, his truest heart, his hidden talents. He held her, grieved with her for the loss of the only father either of them ever knew." Her fingers curled into his hair. "He wants to teach her to fish."

"Oh, Callee…" Joy ripped through Quint, the sweetest, most delectable sensation he'd ever felt. He scooped her into his arms, crushing her to him in a torrid kiss.

Callee broke the kiss, licking her lips, her eyes glazed with desire. "I love you, Quint McCoy, with all of my heart."

He grinned. "Wait'll Mama hears about this."

"She already knows. I stopped there first to check on her."

Quint hadn't thought he could love this woman more, but he did. He pulled something from his pocket. Her wedding ring. He still wore his. He slipped the ring onto her finger. "Welcome home, Callee."

She kissed him again, then said, "Come on, cowboy."

She pulled him from the booth and dragged him to the pie counter, winked at Andrea, and snatched a whole pie from the rack. Grinning, Quint held her hand tight; he wasn't letting go of her ever again. He willingly trailed after her to the door.

"If anyone asks," Callee said over her shoulder, to no one in particular, "we've gone fishing."

THE END

Frozen Sweet Cherry Pie

Pie Filling Ingredients

- 5–6 cups frozen and pitted Bing cherries
- 1 cup sugar
- ¼ cup instant tapioca pudding mix
- 1 tbs lemon juice
- 1 tbs butter

All-Butter Basic Crust Ingredients

- 2½ cups all-purpose flour, plus extra for rolling
- 1 cup (2 sticks or 8 ounces) unsalted butter, very cold, cut into ½-inch cubes
- 1 tsp salt
- 1 tsp sugar
- 6–8 tbs ice water

Combine flour, salt, and sugar in a food processor. Pulse until mixed. Add cubed butter. Pulse 6 or 8 times until the butter is pea-sized and the mixture looks like coarse meal. Next add ice water 1 tablespoon at a time. Pulse until the mixture just begins to clump. If you pinch some of the crumbly dough and it holds together, it's ready. If the dough doesn't hold together, add a little more water and pulse again. Caution: too much water will make the crust tough.

Place the dough in a mound on a clean surface. Shape the dough mixture into two disks, one for the bottom crust, one for the top. Work the dough gently to form the disks. Don't over-knead. You should be able to see flecks of butter in the dough. They will result in a flakier crust. Sprinkle a little flour around the disks. Wrap each disk in plastic wrap and refrigerate from 1 hour to 2 days.

Place frozen cherries in a large bowl and let them thaw for about an hour. Next combine sugar and tapioca pudding mix in a small bowl. Then pour over the Bing cherries, add lemon juice, and toss to blend. Let the filling sit about 15 minutes, stirring occasionally.

Remove a crust disk from the refrigerator. Let it sit at room temperature for 5 to 10 minutes. This will soften it enough for easier rolling. On a lightly floured surface, roll out the dough to a 12-inch circle, about ⅛ of an inch thick. If the dough begins to stick to the surface below, sprinkle some flour underneath. Carefully place the bottom crust into a 9-inch pie plate, pressing the dough gently into the bottom and sides of the pie pan. Trim excess dough, leaving about ½ inch more than the edge of the pie pan.

Pour the filling into the piecrust and spread evenly. Dot with butter.

Then repeat the above process for the top crust and gently place it over the filling. Pinch the edges of the top and bottom crusts together, then trim the excess dough, leaving an overhang of ¾ inch. Flute the edges using thumb and forefinger, or press with a fork, or try something daring like Quint did and use a chopstick for an artistic touch. Slice the top crust in 4 places to allow steam to escape while cooking.

Bake at 425°F for 10 minutes. Lower the temperature to 325°F and bake for an additional 40 to 50 minutes. Fruit and juices should be bubbly around the edges.

Get ready for another helping
of a Big Sky Pie novel!

Please see the next page
for a preview of

Delicious

Chapter One

⁓

When it comes to men, Janey, your mama is as flaky as the crust on my blueberry pie."

Her grandmother's words taunted Jane Wilson as she stared at her ringing cell phone. The screen showed a stunning, amber-eyed brunette, former Miss Montana, every bit as beautiful now as the day she'd been crowned. Rebel Scott, aka her "flaky" mother. If Jane could, she would detour around the coming evening like a highway accident and just avoid the whole mess. But somehow she always got sucked into the mama-drama.

"I didn't forget, Mom," she answered, juggling the phone and two pie boxes into her Jeep. This month's specialty at Big Sky Pie just happened to be Jane's specialty, blueberry pies with buttery crusts that melted on your tongue. "Just leaving the pie shop now."

Her mother laughed, a sound as melodious as perfectly tuned chimes. "Oh, good. I was afraid..."

That I'd changed my mind? That I wasn't interested

in meeting your latest fiancé, a man whose name you won't even tell me? Jane prayed for the courage to do what she meant to do tonight; after all, it was for Mom's own good. "I have the address and the pies. I'll see you around six."

If I don't chicken out by then.

* * *

If I can find something to wear, Jane thought half an hour later, as she shuffled through her closet, keeping in mind her own preference for comfortable clothes and her mother's idea of dinner-appropriate attire. Her mother insisted that she had passed her grace and beauty onto Jane, as well as her singing talent, and that Jane should be competing in beauty contests. *Wishful thinking.* Jane knew better. She would never be a "Miss" anything. On a one-to-ten beauty scale, she was a solid seven. She'd inherited her dad's strawberry blond curls and aqua eyes, and Grandma Wilson's tendency to gain weight just passing by a refrigerator. Could she have chosen a worse profession than pastry chef? Jane smiled. The fact was, the career had chosen her. She'd been baking pies for as long as she could remember.

If getting married was her mother's passion, baking pies was Jane's. Not men or dating. Growing up with a serial-bride mother had soured Jane on love. She didn't need a man to define or complete her. She had a calling.

A calling that was not doing her figure much good, she realized, as she tried on her black sheath and leopard heels. The effect was a longer, leaner look, as chic as Jane ever got, and pulling her hair back in a French braid would highlight the one asset she shared with her mother, her cheekbones; but the image in the mirror showed the dress hugging in a few wrong places, thanks to the fifteen pounds she'd gained at cooking school. The sheath was her only option, however, and it would have to do.

Not that she was likely to gain an ounce tonight given the knot filling her stomach, a knot that grew worse as she soaked in a bubble bath, and after, as she gave herself a pedicure. She might be a mess inside, but she was determined to *look* put together.

* * *

"Love is like-a my cottage cheese pie, Nickola. Some never take a taste, but those willing to give a try…they in for a big delish-a surprise-a." Anna Taziano's advice seemed to pour from the car speakers, startling her grandson Nick as he hit the city limits of Kalispell, Montana. Just back from a business road trip, Nick was suffering the sting of yet another romantic split and longing for some good old-fashioned, family comfort. So much so apparently that he was receiving it from the great beyond.

He sighed with regret. Granna's loss was always with him like a bruise that wouldn't ease. He missed her old-world wisdom, her counsel. *What would she say if she were still here?*

Stalled at a red light, he envisioned her standing in her farmhouse kitchen, her solid little body encased in its proverbial apron, gray hair twisted into a knot on her head as she shook her wooden spoon at him and *tsk*ed. "What I tell-a you, Nickola? You must make-a the sincere, from-a the heart."

Nick smiled wryly, thinking this was probably the root of the problem. His love life had never been sincere, or from the heart. More like a series of hookups based on convenience, the *L* word never entering into the equation. A by-product of his business. He didn't have time for any long-term, serious relationships, so there had been no Ms. Right's in his life, just a lot of Ms. Right Nows.

The light went green, and Nick turned onto a side street, then circled into an alley two blocks over and into his garage. Though the main office for his advertising company, Adz R Taz, was housed in this downtown Kalispell building, Nick traveled a corridor from Spokane to Billings to Cody, and all places in between to work with customers, setting up or improving their advertising campaigns. The result of so much traveling was that he met some interesting women. Mostly through the lens of his camera. Mostly too-thin models.

And he'd been fried more times than a digital image sensor.

It was getting old. Hell, he was getting old. And lonely. If he wasn't careful, he would end up like his dad—an aging workaholic with no personal life. Nick would give anything if his dad could find someone he loved the way he'd once loved his second wife, but the bitch had soured his dad on marriage and skewed Nick's view of it as well. She and her obnoxious little girl, a real pain in the ass.

Nick grabbed his bags from the back of his SUV and started up the stairs to the second-floor loft where he lived and worked. His cell phone rang as he unlocked the door and shoved the bags inside. Still in ad-man mode, he answered without looking at the screen. "Nick Taziano."

"Nicky!" His dad's booming voice instantly lifted Nick's spirits. Damn, he missed his old man. He and Nick had moved to Las Vegas after the divorce. His dad still lived there, but Nick had returned to Montana a couple of years ago, where a man could fill his lungs with fresh, crisp air and let his creative juices flow.

"Dad, I was just thinking about you." Nick shut the loft door and glanced around. Everything looked as he'd left it. The loft was wide open with brick walls, high ceilings, exposed ductwork, and warehouse-sized windows. His work area took up one end wall and consisted of a wraparound counter/desk combo that held his computers, printers, and cameras. "Just walked in the door from a road trip. How're things shaking in Sin City?"

"Wouldn't know," his dad said.

What the hell did that mean? Nick set the briefcase on the work counter, then carried his duffle bag into the bedroom and dropped it on the bed, frowning. "Don't tell me you've finally taken a vacation."

"Even better."

Nick pulled his toiletry bag from the duffle and went to the bathroom. A glance in the mirror confirmed a need to shower and shave, but right now, he wanted a beer. He headed back into the main room to the minifridge, mulling over what his dad considered even better than a vacation. Romeo Taziano loved cars. Old, new, hot rod, classic. An ace mechanic by the time he was twenty, outgoing and honest, he soon owned an auto repair shop, and when they moved to Vegas, he bought a Rolls-Royce limousine and started Black Tie Limo. Over the past fifteen years, he'd acquired Town Cars, Cadillacs, Hummers, stretch limos, and party buses, becoming one of the city's premiere transportation services. The only thing Nick could think of that his dad would consider better than a vacation was a staycation chauffeuring some world-famous movie star around town. "Congratulations."

His dad laughed. "Tell me that after you've heard my news."

"Okay. I'm all ears."

"I sold the business and retired."

Nick's fingers froze on the twist cap of the beer bottle as the impact of this registered. Romeo had meant for Nick to take over the business when he retired, but Nick didn't share his love of cars, and the frenetic energy of Vegas got on his nerves, stifled his creativity. Still, why would Dad suddenly sell out and retire? He wouldn't. It made no sense...unless...God, was he ill? Seriously ill? "Dad, are you feeling okay?"

"Never better, son."

Relief flooded Nick, but it didn't answer his questions about his dad's sudden retirement, and his dad wasn't offering explanations. "I figured you'd keel over behind the wheel of the Rolls before you ever retired."

"Yeah, I kind of thought that might be my fate, too. But things change."

Nick took the beer to his bedroom, sank onto the bed, and kicked off his shoes. "Why is this the first I'm hearing about this? What the hell changed?"

"A lot. In a pretty short time span, too. Look, it's more than we can discuss over the phone—"

"Like hell. I'm not letting you go until you've told me everything."

"I was hoping you'd say that." There was a pause, then

his dad said, "I sold my place in Vegas and bought a condo here."

"Here? As in Kalispell?"

"Yep. On Flathead Lake."

"No shit?" Nick gave a whoop of joy. "Then you're in town?"

His dad laughed. "Moved in this weekend. Wanted to be settled before I told you."

More likely, he hadn't wanted to ask Nick to help him move since he knew Nick had a solidly booked work schedule. Like father, like son. As he took down the address, Nick said, "Hey, I know this place. I did their brochure ads and some online stuff. Dad, I can't wait to see you." They'd had too little time together these past few years. "We have lots of catching up to do. Let me unpack and wash off the road, then I'll head that way."

"Sounds great. Bring your camera. I'm throwing a little get-together, and I'd like to commemorate this new phase of my life."

He wouldn't be having his dad to himself? Normally that might disappoint Nick, but given his dad had moved to town, there would be plenty of father-and-son time. Nick had only one reservation. This new phase might bore the socks off his type-A-personality father. He didn't want to rain on his dad's parade, especially when he sounded so cheery, but it had to be said. "Are you sure you're going to have enough to do with your days now?"

"Well, that's another little surprise I've been saving for you."

Nick wasn't sure he could take another surprise and braced for bad news. "What?"

"You might want to sit down for this one, pal." His dad laughed.

"I am sitting down."

"Your old man is getting married."

Nick's mouth dropped open, but the shock quickly spun to delight. Yes, it was happening pretty damned quickly, but after a two-decade drought, fast seemed almost called for. "That is fanfuckingtastic! Who is this lucky lady?"

His dad was laughing again. "You'll meet her tonight. Party starts at six p.m. Champagne and dinner on me."

Nick hung up, grinning. "Well, Granna, it looks like your son, Romeo, took your advice." He was taking a chance on love. Nick hoped his dad was in for one "big delish-a surprise-a."

* * *

At five forty-five, Jane found herself maneuvering through Kalispell's late afternoon rush hour traffic, summer sunshine a glare on the windshield. A warm breeze swept in through the open Jeep windows and across the pie boxes on the passenger seat, blowing the sweet perfume of freshly baked blueberry pie past her nose. Instead of comfort in the familiar aromas, Jane found only disquiet. Why wouldn't her mother tell her who she was marrying?

Probably worried I'll Google him. Like last time. And the time before that. But wasn't it a daughter's obligation to look out for her mother when the mother didn't seem to ever look out for herself? Of course it was.

Once Jane reached the outskirts of town, she glanced

at the GPS app on her phone, checking the directions. Five miles farther on, she spied the sign for Buffalo Ridge hanging from a massive stone arch and pulled onto a blacktopped drive that led down to a wide-open parking area. Jane's gaze went to the four-story building that stood on the edge of Flathead Lake. The exterior seemed to have been carved from the natural gigantic boulders and Douglas fir prevalent along the lakeside, the visual effect something between a grand hotel and a mountain lodge.

The interior continued the natural theme and yet offered a sense of grandeur in the slate floors and rich decor. There was even a doorman and security. She gave the doorman her mother's name, was checked off his list of expected party guests, and given directions to the condo.

Balancing the pie boxes on top of each other, Jane headed for the bank of elevators, her gaze on the wall of windows that showed views of the lake and manicured flower beds that swept right to the water's edge. The sheer beauty captured her attention...until the heel of her pumps caught on a groove in the slate flooring. She wobbled, but righted herself, clutching tighter to her packages. A fine mess she'd be if she ended up on her butt in the lobby of her mother's new digs, blueberry pie splattered everywhere.

She concentrated on putting one foot then the other solidly on the floor, trying to ignore the splendor of her surroundings and failing. How much did it cost to live in a place like this?

Leave it to Mom to snag another wealthy Romeo. A chill slipped down Jane's spine and triggered an old anger. A man named Romeo had caused the breakup of her parents' marriage almost fifteen years ago. To this day, Jane had never forgiven him. She'd lived a year with him as her stepfather and his evil son as a stepbrother. She shuddered.

If not for *that* Romeo, her mother wouldn't be flaky when it came to men, or have ended up marrying every Romeo since who crossed her path. That man ruined her mother's life. *And mine.*

Jane grappled with the pie boxes, her purse, and cell phone as she stepped into the private elevator and pushed the penthouse button. Just as the door started to close, Tall, Dark, Drop-Dead Gorgeous hurried inside. She reared back and almost dropped the pies, her face heating with alarm.

He reached out to steady her, his cologne stealing through her, a citrusy scent that smelled like...key lime pie? He had a husky, sensuous voice. "Sorry, I didn't mean to startle you."

His deep-dimpled grin reached his warm chocolate eyes, sending a curl of heat through her middle. She couldn't find her voice. She just nodded.

He turned toward the control panel, humming, seeming to be too happy about something to notice her discomfiture. She wished she could find something happy in this situation, wished that she were only a party-goer and not the daughter of a woman who'd lost her last marble.

As the elevator began its ascent, he moved into the corner opposite her and did what men seemed wont to do whenever a woman crossed their paths...checked her out from head to toe. The already too-tight dress seemed to shrink under his assessing eye, making her more aware than ever of how the fabric hugged her curves. A burn, not unlike desire, flamed through her, but of course, it wasn't desire. She didn't even know this guy, or want to know him.

His gaze finally reached her face, his expression belonging to that of a champion poker player. He gestured to the boxes she held. "Big Sky Pie, huh? Best pies in town, I hear."

"They are," Jane said, her voice almost a whisper. As much as she appreciated the compliment, she didn't tell him that she was the pie shop's new pastry chef. The fact that she'd landed this job and got to work every day in the kitchen of her dreams was still such a wonder to her that she didn't want to jinx it by bragging about it. Besides, sharing that tidbit might encourage conversation, and she didn't feel like talking to anyone. Except her mother.

She braced as the elevator stopped, noting from the corner of her eye that he'd taken an expensive-looking camera from his jacket pocket. He slipped the shoulder strap onto his fine-looking shoulders. He must be the photographer for the party. The door slid open, and music and voices hit them in a wave; the party was already under way and promised to be a lively one.

Jane stayed just inside the elevator, a severe case of cold feet washing over her. This was not the time or place for a serious discussion with her mother. Bad idea. She shouldn't have come. She reached to push the down button, but Gorgeous Elevator Guy snatched the pie boxes. "I've been here before. Follow me. The kitchen is this way."

Reluctantly, she trailed after him, wondering where her mother was and who all these people were. A dinner party, she'd said. *Why didn't I ask how many guests were expected?* Two pies would not feed this crowd. The entry tile gave way to a sleek hardwood and a sleeker kitchen. Caterers were preparing hors d'oeuvres on serving trays. Gorgeous Elevator Guy placed the pie boxes on the counter.

She thanked him for the help, but he didn't move off. "I want to see what's in those boxes."

"Blueberry pies." *My specialty.* She removed the pies from the boxes and set them on the counter. The filling, sweet and gooey, poked through the scored top. The crusts were golden brown and clustered with tiny, pie-dough hearts, a sugary glaze drizzled over the tops.

"Wow." He whipped out his camera and took a photo, then turned his lens on her. She raised her hands, warding him off. He grinned, lowering the camera away from her face, but not taking it completely off her. "Camera shy, huh?"

"Something like that."

His camera flashed again. "Great shoes."

This time, Jane couldn't help but return his smile. She thought the shoes were great, too.

She thanked him and was about to attend to cutting the pies when she spied a ghost from her past. Was she mistaken? No. He was older, gray threading his ebony hair, but it was definitely one of her former stepfathers. The one who broke up her parents' marriage. Romeo Taziano. "No, no, no..."

What was he doing here? Coming toward her as though he recognized her after all these years? He may have changed a little, but she had changed a lot. Every instinct she had seemed to cry, "Run. Hide." But there was nowhere to hide, and he was between her and the elevator. She reached for Gorgeous Elevator Guy. "Quick, kiss me."

His black eyebrows arched. "What?"

She didn't have time to explain. She threw her arms around him and pulled him to her, her gaze pleading with his. He stopped resisting, touching his soft, firm lips to hers. A jolt of pleasure unlike any she'd ever experienced flashed through Jane. *Oh, my, key lime pie never tasted so good.* The room seemed to spin away, the voices disappeared, and the music softened to a waltz, until the only thing she heard or felt or was aware of was the man whose arms were around her.

The magic moment snapped at the words, "Well, son, it looks to me like you've found a special lady, too."

Jane recognized Romeo's voice, but who was he calling son? She broke the kiss with Gorgeous Elevator Guy, finding herself a bit breathless. Her hated former stepfather was not looking at her, but straight at Gorgeous Elevator Guy. He released her and spun to greet Romeo with that dimpled smile and a bear hug. "Dad."

Shockwave upon shockwave rolled over Jane. Nick Taziano? She'd been kissing her one-time despised stepbrother, the Tazmanian Devil? *Oh my God.* She bolted for the elevator, darted inside, and punched the button to close the door.

Her mother's face flashed against the narrowing slit. "Jane?"

And then, Nick Taziano's voice reached her, sounding as shocked as she felt. "That was Jane the Pain?"

THE DISH

Where Authors Give You the Inside Scoop

From the desk of Jennifer Haymore

Dear Reader,

When Lady Dunthorpe, the heroine of THE SCOUN-DREL'S SEDUCTION, came to my office, she filled the tiny room with her presence, making me look up from my computer the moment she walked in. The first thing I noticed was that she was gorgeous. Very petite, with lovely features perfectly arranged on her face. She could probably be a movie star.

"How can I help—?" I began, but she interrupted me.

"I *need* you," she declared. I could hear the smooth cadence of a French accent in her voice. "My husband has been murdered, and I've been kidnapped by a very bad blackguard . . . a . . . a *scoundrel*."

I straightened in my chair. "What? How . . . why?" I had about a million questions, but I couldn't seem to get them all out. "Please, my lady, sit down."

She slid into the chair opposite me.

"Now," I said, "please tell me what exactly is going on and how I can help you."

She leaned forward, her blue eyes luminous and large. "My husband—Lord Dunthorpe. He was killed. And his murderer . . . his murderer has captured me. I don't know what he's going to do ." She swallowed hard, looking terrified.

"Do you know who the murderer is?

She shook her head. "*Non*. But his friends call him 'Hawk.'"

Every muscle in my body went rigid. I knew only one man called Hawk. His real name was Samson Hawkins, he was the oldest brother of the House of Trent, and I'd just finished writing books about two of his brothers.

Yet maybe she wasn't talking about "my" Hawk. Sam was a hero, not a murderer. Still, I had to know.

"Is he tall and broad?" I asked her. "Very muscular?"

"*Oui*...yes."

"Handsome features?"

"Very."

"Dark eyes and dark hair that curls at his shoulders?"

"Yes."

"Does he have a certain... *intensity* about him?"

"Oh, yes, very much."

Yep, she was definitely talking about Sam Hawkins.

I sat back in my chair, stunned, mulling over all she had told me. Sam had killed her husband. He'd kidnapped her... and was holding her hostage... *Wow*.

"I need your help," she whispered urgently. "I need to be free..."

"Of course," I soothed.

Her desire to be free sparked an idea in my mind. Because if she truly knew Sam—knew the man inside that hard shell—perhaps she *wouldn't* want to be free of him. She was beautiful and vivacious—she'd lit up my little office when she'd walked inside. Sam had certainly already noticed this about her. Now...all I had to do was work a little magic—okay, I admitted to myself, a *lot* of magic, considering the fact that Sam had killed her husband—and I could bring these two together.

Sam hadn't lived a very easy life. He *so* deserved his very own happily ever after.

This would be a love match born in adversity. *Very* tricky. But if I could make it work—if I could give Lady Dunthorpe to Sam as his heroine—it would probably be the most fulfilling love story I'd ever written.

With determination to make it work, I turned my computer screen toward me and started typing away. "Tell me what happened," I told Lady Dunthorpe, "from the beginning..."

And that was how I began the story of THE SCOUN-DREL'S SEDUCTION—and now that I've finished it, I'm so excited to share it with readers, because I definitely believe it's my most romantic story yet.

Please come visit me at my website, www.jennifer haymore.com, where you can share your thoughts about my books and read more about THE SCOUNDREL'S SEDUCTION and the House of Trent Series. I'd also love to see you on Twitter (@jenniferhaymore) or on Facebook (www.facebook.com/jenniferhaymore-author).

Sincerely,

Jennifer Haymore

❤ ❤ ❤ ❤ ❤ ❤ ❤ ❤ ❤ ❤ ❤ ❤ ❤ ❤ ❤

From the desk of Kristen Ashley

Dear Reader,

As a romance reader from a very young age, and a girl who never got to sleep easily so I told myself stories to get that way (all romances, of course), I had a bevy of "starts" to stories I never really finished.

Not until I finally started to tap away on my keyboard.

One of them that popped up often was of a woman alone, heading to a remote location, not feeling well, and meeting the man of her dreams who would nurse her back to health. Except, obviously (this *is* a romance), at first meeting him, she doesn't know he's the man of her dreams and decides instantly (for good reason) she doesn't like him all that much.

Therefore, I was delighted finally to get stuck in Nina and Max's story in THE GAMBLE. I'd so long wanted to start a story that way and I was thrilled I finally got to do it. I got such a kick out of seeing that first chapter unfold, their less-than-auspicious beginning, the crackling dialogue, Max's A-frame (inside and out) forming in my head.

But I had absolutely no clue about the epic journey I was about to take—murder, assault, kidnapping, suicide and rape, trust earned and tested—and amongst all this, a man and a woman falling in love.

The focus of the book is on Nina's story—oft-bitten, very shy, to the point where she's hardly living her life anymore, feels it, and knows she needs to do something about it even as she's terrified.

But whenever I read THE GAMBLE, it's Max's story that touches me. How he had so much from such a young age and lost it so tragically. How he took care of everyone around him in his mountain man way, but also was living half a life. And last, how Nina lit up his world and revived that protective, loving part of him he thought long dead.

The struggle with this, however, was Anna, the love Max lost. See, I knew her well and she was an amazing person who made Max happy. They were very much in love and neither Max (in my head) nor I wanted to give her short-shrift or make any less of the love they shared even as Max fell deeply in love with Nina.

I didn't know if this was working very well, for Nina was so very much *not* like Anna, but, at least to me, I found her quite lovable. This was good; you shouldn't try to find what you lost but simply find something that makes you happy. But still, it was important for me that the love Max shared with Anna wasn't entirely overshadowed by the love he had for Nina because Anna was in his life, she was important, and being so was part of what made him the man he turned out to be.

In a book that has a good deal of raw emotion, one line always jumps out at me and there's a reason for that. I was relieved when a friend of mine told me it was her favorite in this whole, very long book. So simple but also, by it being her favorite, it told me that I'd won that struggle.

It was Max saying to Nina, *"I see what I had with Anna*

for the gift it was but now that's gone. With this act, are you sayin', in this life that's all I get?"

In a book where grave tragedy had consistently struck many of the characters (as life often hands us our trials), I love the hope in this line. I love that Max finally comes to realize that the beauty he had and lost was not all he should expect. That he should reach out for more.

And he *does* reach out for more.

And in the end, he finds that it isn't all he would get. Being a good man and taking a gamble on a feisty woman who shows up in a snowstorm with attitude (and her sinuses hurting), he gets much, *much* more.

So I was absolutely delighted to take his journey.

Because he deserves it.

From the desk of Nina Rowan

Dear Reader,

What is the worst part of writing a historical romance? Once upon a time, I might have thought it was most difficult to unravel the plot and character motivations, but the more I write, the more I realize the truth. It's the research! And I don't mean that in a moan-and-groan-it's-homework way. I mean that the more I research for the sake of a book, the more I get flat-out distracted by all the little golden nuggets I find.

When I start researching, I tend to trawl the *London Times* archives, which has a searchable database that is so beautiful and easy to use that it almost makes me cry. For A DREAM OF DESIRE, I started by looking up articles about prisons and juvenile delinquency, but got quickly distracted by other things like the classified advertisements. The *Times* was full of ads for polka and mazurka lessons, "paper hanging" sales, tea companies, and job openings for schoolmistresses and butlers. The "prisons" search term appeared in the classifieds in an advertisement for "prisons supply of coal, meat, bread, oatmeal, barley, candles, and stockings." The ad requested that suppliers submit an application to the keeper of the prisons to be considered for the position.

I also get distracted by other articles about criminal court proceedings (a goldmine of story ideas), new laws, intelligence from overseas, and details about royal court life, like the state ball of 1845 at Buckingham Palace, which was attended by over one thousand members of the nobility and gentry and where Her Majesty and the Hereditary Grand Duke of Mecklenburgh Strelitz danced the quadrille in the ballroom, which was festooned with crimson and gold draperies and lit by a huge, cut-glass lustre.

I find that fascinating. But distractions aside, it really is within the pages of the newspapers and magazines published in the nineteenth century that the most vivid details of a story can come to life. When I first started writing A DREAM OF DESIRE, I thought surely the term "juvenile delinquent" was a historical anachronism, but it was used often in Victorian-era *Times* articles about "juvenile destitution and crime."

I've come to accept the fact that rather than being a dedicated, focused researcher, I'm more like a magpie whose attention is caught by shiny objects. But I've also learned to appreciate how much all those little tidbits of information come in handy when crafting a story—what might happen if the hero and heroine were in attendance at Her Majesty's state ball? What if the heroine was having a clumsy moment (or better yet, was distracted by the hero's rakish good looks) and tripped over the Grand Duke in the middle of the quadrille? What if she found herself face-to-face with a rather irate Queen Victoria?

Must go. I have some writing to do!

Nina Rowan

From the desk of Jane Graves

Dear Reader,

I like wine. Any kind of wine. I've learned a lot about it over the years, but only because if you use any product enough, you'll end up pretty educated about it. (If I ate